THE MAGNOLIA BALL III

THE MAGNOLIA BALL III

VOLUME III OF THE MAGNOLIA TRILOGY

THE CONCLUSION

Rebecca Tebbs Nunn

THE MAGNOLIA BALL III
The Conclusion

iUniverse books may be ordered through booksellers or by contacting:

iUniverse
1663 Liberty Drive
Bloomington, IN 47403
www.iuniverse.com
844-349-9409

ISBN: 978-1-4401-9316-3 (sc)
ISBN: 978-1-4401-9317-0 (e)

Print information available on the last page.

iUniverse rev. date: 05/12/2022

Dedication

"The Magnolia Ball III" is dedicated to my sister-in-law Bert Nunn who suggested the title for the third of the Magnolia Series. The title she suggested was "And the Magnolia Blossoms. . .Again! Alas, my editor did not like it, but my dedication stands because Bert and I believe, in our case, that we are sisters-in-law by marriage and friends by choice.

Contents

Foreword

*L*ike the mythical Greek phoenix, a bird that lived for 500 years and then burned itself upon a pyre of ashes only to rise from those ashes anew to live another 500 years, and also like the present-day rock icon Madonna who remakes herself every few years, Bonita prepares to forsake her sackcloth and ashes to blossom once again!

Preface

*H*aving been wrongfully incarcerated in the New Hanover County Jail, Bonita has taken to her bed in Spencer, Tennessee, a humiliated and broken woman. Hannah fears for her employer's life because of Bonita's refusal to eat. The former "Queen of Spencer Society" will see no one and only rouses herself to heed the call of nature or when Hannah insists that she bathe. It seems as though the little Mexican girl who survived living in a two-room mosquito and rodent-infested shack with numerous brothers and sisters and an abusive father, who survived thirty years as a high-priced call girl in Los Angeles, and who survived her fall from social dowager status to pariah in Dorchester County, South Carolina, may at last be fatally and finally crushed after the ordeal in Spencer.

Acknowledgements

*T*HANKS:

To my daughter, Ashley Nunn, an equestrian assisted psychotherapist and clinical psychologist, for making sure my technical terms regarding mental health are correct.

To my husband, Spike Nunn, a retired American Airlines Captain, for providing me with information regarding airlines and their procedures, plus information about small planes, and for assisting me in translating English into Spanish.

To BJ, my hairdresser, for telling me about a barge used for illegal purposes.

To Sandy Williams for providing me with the perfect model for Xandi.

To Martha Howe for being nicknamed "Sugarbritches," and allowing me to use it.

To Nancy Nilsson, Alabama playwright, for her excellent editing.

And finally, a big thank-you to Bonita for providing me with so much fodder about which to write.

CHAPTER ONE

Bonita Defeated

"**S**he gone shrivel up and die. That's what she's gone do if I can't get her to eat a bite," Hannah muttered as she carried yet another untouched tray from Bonita's boudoir down the stairs. Eight months had passed since Bonita's incarceration in the Spencer jail.

Bonita had risen from her bed in those eight months only to relieve herself and on alternate days day for a bath after constant haranguing by Hannah. Each time, Bonita roused herself as if in a trance. She refused to look into a mirror and where she used to love a relaxing soak, she now washed her body as quickly as possible, brushed her teeth with her eyes closed, put on the gown and robe Hannah laid out for her and returned to the safety of her bed. She drank occasional sips of water and ate a few bites of food each day, but she had not had a full meal since her return to Villagio. The once-mammoth woman was visibly shrinking before Hannah's very eyes.

As Bonita languished in Spencer, some five-hundred-miles away in Wilmington, North Carolina, Coach Cliff and his shadow Jim Bolts, the shop teacher at the local high school, were in the Superintendent's office presenting him with his share of the take from the Friday night football game. The high school students called Jim Bolts "Nuts'n" behind his back as in nuts and bolts. They referred to Coach Cliff as an opening in the earth belonging to a beast of burden. (Think about it.) Coach Cliff was damned near an institution in Wilmington. A big, fat, ugly man with a baldhead and a handlebar moustache, he was the winningest football and basketball coach to ever set foot in the county. Anyone who knows anything about North Carolina knows that sports, particularly basketball, absolutely consume most of the population of the state. North Carolina sports' fans are second in their fervor for basketball only to the fanaticism of the Bible Belt Fundamental Baptists in their religious beliefs.

Because of his winning teams, district trophies, state trophies and the presence of college scouts from all over the country at his games to recruit his boys, Coach Cliff resided on a pedestal so lofty he could hardly be reached and was most definitely a legend from his own mouth. He was invited to all the A-list cocktail parties in the seacoast North Carolina town, had been given a complimentary membership in the Wilmington Country Club, and drove a new Cadillac each year purchased for him by the local Sports' Club which was made up of some of the wealthiest men in the county. He lived in one of the newest and finest *noveau riche* developments. His house payments were also subsidized by the Sports' Club.

Coach Cliff existed in such a state of euphoria that several years prior, he had designated his shadow, Nuts'n, to be responsible for the gate at all home sports events. Coach Cliff and Nuts'n regularly skimmed money off the take at the gate and split it. When the Superintendent became suspicious, Coach Cliff cut him in on the deal. The three men pocketed thousands of dollars each season and so far no one was the wiser.

The Superintendent had planned to fire Coach Cliff when he admitted his thievery. Before the meeting where the head of the school systems had laid out his accusation, he had run it by a few Sports' Club members. Superintendent Woodrow Zarot was informed that if he fired the coach, they would be looking for a new superintendent and the coach would be immediately reinstated. It was quite easy for Zarot to accept the coach's offer. Hell, if he couldn't fire him, he might as well get a piece of the coach's action.

Nuts'n had proved helpful too. The super had a new deck, a screened porch, and a gazebo at his home, all built by boys (and a few girls) in Bolt's shop classes and of course all the materials had been purchased with taxpayers' money by the school system. Zarot was now getting ready to propose that Bolt's boys build him a tennis court. The experience the boys were getting was invaluable. They'd be able to move right into good construction jobs immediately after graduating from Wilmington High. None of them were college material anyway.

As the shop crew spent entire school days working at Zarot's home, they missed quite a few classes. Several had failing grades. The super, however, in his magnanimity, took care of that little glitch for Bolt's boys with a few keystrokes on the school's computer.

In addition to coaching and teaching Physical Education, Coach Cliff was the Driver's Education teacher. Many wealthy families in Wilmington sent their offspring to boarding schools where the driver's course was not available. During the coach's summer vacation, he often was called upon to provide Driver's Ed for teenage residents who did not attend public school.

The requirements for Driver's Ed were a certain number of classroom hours and a certain number of hours behind the wheel of the Driver's Ed car actually driving. When a parent contacted the coach about his or her boarding student taking the course, the coach would tell them to drop by his house and pick up a driving book. When he handed the parent the book, he said, "That'll be $25, please."

He accepted only cash.

"Tell your kid to read this in the next two weeks. Then call me and we'll schedule the driving part of the course."

The driving part of the course consisted of two hours with Coach Cliff on a back road with many twists, turns, and hills, a few blocks of town, a left turn, a right turn, hand signals, and a few miles on Interstate 40. Coach Cliff then drove the student home and charged the parents two-hundred-dollars cash, after which the teen could go for his coveted learner's permit.

Superintendent Zarot got a piece of this *flim-flam* also, but Nuts'n wasn't cut in on that scam. Public schools are funded to provide Driver's Ed for all county teenagers and there is no charge levied for the course whether the student attends the local public school or not as long as he/she is a resident of the county.

CHAPTER TWO

Alexa And Norman

"*U*gh. Alexa!" she said as she pulled the slightly sagging flesh on her face upwards. "It's time for another lift."

At age fifty, Alexa had undergone two complete face lifts and was beginning to resemble a frog, but she had heard of a new procedure – the mid-face lift – where the skin was pulled upward on either side at the temples rather than the old sideways pulling that resulted in the frog/toad resemblance.

After her facial work out, Alexa glanced at her Patek Philippe diamond-encrusted watch. "Shit. 7:30. I wonder what time Norman left?"

She rarely saw her workaholic husband, which didn't bother her greatly. He made tons of money and he never flinched when her credit card bills arrived. Alexa's spending habits were legendary. Shopkeepers in Wilmington were said to cross themselves, utter Hail Mary's, and on occasion genuflect when Alexa's chauffeured Jaguar pulled up in front of their establishments.

Norman and Alexa employed a chauffeur, two maids, a cook, four gardeners and a pool boy at their mega-estate twenty miles from Wilmington's docks where Norman's business was located. Norman was the owner and the chief operator of the largest seafood processing plant on the Eastern seacoast. Chances were any oyster, shrimp, fish, scallop, or crab found in any restaurant from Florida to New York had at one time passed through Norman's plant. He employed Mexicans exclusively.

The household staff was also Mexican. Norman was quick to explain to everyone that "His" Mexicans were legal. He made arrangements to get the proper papers for them prior to their arrival in North Carolina. There was an element of truth to Norman's statement. Some of "His" Mexicans were indeed legal, however, the majority was not.

Those who were not legal lived in low-lying barracks-type buildings on the huge estate where he and Alexa resided named "La Reina de la Mar," the queen of the sea, though the mansion and its grounds were more than fifteen miles from the Cape Fear River and even farther from the sea.

The illegal Mexicans were one step above slaves. They lived at the estate, were bussed back and forth to the plant, were never allowed to set foot outside either of those compounds and were charged thirty-dollars each a week for their room and board. As horrid as it sounds, even those conditions were better than those they had left behind. They were able to send money home to their families each month and that's what their working in the United States was all about. One of Norman's foremen, a legal immigrant, collected the letters home with money enclosed in every single one of them from the illegal Mexicans each week and deposited them with the proper postage in the mail slot in Wilmington's main post office.

Norman was a native of North Carolina and had inherited the seafood plant from his father. It was a small operation when Norman took the helm, but he had expanded over the years until his business and physical plant were the Goliath of the seafood industry. Nestled on the banks of the river's edge were rows of buildings, docks, fishing vessels, fueling facilities, and refrigerated trucks all of which comprised *Seafood World*, Norman's empire. A shrewd businessman, Norman had the latest refrigerated trucks and fishing vessels in his fleet as he saved a great deal of money each year by using illegal labor. He also saw no necessity in purchasing buses to transport that illegal labor.

Years earlier through the *good ole boy* network, Norman had struck a deal with his good friend, the Superintendent of Schools. Before dawn, county-owned school buses pulled into a hidden entrance on a back road to *La Reina de la Mar* and picked up the illegal workers and ferried them to Seafood World. In the afternoons, once the school children had been deposited at their bus stops, the buses returned the laborers to the estate. Norman saw that the arrangement was quite lucrative to Woodrow Zarot, the school super, who in turn made sure the drivers were well paid not only for their extra hours, but also for their silence.

Conveniently, the county high school was located half way between Seafood World and Norman's estate and to make sure there were no questions asked about why the buses headed to Seafood World on a regular basis, Norman had made sure there were several newspaper articles about his donation of fuel to the county transportation department for, according to a quote from Norman, "The school buses daily transport our little darlings, our most precious cargo, and the future of North Carolina," and the savings provided by his generosity to the taxpayers of New Hanover County.

Wilmington sits on a bank along the Cape Fear River and though Seafood World was huge, the townspeople had no idea of the enormity of the plant. Through the years, Norman had hired men to tunnel into the high embankment and two thirds of Seafood World was actually underground. That's where the illegal laborers picked crabs, shucked oysters, de-veined shrimp and cleaned fish. Additionally, the sealed area was camouflaged from visiting inspectors.

Norman's tentacles stretched as far as Raleigh, the capital city of North Carolina, and he was always notified well ahead of time of a *surprise* inspection. When one was scheduled, Norman's illegal workers received an unpaid day off. On inspection days, the buses didn't arrive at La Reina de la Mar before dawn. The illegal workers spent the day inside the barracks or in the fenced area surrounding them complete with eight-foot fences topped with barbed wire and patrolled by Dobermans and two armed guards, also members of Norman's household *staff.*

The barracks were out of view of the mansion and although Alexa knew about the illegal tenants, she never ventured to that part of the estate nor did she see the school buses that came and went through the back entrance. An electrified fence encompassed the two-hundred-acre estate that was secreted behind an ornate stonewall that matched the native rock of the sprawling main house. Electrified wrought iron gates stood sentinel at each entrance complete with manned gatehouses – manned by legal immigrants, of course.

Norman had been married to his childhood sweetheart before he met Alexa. They had married a year after they both graduated from Wilmington High and they had over the course of their marriage produced three daughters, all of whom were now married and producing families of their own. Thirty-five years after his first marriage, Norman went on a golfing vacation to Duck Island, South Carolina, with three of his friends. Halle, Norman's first wife, did not accompany him nor did the wives of his three friends accompany them, however the other three men each brought a female companion along for a few days of fun. One of Norman's closest friends who lived in Florida was accompanied by Alexa. Norman was immediately smitten with the pixie-like, slender, blue-eyed brunette twenty years his junior. She was witty, good-looking, sexy, and according to his close friend, could suck the white off rice.

Halle had put on weight, didn't touch up the gray in her hair, and dressed frumpily even though she could have bought anything she wanted. She was all caught up in her humane society activities and her charity work and didn't seem to have time for Norman anymore or sometimes even take notice that he was there.

The pixie flirted with Norman to abandon when her *date* wasn't around and she looked like she'd just stepped off a run-way as each and every one of her outfits was exquisite. When they had a few minutes alone in the Lodge, Norman learned that Alexa was divorced and had a fourteen-year-old daughter. She didn't work, but had a very generous alimony and child-support subsidy.

After the week at Duck, Norman began making frequent *business* excursions to Florida. Within a year, he divorced Halle, gave her *gazillions of dollars*, according to him, and placed a diamond the size of a fifty-cent-piece on Alexa's diminutive ring finger. Two years after first laying eyes on Norman, Alexa and her daughter Jennifer moved into La Reina de la Mar and Alexa assumed the duties of mistress of the manor and whore extraordinaire in the boudoir. Norman couldn't have been happier. At least, for a while.

Three years into their marriage when the buxom Jennifer was seventeen, Alexa was called to the bedside of her ailing emphazemic mother who still lived in the Boston project where the now wealthy Mrs. Norman Masterson had been reared. Alexa stayed with her mother night and day for three months until Mrs. Zambortini took her last tortured breath.

Meanwhile at La Reina de la Mar, Norman and Jennifer were hitting it off splendidly. After dinner each night in the enormous dining room, they had taken to retiring to the master suite to watch television together. It wasn't long before they were lying on the bed rather than sitting in the overstuffed easy chairs. Before too much time passed, Norman, who was feeling and looking his age, began to search for his lost youth in the arms of the younger image of his second wife. One thing led to another and Norman and his stepdaughter became lovers.

During one of their lovemaking sessions, Alexa returned unexpectedly having buried her mother without Norman's knowledge or presence as she never wanted him to discover her background. She walked in on her husband and her daughter doing the nasty.

"What the hell is going on here?" she screeched.

"It's not what it looks like, Alexa," Norman answered.

Jennifer started to cry while grabbing at her clothes that were strewn all over the bed.

"Oh, it's not what it looks like? Then exactly what is it, Norman? You are the lowest form of life! Lower than snake shit, no, lower than that, lower than whale shit in the Mariana's Trench! And you, you little trollop, who the hell do you think you are? Seventeen years old and screwing this old fart! Maybe you were hoping he would drop dead and then we'd have all the money. Well, I'll tell you something dear little daughter of mine, we're going to spend some of your sweet step-daddy's money on you and it's going to begin tomorrow. Your ass is leaving La Reina de la Mar at oh-dark-thirty bound for somewhere as soon as I decide where that somewhere is. Now, I'm going downstairs and fix myself a stiff drink. Jennifer, put your clothes on or don't, I don't really care, and get your ass out of my bed and my room. Norman, you can do the same and don't ever darken the door of this master suite again. I'll have Delilah move your shit out of the closet in the dressing room first thing in the morning. I need more space anyway. From now on, Mr. Masterson, I will be running the show here and if you so much as roll your eyes,

I will disgrace you from one end of this state to the other. Now get out, both of you!"

And they did.

The next morning, Jennifer was sent away to complete her final year of high school at a Swiss boarding school. Norman stayed away from the master suite and was told in no uncertain terms that there would be no divorce or Alexa would expose him to all of Wilmington and its environs as a child molester. Alexa now did as she pleased and Norman worked eighteen-hour-days and he didn't get to leave on any *business trips* or golfing excursions. Tight-assed Alexa ran an even tighter ship.

CHAPTER THREE

Back In Spencer

*D*uring her eight- month *confinement,* Bonita, although severely depressed, never stopped thinking, planning, calculating, and scheming. She just couldn't seem to get her body to physically get up and follow her brain's commands. But Bonita was a survivor and, like the mythical bird, she was about to rise from the *pile of ashes* and remake herself.

Bonita Roberts had gone to Hollywood with Marvin Hamblin at fifteen years of age. For thirty years, she was a thousand-dollar-an-hour prostitute for Enrique Dubre. She was married to Joshua Roberts for eight years before he croaked. A year later after the scandal in Dorchester County, she moved to Spencer, Tennessee. Not quite two years had passed since she purchased Brigadoon, remade it into Villagio, and started the ill-fated Magnolia Ball in Van Buren County. Bonita was fifty-eight years old and she had fantastic bone structure. The woman had been a true beauty in her youth.

Only a few days after Hannah took the uneaten food to the kitchen, she was delightfully surprised when she entered Bonita's room with the breakfast tray mumbling "Another meal you ain't gonna eat, I reckon"

Bonita was sitting up in bed and when she saw Hannah, she smiled,

"Well, what have you brought me?"

Hannah lifted the lid on a plate of scrambled eggs, sausage, biscuits, grits, toast, jelly, and coffee with cream and sugar.

"That looks delicious, Hannah, and I am very hungry. I hate to ask this of you, but I think I need to change my eating habits."

"You ain't got no eatin' habits, Miz Bonita. You ain't had two pounds of food in your belly in the past eight months."

"Oh, Hannah, how you do go on. Would you mind terribly taking this back to the kitchen? I'd like some yogurt, fruit, one piece of unbuttered wheat toast, and a cup of tea with lemon, no sugar."

"I don't mind at all, Miz Bonita if you's gonna eat sumpin."

"I'll eat. I promise."

Hannah fairly flew down the stairs and for the first time in months, she was humming. Once in the kitchen, she fixed the tray. "That chile is gonna be all right. Thank you, Lord Jesus. I seen that same look in her eye I's seen there before. She gone get outta that bed and she gone be fine. O Lord, I wonder where we's gonna be movin' next."

While Bonita was partaking of her breakfast, she instructed Hannah as to what other foods she would be eating. "You'll need to order lots of lettuce, all different kinds, iceberg, Romaine, Bib, radicchio, green leaf, red leaf, and don't forget endive. I want tons of fresh lemons, vinegar, fish and chicken, nothing fried and nothing white. And I want only tea with lemon or water to drink."

"Miz Bonita, you's always eaten steak and potatoes and lobster."

"No more, Hannah. You're looking at a dieter extraordinaire."

"You don't need to lose no weight, Miz Bonita. I bet you don't weigh one-hundred-fifty pounds."

"What?"

"Not one-hundred-fifty pounds."

Bonita, who had tipped the scales at three hundred couldn't believe what Hannah was telling her. Once the maid left, Bonita stood up, pulled her gown up and looked at all the sagging skin where her huge stomach had been. The mounds of fat were gone, but an apron of skin remained. Pulling the gown up even further, she looked at the once pendulous breasts that had filled a double F cup to overflowing. They resembled two huge sweat socks with lumpy potatoes in the toe portions hanging almost to her waist. She reached down and pulled up the cellulite-ridden skin on each of her thighs. She checked the bag of flesh hanging from each arm. Finally, she made her way to the Cheval mirror. Her double chins were gone. In their place was a horribly wrinkled, wattled neck. She looked at her once broad and unlined face – that had been stretched to its limit by fat – and saw that it was haggard and drawn with sagging jowls and deep lines galore.

Bonita removed her nightclothes and stared at her body in horror. She went into her pink bathroom and stepped on the scales. One-hundred-and-forty-seven pounds. She hadn't weighed below two-hundred-and-fifty in years. She slipped back into her gown and rang for Hannah. "Call Raven. Tell her I want her here first thing in the morning."

Raven was taken aback when she received the call from Hannah saying Mrs. Roberts wanted to see her. Raven had been to Villagio any number of times only to be told by Hannah, "Miz Bonita won't see nobody."

Often Hannah had called Raven in tears, so worried was she about Bonita's not eating and losing so much weight. Raven suggested more than once that Hannah call a doctor, but Hannah said Miz Bonita would kill her.

"I'll be there at eight tomorrow morning. What happened, Hannah?" Raven asked.

"This morning, I went to her room with a good breakfast. For the first time since she come home, she was sittin' up in bed and she was smilin'. She told me she didn't want what I'd fixed, but she wanted yogurt, fruit, wheat toast and green tea. I fixed it and she ate every bite. I's got to call in an order to the grocery store for chicken, fish, vegetables, and a bale of lettuce, and she ain't gonna be eatin' nothin' white. She been up, too. I heared her walkin' 'round upstairs. Then she told me she wanted you to come tomorrow mornin' first thing."

"Sounds like she's going to recover, Hannah. I'll be there. I'll see you in the morning."

Upon her arrival the next morning, Raven realized she would not have recognized Bonita Roberts if she had seen her anywhere but in her bedroom at Villagio. Bonita was a mere shadow of her former self with sagging skin hanging from her body like bag worms suspended from a diseased oak tree. Her once almost smooth face was lined, her platinum blonde hair was dark brown, and she had on no make-up! Raven had never seen Bonita without her de rigueur florescent blue eye shadow and pink lipstick.

"Hello, Raven. How nice to see you, dear. How is your father?"

"Do you mean the man I live with or Alphonso?" Raven asked, but there was no bitterness in her voice.

"Well, both," Bonita responded with a laugh.

"The man I live with, who will always be my father in my mind, is recovering slowly, but he's gone through a major depression. He really loves my mother, you know? And Alphonso and mother are deliriously happy in La-la Land."

"Well, that's good news on both fronts. I'm glad to hear your father is starting to feel better and of course, although I miss Alphonso terribly, I'm pleased he's happy too."

"Hannah said you had work for me?"

"I do. Have a seat. First of all, I want you to do research on that computer of yours and find me the finest exercise equipment available. I will be transforming the upstairs ballroom into a gymnasium. Then I want you to find me a nutritionist, a personal trainer, order workout clothing and check into the best plastic surgeons in the country. Bonita has decided to live."

"I'll get on it right away."

"And lastly, Raven, after I start my work-out routine and get on a proper diet, I'm going to want you to teach me how to use that computer thing."

"It'll be a pleasure, Mrs. Roberts."

"Well, all right, you best go downstairs and get started. I'm going to get this bag of bones out of bed and take a bath and I may even venture outside for a little walk around the grounds."

"That's a wonderful idea. I'm so glad you're feeling better. Hannah and I have been so worried about you, Mrs. Roberts."

"Thank you, dear, but believe me, you're the only two people in the world who have worried about me."

"That's not true. Hannah says folks have come to visit and you wouldn't see them."

"Those old biddies who came snooping around here weren't concerned about me at all; they just wanted to nose around and see what and how I was doing so they could have more fodder for their morning bridge groups or their luncheon dates."

"I've lived in this small town all my life, Mrs. Roberts. True, the folks here are nosy, but they're nosy out of love and they really do want to help."

"Then I'm happy for them, but they won't have Bonita Roberts to gossip about much longer. As soon as I get this body and face back in shape, Hannah and I, and you too, if you'd like to go with us, Raven, are moving on to greener pastures."

"I'll take that under advisement and think about it, Mrs. Roberts, but if it's anytime soon, I probably will have to say no. Daddy needs me to help him with the stores and I'd really worry about him if he had to come home to an empty house every night."

"Oh, it'll be a while yet. One can't undo years of overeating and overindulgence in a few months. Keep it at the back of your mind."

"I will and thank you for the invitation and the opportunity."

"No thanks necessary, Raven. You've been invaluable to me. Now, run on downstairs and get to work and find me all the things I need so we can get started on the Bonita make-over."

"Right away," Raven said as opened the door and left Bonita alone.

Bonita picked up her hand mirror from the bedside table and stared at herself for a few moments.

"Well, Bonita, old gal, it's begun. The little Mexican gal from Texas is about to shed another cocoon and fly once again. And this time, there'll be no stopping her."

CHAPTER FOUR

Hank

*H*ank was pure and simply a ladies' man. Although he had earned a college degree, he had never held a real job; however, he managed to get by always having a ready supply of the best Scotch, expensive and illegal Cuban cigars, hand-tailored clothing and a flashy car. His living accommodations changed frequently depending on his lady du jour.

Like John Kerry, the erstwhile wealthy Senator who pretended to care about the poor during his failed Presidential campaign, Hank only courted and/or married the super-rich. He had married the first time at twenty-three. Helena, his first wife, was heiress to the Reynolds Metals of Virginia fortune and she supported him in high style. They traveled between the Reynolds' homes in the Caribbean, New York City, the South of France and London. During their rambling days, Hank managed to impregnate Helena three times and with each child, their traveling entourage grew with a nanny for each of the progeny.

Eventually, Helena grew tired of the constant movement and wanted to settle down in one place. Daddy Reynolds built the young family a mansion in West Palm Beach. The Reynolds connection guaranteed membership in all the best clubs and Helena and Hank Asbury, a distant relative of Jackie Bouvier Kennedy Onassis, became one of the most desirable couples in the fabulously wealthy enclave.

Hank was the quintessential gentleman. Tall and slim with a head of thick black hair and aquamarine eyes, the man was beyond handsome. His good looks were enhanced by his impeccable manners. Any lady within his vision and periphery who removed a cigarette from her sterling silver cigarette case, was the recipient of Hank's proffered light from his engraved gold, Cartier lighter. He held doors and chairs for Helena and any other ladies if their companions did not. He walked unescorted ladies to their cars and he always stood immediately when a lady left and/or returned to his table. Hank did everything but click his heels!

Hank loved Helena. Of course, he did. Hank loved *all* women and eventually he tired of golfing, handball, cocktails at the club, dinners where he and Helena entertained or dinners out every evening either at the club or at someone else's mansion. He began to dally with some of those women who were irresistible to him. Helena felt something missing in the relationship and hired a private investigator. A messy divorce ensued where Helena obtained custody of the children and the mansion, but Hank walked away with a quarter of a million dollars in 1980 – a tidy sum.

Hank bid his children good-bye and made reservations for a world cruise. On the third night out of the harbor, he asked a lovely young lady to dance in the ship's ballroom and within three months, he was married to a recent divorcee who happened to have received a five-million-dollar settlement when her Hollywood producer husband found someone even younger and prettier than she to attach to his arm.

By the time Hank moved to Wilmington, North Carolina, he had been married four times and each time a marriage ended, always because of his indiscretions with other women, Hank left with a new stack of jack.

Occasionally, he saw his children, but there was really no emotional closeness, as he'd never really gotten to know them, as they had been almost entirely reared by nannies.

He had vacationed in Wilmington following his fourth divorce and liked what he saw, so he bought a small home on the waterfront and presently was *between engagements*. He spent his days golfing, fishing, enjoying cocktails and dinner at the Wilmington Country Club or some of the other fine waterfront restaurants. Several Wilmington widows, divorcees, and even young single gals were quite interested in the extremely handsome, dashing, and obviously well-fixed fifty-eight-year-old roué, but at the moment Hank had yet to find his next *true love*.

CHAPTER FIVE

Joey Scappaticcio

*T*he Wilmington Harbor was controlled by Joey Scappaticcio, a native New Yorker and a former union organizer. Joey had married a Wilmington girl who attended Cornell University in New York. After their wedding and honeymoon, they lived in Great Neck, Long Island, but Mrs. Scappaticcio was never happy in *Yankee land* and insisted on returning to Dixie. Reluctantly, Joey agreed for he loved his Southern belle to distraction.

They moved to Wilmington and Joey, as he was called by everyone in Wilmington, started a trucking business and his trucks naturally spent a lot of time at the docks loading and unloading. Joey got to know everyone of importance on the docks. One thing led to another and now he let his second in command run the successful trucking firm while he, as the dock master, sat in his glass enclosed office three stories above the Wilmington Harbor so he could watch and see everything happening there.

Nina, Joey's wife, had expensive tastes and managed to spend all of Joey's handsome salary, his earnings from the trucking company, and then some. Thus, Joey was always looking for ways to make more money. He had entered into a few shady deals with Norman Masterson involving the illegal Mexicans. Occasionally, he looked the other way when drugs were off-loaded, but if his palm weren't greased sufficiently, he called the local police. The cops thought he was a stand-up guy because he turned in the drug dealers. Joey was considered to be a model citizen even though he was a New Yorker with that horrible accent, an Italian, and a Yankee. His other saving grace was that he was married to a native North Carolinian from a fine family with a good name.

CHAPTER SIX

Bart And Kim

*C*aptain Andrew Bartlett, "Bart," was an international commercial pilot for American Airlines. Although he resided in Wilmington, he flew out of Kennedy Airport in New York, his home base. With his seniority at the company, he was never on reserve, where he could be called out on two hours' notice. His schedule each month was carved in stone. He flew out on Tuesdays to Bangkok, Thailand, returned on Sundays, and was home for at least nine days before he repeated the sequence.

Bart kept his Beech Baron aircraft tied down at General Aviation at the Wilmington Airport. On the Tuesday mornings he was scheduled to fly, he flew to JFK in his own plane and on the following Sunday after his commercial flight, he flew it back to the seaport town. Often, Bart's wife Kim, a Thai native, accompanied him on his trips either to visit her family who still lived in Thailand or to buy wares for her exclusive gift shop in Wilmington. Kim's business was flourishing. She not only sold to locals and summer people, but she also did a bang-up business over the Internet with contacts all over the world.

Besides Bart's airline job and Kim's gift shop, they owned a barge anchored in the Cape Fear River off Wilmington's coast. Clients were motored out to the lavishly remodeled barge in a pontoon boat. The barge had a Thai motif and was a combination nightclub and restaurant *splendiloquent* with absolutely disgraceful prices, outrageous entertainment, an extremely strict dress code, and a whorehouse on the upper deck. Only *those in the know* whose lips were sealed knew about or had visited the upper deck and it was certainly to their benefit not to notify any authorities. It wouldn't have made much of an impact if someone had complained to or voiced their suspicions to the authorities as Kim saw that the Chief of the Wilmington Police, the New Hanover Country Sheriff, and all visiting legislators from the capital city of Raleigh were given complimentary visits to the upper deck. Even the Governor of North Carolina had been Kim's guest. Of course, a large amount of cash changed hands each month. Kim paid the local gendarmes handsomely for not only their silence, but also for their protection.

Kim advertised that her upper deck was composed of suites for rent and an exclusive spa, however when one, not *in the know,* called for reservations, there was never a vacancy. Kim would, on occasion, conduct tours of the upper deck. She would show interested parties a few of the suites and the main lounge, but tour guests could not be permitted to view the spa as the privacy of the registered guests had to be protected at all costs. Any *working girls* present were introduced by Kim as masseuses or skincare specialists.

The *ladies* employed on the upper deck ranged in age from eighteen to thirty and were beautiful beyond belief. Kim saw that they were outfitted in only the best and most expensive clothing. She paid them well and had them examined monthly by a doctor who was no longer licensed to practice medicine in North Carolina. She paid the doctor under the counter. Girls stayed on the barge and only went ashore every two months when they received an expense paid two-week vacation to Thailand and home.

Bart ferried the *ladies* back and forth to JFK and often they flew on his commercial flights to visit their families. There were no defectors as they made more in a night than many of their families made in half a year. The girls took home scads of money every two months.

By 2006, the barge restaurant/night club/*whatever* had been in business for two years and was providing the Bartletts with more income than Bart's two-hundred-and-fifty-thousand-dollars a year airline job and Kim's half-million-dollars a year Thai gift business.

CHAPTER SEVEN

Other Roberts' Family Members

*T*wo people to whom Bonita rarely gave a thought were still very much alive and kicking. One was the original Mrs. Joshua Roberts. Seventy-two-years of age, Jillian Roberts lived on the family estate in Greenwich, Connecticut. Joshua had generously allowed her to keep it when he divorced her to marry Bonita. He had also given her a ten-million-dollar settlement. So other than losing the man she had loved her entire life, Jillian was in good shape.

The second was the daughter of Jillian and Joshua who was now forty-five years old, only thirteen years younger than Bonita. Joshua had mentioned the child Donnice once in passing to Bonita but he had not kept in touch with her after their marriage, as far as she knew. While Jillian had unhappily but without confrontation accepted Joshua's desire for a divorce, Donnice was embittered by her father's unfaithfulness, his lack of taste, his rejection of her mother, and his marriage to a whore, albeit not a *two-bit* one.

Donnice, who became Princess Donnice when she was married briefly to Prince Macmillan of Germany had retained the title, her diamond tiara, the Macmillan surname, and several of the family's millions after the divorce. She was also the recipient of an extremely generous trust fund from Joshua and she had used a sizeable amount of her money to track Bonita's every move since her marriage to her father. Donnice moved in elite circles because of her title and never alluded to her maiden name or her late father's publishing empire.

The attractive woman had laughed with glee when Bonita was disgraced in Montiac at the Magnolia Ball. She clipped every report from every newspaper she could find with a report about the drug deal gone bad and the scandal resulting from Bonita's real identity being blabbed to everyone by Anthony through Celestine at the Ball.

Two private investigators retained by Donnice had followed the burgundy Rolls Royce at a discreet distance when Alphonso drove Bonita and Hannah out of Montiac on their way to Spencer, Tennessee. Donnice received bi-weekly reports of Bonita's doings and was even more delighted when she was incarcerated in Spencer. Her merriment was somewhat diluted when it came out that Bonita was not directly involved with the child pornography computer scam, but the fact that Bonita had once again been disgraced made Donnice ecstatic.

But that was then and this was now and for sometime, Donnice had not been pleased, as her bi-weekly reports for the past eight months had been worthless. Bonita had not left the house and no one had been allowed in to see her. The most exciting aspect of each report was the weekly grocery delivery. Ah, but now, something was definitely going on at Villagio.

CHAPTER EIGHT

The Delivery Man Cometh

*B*y Monday, Villagio was abuzz. Four local men Raven had hired were moving the ballroom furniture to the attic. Hannah hurried to answer the ringing bell at the impressive front door of Villagio.

"Yes," she said as she opened the door.

"Where you want this stuff?" a burly truck driver asked.

"What is it?" Hannah asked.

"Exercise machines."

"Take it around back. I guess you can put it on the elevator. It's going to the ballroom on the third floor."

"Yeah, I figured it would be going up some steps," the deliveryman said as he headed back to his truck.

As the deliverymen reached the ballroom, they had to negotiate around the men who were still moving the furniture out. The truck driver and three other men worked the major part of the day hoisting a treadmill, a bow-flex, a rowing machine, a step machine and various other Nautilus equipment all of which resembled torture devices from the Middle Ages to Bonita's third floor ballroom.

Hannah showed Bryan, the personal trainer, to his suite while Felice and Javiar, two nutritionists Raven had located and flown in from California, were cleaning out cupboards and pitching everything that contained a calorie. Hannah was not a happy camper. These two had taken over her kitchen and three times daily prepared the nastiest looking stuff she had ever seen.

Sprouts, nuts, berries, sticks, and all kinds of weird blender stuff, that's all they know how to fix, Hannah thought, *and Miz Bonita's payin' em a fortune!*

"That chile gotta eat somethin' more than what you folks fixin'. She ain't hardly eat at all for eight months."

Felice said, "She's getting plenty to eat, Hannah, but now she's eating healthy. All that steak, lobster, gravy and biscuits she was eating before she fell ill is what made her so huge."

"That's what she likes."

Javiar responded, "Well in order to stay healthy and in shape, we can't eat what we like, Hannah."

Hannah harrumphed. *Those two looked like shadows they were so thin and then that personal trainer had muscles and sinews standing out all over his body and Hannah was sure he was going to kill her mistress with all those exercises he had her doing six hours a day. Miz Bonita had never done no exercise except that required by her former profession in Beverly Hills. Now she was crunching and scrunching and running in place and jumping rope.* Hannah had no idea what Bryan, the personal trainer, *was going to have Miz Bonita do with all those torture machines the movers were hauling to the ballroom.*

Bonita meanwhile was oblivious to the chaos as she tried on first one outfit and then another of the mountain of workout clothes delivered the day prior. She particularly favored a black spandex full-body suit that molded some of the sagging skin into an almost shapely body. Bonita sat on the side of her bed and slipped on sweat socks. "Why I haven't worn a pair of socks in forty years!" she exclaimed aloud, but what really amazed her was that she had bent over to put the socks on without feeling faint. She hadn't been able to bend over without constricting her internal organs in an age. She pulled on the legwarmers and then the tennis shoes. She slipped a black sweatband on her head and wrapped the five-pound weights around each appendage securing them with Velcro tape. Bonita was ready to rock and roll and grunt and sweat!

Right then, Bryan, whom Bonita had interviewed a week before and who had already been to Villagio for workouts with her, tapped on her door.

"Come in."

"Hi, Bonita. Now that we've got the equipment . . . well, look at you, don't you look precious? The black body suit is you, darling. I'm glad you're all dressed because I just want to take your measurements to see what we're starting with here and then you and I are going to get to work and find that fabulous body hiding in there."

Bonita smiled, "Oh, I hope we can find that body wherever it is, Bryan."

"Have no fear. The Bryan is here!"

Bonita had watched with shining eyes as the fifty-thousand-dollars plus pieces of machinery were taken to the ballroom and placed where Bryan specified. Bonita loved Bryan. He made her laugh and he made her work, but it was almost fun with him prodding and pushing her. The woman who for thirty years of her life had slept until noon was now awake and dressed in leotards and tights by six each morning. At precisely six-twenty, Hannah brought her a morning energy shake prepared by Felice containing eggs, malt, and vitamin supplements stirred into no-fat milk. It tasted horrid, so each day, Bonita held her nose and drank it down. She could almost accomplish it without gagging by now. At six-thirty, she was in the ballroom with Bryan who started her on stretching exercises in time with hip-hop music.

When Bryan had first arrived, Bonita told him Raven had ordered all manner of workout machines to arrive the following week and they were to start her exercise program then. Bryan would have none of that.

"No, Cherie, we start right away. Got to tone those muscles under all that yucky, ugly, baggy flab," and then he chucked Bonita under her chin.

"Such beautiful bone structure, such lovely skin. There's a gorgeous woman hiding in there, Bonita, and we're going to watch her emerge from that ugly old cocoon where she's hiding and be transformed into a fabulous butterfly again. *Bryansie* is going to do that for the fair Bonnie and we start today!"

No one had ever called Bonita by a nickname or chucked her under the chin, but gay Bryan had a way about him that Bonita adored and she loved how he referred to her and to himself in the third person. *Bryansie? What straight man would ever call himself such a silly name?* Bonita thought and chuckled.

Even though Bonita knew that Bryansie was as queer as a three-dollar-bill, she did love his physique and she believed he would pull the butterfly tortured, screaming, perspiring, and hating every minute of it, from the cocoon.

Once the machines were in perfect position and ready to go, Bryan wrote out an exercise plan for Bonita. She would stretch, crunch, jump rope and do ten laps around the ballroom before progressing to the machines where they would work for five hours until lunchtime. Bryan gave Bonita an hour off at lunch at which time Felice and Javiar took over her health regime with a yummy lunch of nuts, berries and a dab of yogurt accompanied by another energy shake. The lunch shake was always green. Bonita didn't want to know what was in that one. Bonita always had her lunch; such as it was, in the kitchen and that completely flabbergasted Hannah. *Why Miz Bonita ain't hardly been in the kitchen five times in all the years I done worked for her and now she be sittin' at the counter eatin' her lunch, if that mess can be called lunch.*

Felice and Javiar insisted that Bonita had to drink the lunch shake immediately after it was blended as it contained miso and they were alive and had to be consumed right away. Hannah was sure they were feeding Bonita some kind of bugs.

Bonita knew Hannah was at loose ends because she was no longer required to prepare meals. That's why she had prevailed upon Felice and Javiar to allow Hannah to bring her the morning shake.

"Hannah's been with me for eons and I depend on her. I can't have her thinking I don't need her," she explained to the new employees.

Bonita further insisted that Hannah be allowed to prepare and serve her the evening meal. Felice and Javiar had never heard so much grumbling as when Hannah cooked tofu one hundred different ways.

"When you gone let Miz Bonita have some meat? This paste stuff ain't enough to keep body and soul together."

"Friday night, Hannah. Friday night, your Miz Bonita can have tuna."

"Oh and I knows jest how she like it too. I'm gonna blacken it and make a nice Béarnaise sauce."

"No, Hannah, she can have a four-ounce serving from a can and it has to be water packed tuna."

"Miz Bonita don't eat no tuna outta a can."

"She does now," stated Javiar.

Hannah was horrified, but she *was* noticing that Miz Bonita was beginning to have some definition in her arms and legs and she seemed to feel wonderful. Hannah couldn't wrap her mind around that what her mistress was consuming might be helping.

Bonita was diligent as was her entourage. After lunch, she rested for thirty minutes and then Bryan took her through two more hours of stretching and yoga in the afternoon. At three every afternoon, Demitra, the masseuse, arrived and pounded and pummeled Bonita for an hour after which Bonita showered, applied a little makeup, combed her now dark hair and slipped into a size ten caftan with matching mules and went down to her lavish dining room where Hannah served her a carrot juice cocktail on the rocks.

Raven met with Bonita during *cocktail hour* to report on any errands Bonita had assigned her for the day. It was also at that time that Bonita gave Raven the schedule for the following day and began her computer learning sessions.

"Mrs. Roberts, you look fantastic! Your skin is positively glowing!"

"You mean my wrinkles and jowls?" Bonita asked with a laugh.

"No, you have lovely skin."

"It's going to be lovelier, Raven. Bryan says after he whips me into shape for six months or so, I'll be ready to go under the knife. What have you found out about plastic surgery for me?"

"All my research and the doctors to whom I've spoken point to Dr. Kamlash Vyas. He's from India and his office is in Beverly Hills. He's the reigning plastic surgeon in the United States and the only one who specializes in the total body lift, which is what you told me was a requirement."

"Then book him for six months down the road."

"I'm afraid that's impossible, Mrs. Roberts. He's booked through 2010."

"Get his phone number."

"I have it right here."

"I'll call myself tomorrow."

"Well, I wish you luck. I've already used your name, the name of the publishing company, and anything else I could think of to influence his scheduler to get you an appointment."

"I appreciate all your research, Raven, and your efforts, but if you want something done, you don't deal with schedulers or secretaries or receptionists, you go right to the top. I plan to speak to Dr. Vyas himself."

"How are you going to do that?"

"I'm not exactly sure yet, but it'll come to me," Bonita said with a Cheshire cat grin.

Raven returned the smile as she thought, *Hannah was right. Mrs. Roberts is definitely back! She may not resemble the old Bonita in looks, but that steel will of hers is intact.* Raven had no doubt that Bonita would not only speak to Dr. Vyas on the phone, but that she would also get an appointment with him.

CHAPTER NINE

Princess Maximillian

Something was definitely going on at Villagio. Donnice read with interest from the private detectives' report about the arrival of Bryan, Felice, and Javiar and the fact that they had taken up residence in the Spencer mansion. She made note of Demitra's arrival each day at precisely three o'clock. Bonita was having daily massages and had employed two nutritionists and a personal trainer. *What is she up to now?* Donnice wondered.

She didn't have to wonder for long because in the next report, Donnice was able to put two and two together. The exercise equipment had arrived. Donnice quickly calculated Bonita's age. Talking to herself aloud, she said "Hell, she's only fifty-eight, thirteen years older than me and she was a looker when Daddy married her. She must be getting herself in shape for something and planning to lose all that weight she gained. It won't be long before she makes a move. I only have to continue to be patient. I think the time is rapidly approaching to bring her down."

Donnice dropped the latest report on her Oriental mother-of-pearl desk and retired to her boudoir to dress for the evening. She was attending a dinner at Maxim's in Paris where she currently resided – a dinner in honor of Fergie, the Duchess of York. Donnice, an international socialite, was a favorite of the British Royals and other various and sundry Euro-trash.

Her girl had laid out a smashing one-shouldered emerald green sheath with a rhinestone buckle atop the shoulder to cinch the chiffon cascading down the back of the gown. Donnice decided she would wear her tiara, the Macmillan family tiara, damn them, and she would upstage the duchess. After all, she was a princess!

CHAPTER TEN

The Appointment

*B*onita had kept track of all her *Johns* during her thirty-year tenure with Enrique Dubre. She remembered each and every one of them. Some were gentlemanly, others a little rough around the edges, but all had been kind and good to her. Bonita had never had anyone who wanted really kinky sex and she had never been abused or beaten by any of her clients as some of Enrique's other *girls* had been. Of course, Bonita was Enrique's highest-priced call girl, so he was unusually careful about the men he sent to her.

Bonita had not reacted when Raven mentioned Dr. Kamlash Vyas, but she knew she would be able to get an appointment with the famed surgeon. After all, she had "known" him intimately many years before. She recalled the young Indian medical student who was so shy and a virgin. A group of his friends had put up a great deal of money for students – a thousand dollars! – to have Kam, as they called him, lose his virginity. Enrique had sent the young medical student to Bonita, who at the time, wasn't a great deal older than Kam. The medical student and Bonita had talked at length and then she had very gently freed the young man from what his friends told him was an unusual ffate, his virginity

Kam had come to see Bonita only one other time several years later when he was a doctor and could afford her fee. He told her how much their encounter meant to him and kindnesss and gentleness with him as he was so shy and had absolutely no idea what to do. On his second visit, Kam had paid the thousand-dollars merely to talk to Bonita- he did not require her services. Bonita had been deeply touched. Bonita picked up her phone and dialed the surgeon's number.

"I'd like to speak to Dr. Vyas, please," Bonita said to the answering receptionist.

"The doctor is not available. I'll be happy to take your name and number, but I assure you, Dr. Vyas is quite busy and it may be some time before he is able to return your call. Is there some way I may help you?"

"Yes, I want to make an appointment to have extensive plastic surgery done."

"Oh, an appointment. Well, I can handle that for you. Dr. Vyas doesn't schedule appointments. The bad news is that we're all booked through 2010."

"Is Dr. Vyas in the office now?"

"Yes, he is, but he's unable to come to the phone. Now if you'll simply give me your name and phone number."

"Is the doctor somewhere where you can speak to him?"

"He's in consultation with a patient who's having surgery in a few days."

"Could you be a dear and just buzz him and tell him Bonita's on the line?"

"He doesn't like to be disturbed when he's in consultation with a patient."

"I can assure you he won't mind. Please buzz him and tell him it's Bonita."

"Bonita, he's going to be very upset with me if I do that," the receptionist responded.

"I promise you this, young lady, if he finds out that I called and you didn't buzz him, he's going to be even more upset with you."

"Dr. Vyas here. Yes?"

"Dr. Vyas, I'm sorry to disturb you, but there's woman who says she must speak to you about an appointment."

"Sherry, I don't handle appointments. What is the meaning of this?"

"She said you'd be upset if I didn't buzz you. Her name is Bonita."

"Bonita?"

"That's what she said, Doctor."

"Tell her I'll be right there." Turning to his patient, he said, "Excuse me, Mrs. Jacoy. I have an emergency phone call. I'll be right back with you."

Dr. Vyas left his office and went to the front desk. He took the phone from the receptionist

"Bonita, how are you?"

"Hello, Kam. I'm well, thank you, but gravity is winning. I've lost a great deal of weight and I need your services as soon as possible."

"I can't imagine that you would ever need my services, Bonita. You are such a beautiful woman."

Sherry couldn't believe her ears. Not only was Dr. Vyas not upset with her, he was

telling this Bonita woman how beautiful she was.

"We haven't seen each other for years, Kam. Believe me, I need your services."

"Where are you?"

"On the East Coast, but you tell me when you can see me and I'll be there."

"How about next week?"

The receptionist interrupted, "Dr. Vyas, you can't see her next week. You're completely booked."

"Shush!" Vyas directed to Sherry. "Let's say Wednesday morning at nine o'clock in my office."

"That will be fine, Kam. Thank you so much."

"Not at all. I'm so looking forward to seeing you again, Bonita. I'm going to turn you over to Sherry now and she'll give you all the information you need. I hate to run, but I was in the midst of a consultation and I don't want to leave my patient waiting."

"I understand, Kam, and I'll see you Wednesday."

"It's a date, Bonita. I can hardly wait 'til Wednesday." The doctor gave the receiver to Sherry and said, "Book Bonita for nine o'clock Wednesday morning."

"You already have a nine for Wednesday."

"Then change whoever it is to another day."

"Dr. Vyas, you don't have any time another day. You're completely booked."

"I operate; you schedule. Figure something out, but Bonita has an appointment here Wednesday at nine o'clock in the morning."

"And what is her last name?"

"I have no idea. Just Bonita. That's enough," and he walked back to his office.

Sherry set about figuring how she was going to manipulate patients so Bonita could have her appointment, which the good doctor had left no doubt about.

Bonita called Raven and told her to make reservations for the entire entourage in Los Angeles.

"We'll leave Monday. My appointment with Dr. Vyas is for Wednesday morning at nine. I want to have a day to recover before I see him."

Raven smiled. She didn't know how Bonita had done it and she wasn't about to ask her, but she'd never doubted Mrs. Roberts would get what she wanted.

"I'll take care of it right away." "You come too, dear."

"Let me check on how things are with dad and then I'll let you know." "Suites for everyone Raven or one large suite for all of us. Perhaps a penthouse suite?"

"I love it, but I've stayed there many time. I'd like a change."

"I'll get right on it."

"And Raven, I'll need some clothes. None of mine fit anymore." "Right."

Raven made the hotel and plane reservations, called New York to have haut couture clothing Fed-exed over-night to Spencer and then spoke with her father. After only a few minutes, she knew she would not be going to Los Angeles. After all, that's where her mother and Alphonso were living. Her father seemed so "Down in the dumps" that Raven didn't mention anything at all about Bonita's invitation to him.

Hannah, Felice, Javiar and Bryan would be accompanying Bonita. Raven would stay at Villagio to run things there and Bonita would communicate with her via e-mail. When Bonita had not been exercising, she had through Raven's tutelage, mastered the computer and could surf the net with experienced hackers.

During her long recuperation, Hannah would be on hand to care for her while Felice and Javiar prepared her nutritional meals. Bryan would put together a mild exercise program for her as she entered recovery periods through possibly many bouts of surgery.

Donnice's investigators took note of the mass exodus from Villagio when Bryan drove the Rolls to the front door. He and Javiar loaded the over-sized trunk with luggage for five people. Felice got in the front seat and Hannah and Javiar slid into the back. Bonita, looking trim in a loose, black jump-suit, a black turban, and Jackie O sunglasses emerged last and settled in the back seat. At least, the investigators thought it might be Bonita. She certainly didn't resemble the woman they'd been tailing for lo these many years, but there was no on else it could be. The lady clad in black had to be Bonita Roberts and she must have lost two hundred pounds.

The Rolls pulled out of the Villagio driveway and headed for the Spencer Airport where Raven had arranged a private chartered jet to take Bonita & Company to Beverly Hills. A limousine in Los Angeles would transport the entourage to the Beverly Hilton penthouse suite with its gourmet kitchen, five bedrooms, six baths, expansive living room, library, formal dining room, exercise room, and full sized terrace. Bryan had advised Raven of his requirements for the exercise room and the staff at the hotel had made it happen. A hotel masseuse had been notified that she would be required in the suite frequently.

Raven had made arrangements for rental cars – one for Felice and Javiar to use for their grocery shopping and one for Bryan to drive Bonita to and from her appointments with Dr. Vyas.

Wednesday morning, Bonita left the suite and descended to the third level-parking garage in the suite's private elevator. She was helped into the rental car by Bryan and headed to her first appointment with Dr. Vyas.

"Good morning, Bonita. It's so good to see you," Kamlash Vyas said as he rose from his desk and crossed to Bonita and gave her a big hug. "Why you look fantastic! What is this about needing all kinds of surgery?"

"It's wonderful to see you again too, Kam. Believe me, the clothing conceals a myriad of sagging flesh."

"You certainly could have fooled me. The face may need a few tweaks and tucks, but the body looks marvelous! Do have a seat and tell me what this is all about."

"Thank you, Kam. Several years ago, I left my profession. I married Joshua Roberts of Roberts' Publishing. We moved to South

Carolina and I began to pack on the pounds. After Joshua passed away (and here Bonita actually touched a tissue to her eyes as if she had ever cared about old Joshua after his stroke, or perhaps even before it) I moved to Tennessee and probably gained another twenty-five. There was some unpleasantness about a year ago and I took to my bed. I guess I was in the depths of depression, but I got up very little and I had no appetite. I hardly ate at all. Finally, when the dismal clouds dispersed, I found myself weighing less than half of what I once did and the elasticity isn't what it used to be. I have sagging skin everywhere. I have, however, been working with two nutritionists and a personal trainer trying to get some muscle tone back. I think I'm going to need a great deal of your expertise, Kam. I want the flabby skin all over my body removed and I want a neck, chin, and face lift."

"Why don't I show you to an examining room and then we'll take a look and afterwards we'll talk about possible procedures and corrections. How does that suit you?"

"Perfect," responded Bonita.

Once the nurse closed the door, Bonita removed her clothing and sat on the examining table in a paper top and a *blanket* over her lower region. Dr. Vyas and his nurse tapped on the door and entered. The doctor performed a thorough and complete examination of Bonita in the sitting, standing, and prostrate positions front and back. During all this, he took measurements and called out numbers to his nurse. Finally after an hour, he said, "All right, Bonita, you get dressed and come back into my office and we'll talk."

When Bonita was back in the doctor's office and seated, he said, "Bonita, we're going to need six to eight months and probably five or six surgeries to take care of the excess skin. You need a complete body lift."

"Six to eight months and five to six surgeries are acceptable, Kam. When do we start?"

"First is a tummy tuck. On the operating table, I'll prop you into a sitting position and pull all the skin down toward your groin. I'll remove the skin and tighten your abdominal muscles. You'll have what we call the bikini scar. In other words, a bikini bottom will cover it."

"I'm not sure I'll be wearing a bikini, Kam. What is the recovery time for the tuck?"

"Six weeks minimum. Once you're back on your feet after that major surgery, I'll do your legs. You'll have scars in the groin and behind the knees, but they'll fade and be hardly noticeable. All the excess skin on your legs will be removed. Your exercise regimen has paid off – you have excellent muscle tone and once we remove the skin, your legs should look like they did when you were in your thirties."

"Wonderful! Next?"

"About a month after the leg surgery, I'll do your arms. Scars will be in the armpit and inside your elbows and once again will fade. A month after that, we'll perform two procedures. I'll lift your derriere and take care of the remaining excess skin on your back and at your waist. That'll take another minimum six-week recovery period. Unfortunately, the scars will be in the waistline so the bikini may be out then."

"That's not a problem. I'm not interested in wearing a bikini, Kam."

"But you'll look ravishing in a one-piece suit."

"Good! And then?"

"Then I'll reduce the breasts and excess skin, and lift them. You'll never have to wear a bra again!"

"I've always had large breasts and I've always had to wear a bra."

"You'll still have large breasts, but won't need a bra. When I tighten the muscles underlying your breasts, they'll look like they did when you were twenty."

"Kam, you are truly amazing!"

"Not at all. I merely return God's creatures to their former youth and beauty. It's important though that all during these procedures you neither gain or lose any weight and the same is true after we finish everything."

"I can do that. I'm never going to be obese again!"

"Good. Last, we'll life the area above the breasts and perform the face and neck lift. You have excellent bone structure and still a great deal of elasticity in your skin. I predict when we're finished, you'll appear to be in your late thirties."

"That's incredible, Kam. I'm fifty-eight! And I don't tell that to just anyone."

"I'm going to take twenty years away, Bonita. That's not too long after we first met, is it? In eight months at the outside, you'll be able to pass for thirty-eight. No one will believe you if you tell them you're fifty-eight," Kam said with a smile.

"When do we start?"

"I can perform the first procedure Monday at eight in the morning. You'll need to be here at six for prepping. Is that a problem?"

"Not at all."

"My nurse will give you all the instructions for pre-op. You'll stay here for two nights following the tummy tuck procedure and have twenty-four hour care."

"That sounds fine, Kam, and I want you to know how much I appreciate your taking the time to see me. I've heard about your wonderful surgeries and your sterling reputation and I know you were booked through 2008. Thank you."

"I seem to remember your doing something for me once."

"Yes, and I charged you, so I'm not expecting any favors of the monetary kind."

"Would you like to discuss the cost?"

"Not especially. I want everything done."

"All right then. You can speak to my book keeper at the reception desk and because you want no favors, I do require a payment up front."

"Of course. I'll take care of it on my way out," Bonita said as she stood.

"I'll see you Monday bright and early, Bonita."

"And it'll be my pleasure, Kam."

They said their good-byes and Bonita went into the reception area where she received her written instructions and where she wrote a check for $25,000 toward her future procedures. Bonita returned to the Beverly Hilton happier than she'd been in years. Her complete make-over was about to begin.

CHAPTER ELEVEN

Ralph, Maggie, And Luzanne

*H*e had inherited his daddy's investment banking firm after working with his father for fifteen years until daddy first retired and secondly passed away. Ralph Reddington was a large man. He was dull, uninteresting, with a pasty complexion, kinky black eyebrows, dishwater colored eyes, and rather large red lips. Brad Pitt he was not, but he had a shit pile of money.

Ralph had married Maggie whom he met his second day at Yale. They dated all through college and one week after graduating in Connecticut, they were wed in San Francisco, California, Maggie's hometown. They honeymooned in Venice and set up housekeeping in Wilmington where daddy's and now Ralph's firm was located. Over the next several years, they had four children, two boys and two girls.

Maggie had everything money could buy, but she was an unhappy person. She hated the East Coast and everything Southern. She didn't seem to fit in with the tight-assed East Coast types and had a difficult time making friends with the syrupy sweet Southern women who seemed to have two first names, so she spent her days riding herd on her children with little or no help from Ralph. Ralph had suggested several times that they hire a nanny or governess, but the only ones available were Mexican and Maggie didn't speak Spanish, so she had nixed that idea. Finally, after years of desperation, Maggie took to the bottle. By the time the children were pubescent, on the rare occasions Ralph returned from the office when anyone was awake, he found Maggie either drunk or passed out.

Ralph then hired maids and nannies and tried to get Maggie to seek help, but she was in denial and said she could control her drinking if only Ralph would spend more time at home. He'd promise that he would and he's say he was going to spend evenings and weekends with her and the children, but after a few weeks he was always back to coming home late, missing dinners, and was either at the office all during the week and/or playing golf with perspective clients on the weekends. When Ralph kept his word and spent time at home, Maggie controlled her drinking, but when he jumped back onto his workaholic bandwagon, Maggie fell off of hers with a bang!

Eventually, Ralph thought, he had all avenues available to help Maggie. He filed for divorce and with his money and his ability to hire a veritable staff of the best attorneys, he not only divorced Maggie, but he also paid her a very small settlement considering his immense wealth, and he got custody of the children.

The four teenagers were then reared by a series of nannies and fed by a series of cooks and their rooms were cleaned by a series of maids. Ralph continued to work and to make money, money, money! His children had every luxury, every electronic device, a swimming pool, a tennis court, stables in which resided thoroughbred horses, the latest clothing, a playroom that boggled the mind and an absentee father. The environment was perfect for one or more of them to develop severe mental problems. Additionally, they could only see their mother at their home and only once a month for a few hours. Maggie, by court order, had to be accompanied by a chaperone and could never visit with her children alone. Ralph's attorneys had managed to have Maggie declared unfit.

While Maggie and Ralph were students at Yale, Luzanne (rhymes with Suzanne) was a student at UCLA. Majoring in Italian, Luzanne was selected to spend her junior year abroad. Within a few days of her arrival in Rome, Luzanne impulsively married a dashing Italian who swept her off her feet. Nine months and one day after the wedding, their son Phillipe was born. Luzanne and Guido were ecstatic however, Luzanne's state of euphoria was short-lived. Once she was no longer pregnant, Guido became an absolute tyrant. He screamed and yelled if anything in the tiny house they rented was out of place. He expected to sit and have Luzanne wait on him. He complained about her horrible cooking. He ridiculed her for still being fat after having the baby. He told her she was lazy for not exercising and getting her figure back.

Luzanne was overwhelmed. She was taking care of a baby, nursing him, getting up in the middle of the night. and Guido expected her to be svelte already when the baby was only eight weeks old. Also, he wanted the house to be immaculate, for her to have a three or four course meal ready when he came home each evening, and then he expected her to step and fetch for him until he was ready for bed at which time he demanded sex. At that time, she was supposed to transform herself from Guido's personal maid into a sex siren in a lovely negligee who was ready to make love half the night. Guido became very angry when she left him during the night to soothe the crying baby or when she fell into bed exhausted and told him she was too tired to make love.

"What's the matter with you, Luzanne? You were hot to trot before our marriage. You don't love Guido anymore?"

"I love you, Guido. I'm tired. I've cleaned, cooked, and taken care of the baby all day. I was up half of last night with him. I'm just too tired to make love tonight."

"You're too tired every night. What did you clean? This whole house is a mess. There're bottles in the kitchen, dirty baby clothes in the bathroom, newspapers on the coffee table – *you call this house clean?* As for cooking, that slop you served me tonight wasn't fit for a pig." With that he stomped out of the bedroom and slammed the door, which in turn woke up Phillipe.

Luzanne staggered to her feet to shush the crying baby as she heard Guido bang the front door. This had happened before. He was probably on his way to the neighborhood trattoria. He'd drink and then come home and demand sex. There would be no telling him she was tired then. He wouldn't take no for an answer. She had to get out of this situation.

When Phillipe was six months old, Luzanne called her mother in Valencia, California. Luzanne's father had disappeared when she was two. She barely remembered him. Her mother had never been much help to her financially or emotionally, but Luzanne didn't know where else to turn. She somehow convinced her mother to wire her enough money to get a flight to California. After she went to Western Union and got the money, Luzanne packed two small bags, one for her and one for the baby, and called a cab for the airport. She didn't clean the house before she left nor did she wash the breakfast dishes. She did pick up a single cup and throw it into the sink and she smiled as she heard the cheap china break. She didn't lock the house and she didn't leave Guido a note.

The next time Guido heard from her divorce papers were served oh him. He refused to give Luzanne a divorce and demanded his son back. She didn't realize how important a son is to an Italian male.

Luzanne was a beautiful honey-blonde with long flowing hair and emerald green eyes. She also possessed a modicum of acting talent that she had displayed on stage while a scholarship student at UCLA. Once back at her mother's she got a night job as a cocktail waitress and made money pretty quickly, no doubt because of her good looks. Soon she and Phillipe moved into an efficiency apartment and Luzanne hired babysitters to stay with the child while she continued to work nights.

Once she got enough money together, the pretty blonde went to an expensive professional photographer, got a few head shots made and starting going to auditions during the day. Almost immediately, she got signed for a Tidy Bowl commercial; not the glamorous role she craved, but any commercial would help pay the bills. Tidy Bowl was followed by Purina Dog food, Mr. Clean, and Oreck vacuum cleaner ads. Pretty soon, Luzanne was able to move young Phillipe and herself into a one-bedroom apartment in a better part of town and miles away from the cheesy efficiency she'd had in the Valley. Luzanne and her young son now lived in LA – close to the action.

As luck often works for beautiful folk, Luzanne, through promotional parties, and a little help from her agent, plus her gift of guile, (the woman could talk buzzards off of roadkill) she met some of Hollywood's leading men and was seen on the arms of George Clooney, Matt Damon and Ben Afleck and she was cast in a B movie and then another. Her second movie role took her to India. Luzanne took Phillipe with her. They took a weekend trip to Nepal and at a temple, monks spotted Phillipe, a beautiful blonde, blue-eyed child. The monks gathered around him and admired him, after which they informed Luzanne that her Italian-American son was the reincarnation of an earlier Dahli Llama and was destined to become the new Llama at the age of twenty. Luzanne thought that was all a crock, but she was thrilled to receive so much attention and for Phillipe to be in the limelight too.

Upon her return to the United States after being on location in India, Luzanne attended a studio gala where she met a rather dull gentleman by the name of Ralph Reddington, who was in LA on business. She wouldn't have given him a second glance under ordinary circumstances if her agent hadn't told her Ralph was an investment banker, often an "Angel" (the name in the trade for producers who provide the money) for movies, worth millions and millions of dollars and recently divorced.

Luzanne originally feigned interest in Ralph with the idea of convincing him to produce a movie with her in the starring role. She soon realized that Ralph loved her attention. Perhaps there was more potential there than a movie. Ralph began to call Luzanne, to make frequent trips to California, to take her to the best restaurants where everyone seemed to know him, to buy her expensive gifts from the big three Harry Winston's, Cartier's, and Tiffany's, and to confide in her about his horrid ex-wife and his love for his four children of whom he had custody.

Luzanne commiserated with him as she told him of her trials and tribulations as a single parent and how much she loved children. Ralph suggested that she might want to meet his four teenagers. Luzanne said she would be delighted to meet them and was thrilled that Ralph would ask. She made plans immediately to travel with Ralph to Wilmington for a weekend. The teenagers loved Luzanne immediately and she took to them like black on tar or at least that was the impression she gave. Ralph met Luzanne's son Phillipe upon his return to LA, and the wedding was set for early June.

Luzanne and Phillipe were to move to Ralph's elaborate Wilmington estate and to reside with Ralph, the four teenagers, Justin, Phillip, Mindy, and Leslie, Cossack, a one-hundred-pound German Shepherd, Emilia, the Russian housekeeper, Paula (pronounced Pa-U-la), the Hungarian cook, and Maureen, Ralph's personal live-in assistant. Everything appeared to be perfect!

It was a totally new world for Luzanne with the luncheons, teas, galas, sweet tea, sweet milk, as opposed to buttermilk, the colloquialisms such as a "Mess" of collard greens, "Yonder" – wherever that was, "Directly" as in "I'll be back directly," "By and by," – whenever that was, "Right near," and a "Right fer piece," grits, sliced tomatoes with breakfast, "Bless her/his/ or your heart," and the men and women with two names or the women with men's names.

There's a reason for the names in the South. Those not from "God's Country" find it difficult to understand why Southerners name their offspring Billy Bob, Jimmy Joe, Myrtle Sue and Martha Lou. Most often it has to do with heritage. Southerners are very much into family and heritage. In the case of Billy Bob, his daddy's name is probably William and one of his grandfathers either maternal or paternal, was or is named Robert. Now, it would be confusing to have two Williams or two Roberts in the same family, because in the South, families get together all the time for sumptuous dinners, picnics, cookouts, christenings, weddings, first Communions, engagement parties, anniversaries, birthdays, Memorial Day, Fourth of July, Labor Day, Thanksgiving, Christmas, Easter, and even Ground Hog's Day. Southerners will use any excuse to fry up the chicken, make mounds of sweet and sour potato salad, and deviled eggs by the dozens. Therefore; William Robert is shortened to Billy Bob so there won't be any confusion at all those family get-togethers.

Martha Lou may be named for two aunts, but again two Marthas or two Lous would cause problems, so the little girl is dubbed Martha Lou, sometimes hyphenated, sometimes not, and she is addressed by both names. Simple, isn't it? And not so stupid when one thinks about it.

Outsiders, or "come-heres" as they are called in the South, also wonder about females having names like Potter, Hunter, Harper, Paxon, Bailey and the like. There's an excellent explanation for this practice too. Again, remember that the family and heritage are very important in the South. Often a Southern mother will convince her husband to allow her to give her maiden name as the first name for a female child especially if the first child was male and is a junior. This is especially prevalent when the mother is the last of her line and she has no brothers to carry on her proud family name. A Southern mother may also insist upon this when she and her husband produce one girl baby after another with no boys in sight.

Of course, often a second son in a Southern family will have momma's maiden name as his middle name. Rest assured, however, that the true Southern female will make sure her maiden name reaches into at least one generation beyond her – one way or another.

Luzanne had trouble when acquaintances she made in Wilmington referred to someone as a redneck, a good ol'boy, or po' white trash. She had no idea what the distinctions between the three were, but obviously the natives did. And all of them seemed to be related. Before telling a story, the family tree had to be climbed up one side and down the other. Luzanne was frequently lost before the actual story ever left the lips of the Southern belle who was telling it. The women in Wilmington called everyone they met either Honey, Darlin' or Shugah and they made sausage gravy for breakfast and homemade biscuits like they were going out of style. Luzanne didn't understand why they didn't all weigh three hundred pounds.

The California gal had a bit of adjusting to do; however Ralph did also, as the first thing Luzanne said after she had unpacked her suitcase was that they couldn't have a Phillipe and a Phillip in the same household.

"Why not? Those are their names."

"It'll be confusing because now there are four of your children and only one of mine. I think Phillipe should be able to keep his name, but your Phillip could simply pick another name that he likes and we'll call him that. It's not like we're going to legally change his name or anything."

"That has to be one of the dumbest ideas I've ever heard, Luzanne."

"I see, married five weeks and suddenly, I'm dumb."

" I don't mean you're dumb. The idea just seems ridiculous to me. Phillipe and Phillip are not the same names, close but not the same."

"Well then let's ask Phillip. Maybe he'd like another name. What do you think?"

Luzanne crossed to Ralph and put her arms around his neck and said, "It's really important to me, Ralphie. Can't you do this one little thing for me?"

"I can't see why it's so important, but if it will make you happy, we can ask Phillip, but we'll only do it if he agrees, all right?"

"Okay."

After dinner, Luzanne and Ralph asked Phillip if he would step into Ralph's study with them. When they were all seated, Ralph said, "Phillip, Luzanne has an idea. Your name and Phillipe's are pretty close and she thinks it might be confusing so she wondered if you might like to pick another name that you'd like to be called."

"What? You want me to change my name?"

"No," answered Luzanne, "Not change it, merely pick another name to be called by. Your name would still be Phillip, but we wouldn't call you that."

"Cool. Let's see. I want my name to be. . . hmmm. . .Night!"

"Knight? Like Sir Knight?" asked Ralph.

"No, Night. As in opposite of day."

"Well, that's a silly name," countered Ralph.

"I don't think it's silly at all. Why did you pick Night?" asked Luzanne.

"I like night. It's dark, spooky, and cool things happen at night. It's so much better than day. That's it. My new name is Night. Can I go tell the rest of the gang?"

"I guess, but won't it be strange to say 'Good night, Night?'" asked Ralph.

"Oh, dad, now you're being silly!" *Night* said as he ran out of the study yelling, "Hey, guys, guess what? I have a new name. From now on, call me Night."

"I think that went very well, don't you, Ralph?" Luzanne asked.

"Night. Where in the hell did he come up with a name like Night? I can see my clients now when I tell them I have a child named Night."

"Don't tell them then. Your son's name is still Phillip for real and how many times do you tell your clients your children's names?"

"You do have a point."

Phillip became Night and Philippe remained Phillipe. Luzanne had won the first of many battles, but would she win the war?

CHAPTER TWELVE

Miss Twyla

*E*ven with Donnice's seemingly unlimited supply of money, she would have depleted it rather quickly if her private detectives followed Bonita 24/7 so, it was indeed fortunate for her that she had an ace in the hole. That ace was named Miss Twyla, executive secretary at Roberts' Publishing in New York City. Miss Twyla had worked for Roberts' Publishing since she was eighteen years of age, however no one had the slightest idea how old she was at present. Twyla had been hired by Joshua Roberts himself when he first went into business and she had watched and participated in Roberts' Publishing metamorphosis from a fledging company into one of the largest and most prestigious publishing companies in the world.

For most of the time she was employed by Joshua, she and her boss had engaged in a torrid affair. Joshua was extremely generous with his paramour. He gave her expensive gifts, paid the rent on her apartment in the lower East side, gave her a generous allowance in addition to her salary and took her to the finest dining establishments in *Gotham*. Once he met Bonita, however, he no longer sought Twyla's company although he still paid for everything. Joshua told his secretary/lover about Bonita, as he wanted to remain on friendly terms with his long-time employee. Twyla seemed to take Joshua's news well, but her heart was broken and she was never the same again.

When Joshua married Bonita and retired, Twyla figured her days at Roberts' Publishing were over, but Joshua made sure her position was left intact. Twyla had been Joshua's personal assistant and executive secretary, so when he was no longer there, she was left with little to do. She sat at her desk everyday outside Joshua's empty office. She made coffee in the morning, put fresh flowers on her boss' empty desk and ate lunch in the executive dining room each day.

Miss Twyla was a creature of habit. She rose every morning at six, showered, brushed her teeth, combed her hair and then fed her two cats, Tristam and Isolde. Then she sat at her small table in her kitchen and ate her two pieces of butter less wheat toast with unsweetened strawberry jam and her cup of green tea. After rinsing the dishes, Miss Twyla retired to the bedroom and dressed. She wore expensive tailored suits every day with soft crepe blouses that tied at a bow at the neck. Her wardrobe included matching shoes and purses for each of her outfits. Once she had put on her shoes, she applied peach foundation, ruby red lipstick, a tiny bit of blue or green shadow, and then brushed on translucent powder. Even at her advanced age, Miss Twyla was an attractive woman. She was five feet seven inches tall and weighed about one hundred seventeen pounds. Although not voluptuous, she was quite trim and stylish looking. Her rich brown hair had a few natural streaks of gray and her green eyes that Joshua had always referred to as "Cat's eyes," were still quite clear.

After dressing, Miss Twyla opened her door, picked up her newspaper, and left for work. A car provided by Roberts' Publishing waited for her outside the apartment building and she rode to work in style. At the end of each workday, the car returned her to her apartment. On Mondays, after riding home, Miss Twyla went into her apartment and collected suits to be dry-cleaned and walked two blocks to the drycleaner who had taken care of her clothes for decades. She dropped off her clothes to be cleaned and picked up those from the prior week and walked back home.

Once back home, she fed the cats, then removed her office attire, put on a robe and slippers, removed her make-up and micro waved a Lean Cuisine meal. She ate at the little table and then watched television for a few hours before retiring.

On Tuesday evenings, she walked to the grocer, a block in the other direction from the dry cleaners, and bought her provisions for the week. Wednesdays, she walked to the drug store. a few blocks beyond the grocer's, and purchased any necessities there or had her prescription for cholesterol medicine filled once a month.

Thursdays, she indulged herself by having the driver take her to Bloomingdale's, Macy's or a new boutique she had learned about and leave her there. She shopped and looked around the stores sometimes purchasing and sometimes not and then treated herself to a light dinner at the Russian Tea Room after which she took a taxi back to her apartment where she always apologized to Tristam and Isolde for feeding them late. On Fridays, after returning home, she fed the cats, changed into casual clothing and walked three blocks to the neighborhood cinema and watched the latest art movie featured there. Ingemar Bergmann was her favorite director and she had seen most of his artsy films numerous times. Her schedule never changed unless she was sick or incapacitated for some reason and that occurred hardly ever.

When Miss Twyla had the opportunity she had her knitting needles in hand. Tristam and Isolde were Persian cats and shed profusely. On a daily basis, their owner collected their precious fur and stored it in a cloth bag. Usually after six months she had collected enough fur to send away to a company who spun the cat fur into yarn. Miss Twyla knitted exclusively with the cat fur yarn. She made hats, very ugly hats, and once a month she delivered them to a store in the neighborhood operated by the local chapter of the SPCA.

Not a single one of her hats had ever sold at the store, but the SPCA volunteers didn't want Miss Twyla to know that so on the second Tuesday evening of each month prior to her grocery-buying when Miss Twyla took her ugly hats to the store, volunteers made sure the hats from the previous month were removed or sometimes they left only one. Miss Twyla always checked the hat inventory and was delighted that her cat fur hats *sold* so well. Actually, the volunteers gave the hats to Good Will every few months. It was a good arrangement for everyone. Miss Twyla felt she was doing a good deed; the volunteers made her happy by hiding or giving away the hats as Miss Twyla also wrote generous checks to the SPCA every few months; Good Will was happy as they distributed the hats to young children in the tenements of the city; and the children were happy to have them because even though the hats were ugly and definitely not a fashion statement, they were warm.

Miss Twyla knitted when she watched television, when she sat in the chauffeured car on the way to and from work, and while her hair was being set at her weekly Sassoon appointment. She also spent a great part of her workday knitting. Miss Twyla was almost never seen without her knitting satchel, her needles and her cat fur yarn.

On the weekends, she cleaned her small apartment, gave the litter box an extra good cleaning, its third one each week, and then put collars and leashes on Tristam and Isolde and took them on a thirty-block walk. Miss Twyla had leash-trained the cats when they were kittens and they were always quite excited about their Saturday walk. She always received a lot of looks, stares, and questions from passers-by when she walked the kitties. After the walk, Miss Twyla brushed the cats and then immersed herself in a long soak in a bubble bath. At precisely two o'clock every Saturday she left her apartment and walked six blocks to one of the many Vidal Sassoon salons in New York City, and had a facial, a massage, her hair shampooed, blown dry, and set, followed by a manicure and pedicure. She left the salon by six and walked home, called in an order to a nearby Chinese restaurant, changed into to her robe and slippers and poured herself a glass of wine, but she never had more than one. By about the time she finished her wine, the Chinese deliveryman was at her door. She paid him and then removed the food from the cartons and put it on a china plate that she placed on her kitchen table set with sterling silver, crystal, and a silver chandelier complete with lit candles. She ate, cleared the table, washed her dishes and retired to her bedroom where she removed her vibrator from a dresser drawer and proceeded to pleasure herself for several hours. On Sundays, Miss Twyla slept in and didn't arise until eight unless the cats created a big ruckus demanding their breakfast they were accustomed to eating at a little after six. Miss Twyla followed her same routine as on weekdays except she retrieved the Sunday paper and placed it on the hall table and then left to walk to church. She attended a Presbyterian church several blocks away. After the services, she didn't attend the coffee reception, spoke to no one, never shook hands with the pastor and had done no more than nod to any of the other parishioners. She walked home, undressed, ate a tuna sandwich for lunch, read the New York Times, worked the crossword puzzle using her Mont Blanc pen, watched a movie on the Lifetime channel, ate her dinner, decided what she would wear the work the next day and got ready for bed.

The executive secretary had no family as her parents had passed away long ago and she was an only child. She also had no friends as she had dedicated her life to her position at Roberts' Publishing and to Joshua until his defection into Bonita's arms and his subsequent death. Her phone never rang unless it was a telemarketer or a wrong number and she made no calls from it except to order her weekly Chinese dinner.

At work, Miss Twyla did little. Some old Roberts' clients still came to see her when they were in the city and many of them brought her gifts. Occasionally, one of the other executive secretaries who was very busy would ask her to help with typing or copying something but not often as Twyla had never moved into the computer age. Her Selectric typewriter still sat on her desk.

Upon Joshua's death, Twyla had known for sure her employment at Roberts' Publishing was coming to an end. To her surprise, her ex-boss and ex-lover had provided for her in his will. She was to remain in her position for as long as she wished. Robert's Publishing would continue to pay her rent, provide her with an allowance and pay her salary. Additionally, Joshua left her a sizeable amount of cash.

So Miss Twyla, as she was called by everyone, continued at Roberts' Publishing doing practically nothing; however, because she was in the office everyday, she managed to stay abreast of the happenings. She paid particular attention to any contact Bonita made with the company and as soon as she found out what Bonita was requesting, she called Donnice at the speed of light. Miss Twyla also had access to the company books and checked rather frequently to see if there had been any unusual expenditure on Bonita's behalf. She was quite thrilled to call Donnice and tell her of a rather large check made out to a Dr. Vyas, a plastic surgeon in Beverly Hills. And Donnice was quite thrilled to receive the news. She contacted her private detectives immediately and told them to find out where Vyas' office was and to watch for Bonita's visits there.

CHAPTER THIRTEEN

Bonita Goes "Under The Knife"

*A*nd so Bonita "went under the knife" as Southerners always refer to surgery of any kind. It sounds so much more dramatic, serious, and life threatening than just the simple word *surgery*. She was "On the table" for four and one-half hours while Dr. Vyas suctioned out several ounces of fat - only ounces as Bonita had lost so much weight. The fat went into a clear jar. Human fat looks for all the world exactly like chicken fat. As humans are in no way related to chickens, fat must be the same in all of God's creatures – ugly, yucky, yellow slime in its raw, uncooked state. While Bonita was "Under the knife," Bryan and Hannah sat in the private waiting room. Hannah was quite nervous and extremely worried about *Miz Bonita*. Bryan was talking a blue streak in an attempt to ease her anxiety.

"So, Hannah, aren't you excited about how *Sugarbritches* is going to look after this surgery?"

"I 'spect you's referrin' to Miz Roberts?" Hannah asked.

"I am."

"How come you call her all them names? That ain't very respectful, you know. She's your boss lady."

"Hannah, she loves for me to call her those names. Besides I can get away with it."

"I noticed that, but nobody else ever called her any of them cutesy names," Hannah huffed.

"It's because I'm non-threatening to her, Hannah."

"What does that mean?"

"I'm not into women, Hannah. I mean I like women. I like their clothes, their shoes, and their make-up. I love to talk to them about fabrics, decorating, hair-styles, and all that, but I don't plan on marrying a woman or making love to one."

"Hesh your mouth, boy. Don't be talkin' to me 'bout makin' love. I don't want to hear any that trash."

"I'm sorry. I didn't mean to offend you. I was trying to help you understand why Mrs. Mrs. Roberts doesn't get upset with me when I call her names."

"What does that have to do with makin' love to women?"

"I'm gay, Hannah. Women are not threatened by gay men."

"You mean you happy all the time?"

"No, I mean I like men, not women."

"O Lawdy, you one of them queers?"

"Hannah, *queer* is a horrid word. Men who like other men prefer to be referred to as homosexuals or gay men, not as queers. That's so vulgar!"

"Yeah? Well what them queers do is vulgar too!"

"Now how do you know that?" Bryan asked.

"I jest know. Two men in bed together makin' love jest ain't natural. God never intended no such thing to happen as that."

"You have a personal phone line to God, Hannah?"

"No, I ain't, but if I did, I know He'd tell me he don't like no queers."

"Then you don't think God likes me, Hannah?"

"Well, you's likable, so maybe He do, but He sure don't approve of what you doin' and I know that as well as I'm sittin' here."

"All right. I guess we've exhausted that. Tell me why you remain in a subservient position, Hannah."

"You think I don't know what that word means, don't you? I know what it means and I know how to speak properly too, Mr. Homosexual. I talk the way I do because that's what Mrs. Roberts expects of me. She loves the way I slaughter the language and the funny things I say. And I'm not any more subservient than you are, Bryan. I've been taking care of Bonita since she was sixteen years old. She's my baby."

"Hannah, you amaze me. I cannot believe that you affect that Ebonics' speech just to please your employer. You're pretending to be something you're not."

"Take a lesson. Maybe you should do the same thing."

"Then I wouldn't be true to myself or anyone else. And you're not being true to yourself or to Mrs. Roberts either."

"That's my business, isn't it, Bryan?"

"So you must have lived in Spain?"

"Did I say I lived in Spain?" Hannah asked.

"No, but Mrs. Roberts is of Spanish descent and I assume she came to this country from Spain."

"There are more countries than Spain she could have come from being of Spanish descent, you know?"

"Well, of course, but how did you first meet her?"

"That doesn't make any difference. I've been with her since she was sixteen and I'm not subservient. I love her as if she were my own child," Hannah replied.

"But you never take a day off."

"What would I do if I took a day off? I go where I want when I want to go. She provides a car for me if I want to go shopping. She gives me clothes, food, magazines, a color television, a nice room wherever we are, and pays me a handsome salary."

"Do you have any family?"

"Mrs. Roberts is my family."

"What about friends?"

"Of course I have friends, Bryan. Don't you?"

"Many, but when do you ever see yours?"

"When I want to. What is this? Twenty questions about Hannah Browne."

"Hannah Browne. I never knew your last name."

"Because usually people don't ask or need to know the last name of subservient people, Bryan. By the way, what is your last name? Gotcha, didn't I?"

"I guess you did. Wilcox."

"Well," Hannah said extending her hand, "I'm happy to meet you, Bryan Wilcox."

"It's my pleasure, Hannah Browne."

"Now, I want you to hesh up a minit, so I's can concentrate on Miz Bonita."

"How easily you slip back into the jargon, Hannah."

"Comes from lots of practice, now hesh up."

"I think I'll go walk around and stretch my legs a little. Will you be all right by yourself for a little while?"

"O lawsy me, I don't know, but I'll try to hold myself together. 'Course I'll be all right, Bryan. Get on outta here."

After Vyas had suctioned, he sat Bonita up with the help of two nurses as Bonita was out cold, and rolled all the excess skin from under her breasts down to her groin and cut it off in slices resembling the Thanksgiving turkey, albeit it was all white meat. He finished the removal of all the stretched skin that had once covered Bonita's apron of fat that had hung half way down her thighs. Then, he turned his attention to Bonita's previously mammoth thighs. There was quite a bit of crepe-like skin there too. Vyas moved to the lower part of his incision in Bonita's groin and picked up the liposuction canula and removed the residual fat from her thighs. Then he pulled the skin of her upper legs taut and removed the excess.

Bryan had been gone about a half hour. When he returned to the private waiting room, he said to Hannah. "Boy, Vyas must be a magician. There are some *yayboos* downstairs waiting for appointments that look like they could stop Big Ben."

"And what is a *yayboo*?"

"A *yayboo*, Hannah, is a woman who when you look at her body, you say "Yay!" 'cause she's so hot, but then when you look at her face, you go "Boo!" 'cause she's so ugly. There's one down there with a body like Jayne Mansfield, all natural I'm pretty sure, but her face is nasty. She's got these close-set eyes and big glasses on so she looks like a fly looking at you through a Coca-Cola bottle, skinny lips, a lantern jaw and a Neanderthal forehead – she was hit hard with the ugly stick. I mean her face is coyote-ugly. You know what coyote-ugly means, right?"

"No."

"When someone is coyote-ugly and you wake up with them the next morning, you'll gnaw your arm off to keep from waking her up."

"That's ugly! Did you see anyone out there who knows anything about Miz Bonita?"

"Nope. Downstairs, all you see are people waiting and the receptionists. There was a great looking guy down there though. I mean he was like a nine on the hot scale. I can't imagine why he'd be looking into plastic surgery."

"Bryan, calm yourself. Maybe he's the husband or boyfriend of one of the prospective patients and he's not here for himself."

"You're absolutely right, Hannah. That is a possibility and one I didn't even consider. I guess that means he may not be available."

"Bryan, you don't go around trying to pick up men in doctors' offices, do you?"

"I'm not overt about it, but I try to pick up men anywhere I can – not pick them up, but meet them at least."

"Lawsy mercy. I don't want to talk about this anymore."

"You asked."

"It was a brain cramp. Sorry I asked. I don't want to hear nothin' else about it."

"All right, Hannah. Then what shall we talk about?"

"Why don't you read a magazine? Why do we have to talk?"

"I'm trying to help. I know you're nervous about Mrs. Roberts, so I'm trying to keep you occupied by talking and then the time will pass quicker."

"Ain't that sweet? Thank you. Right now, I'd jest like to close these old eyes if that's all right with you."

"Okey-dokey. I'll be as quiet as a church mouse. You meditate."

In the operating room, Dr. Vyas surveyed his work and was quite satisfied with how well the procedure had gone. He began the tedious process of stitching Bonita back together. He was world-renowned for his plastic surgery and he knew the secret was in the minute stitching of which he was capable. He clamped Bonita's surgical opening with four staples and hundreds of tee-ninesy stitches.

He was done at last.

For the last hour and a half of the operation, scrub nurses had wiped the doctor's forehead over fifty times as the perspiration appeared again and again, so complete was the surgeon's concentration. When he tied off the final and the anchoring stitch, he backed away from the operating table and walked out of the sterile area where he removed his optic microscope, his mask, and his surgical gloves. His assistant, Dr. Mustafa, would apply the padding and bandages to Bonita's incision.

Dr. Vyas walked into the private waiting room to the overwrought Hannah and to Bryan, Bonita's personal trainer.

"Is she alive, Doctor?" asked Hannah.

"Of course, she's alive, and she's doing very well. Her bandages are being applied now. Shortly, we'll move her to the recovery room and in about an hour or so, she'll be ready to be moved to the eighth floor of the hospital to a private suite. Everything went perfectly. Mrs. Roberts has a completely flat abdomen and her upper legs look like those of a twenty-year-old."

"How long is she gonna be laid up?" Hannah asked.

"Oh, we'll get her up for a short walk this evening. It'll be painful, but she needs to start moving about. We'll keep her here for two nights and by the time she's ready to leave, she'll be able to walk about – no stairs, however. She will need to rest as she's had major surgery. She's to have no exercise for six weeks, but in another week or so, she'll be able to resume most normal activities. Now, if you'll excuse me, I'm going to retire to my office for a bite to eat. I have another surgery scheduled in forty-five minutes."

As the doctor turned to leave, he extended his hand and said, "It's good to see you again, Hannah."

"It's good to see you too, Kamlash. It's been a long time, but you've done real good."

"Thank you, Hannah."

After the doctor left, Bryan closed his mouth and said, "How do you know him, Hannah?"

"Maybe I had some surgery?"

"Come on, Hannah. How do you know the famous doctor?"

Hannah smiled at Bryan and said with a wink, "Oh, you know how it is, Bryan, we subservients get around."

Hannah stood and picked up her purse and said, "This place is like a factory, ain't it?"

"Exactly like a factory. Shall we go and get a bite to eat and come back in an hour or so to see Sugarbritches?"

"That sounds like a good idea, but I don't want to eat none of them sprouts and berries and nuts and stuff you eat. I wants me some meat loaf, mashed potatoes, gravy, biscuits and turnip greens."

"Then I guess we better go to the cafeteria. I don't think we'll find that fare in the bistros on Rodeo Drive."

"Oh, there's some places on Rodeo Drive that serves soul food, Bryan. You want me to take you to one of'em?"

Bryan extended his arm and Hannah took it.

"You never cease to amaze me, Hannah. So you've spent some time in LA before this trip?"

As they exited the waiting room arm in arm, Hannah said, "As I said afore, us servant folks get around. You gay boys need to take some notes. Stick with me, boy, and I'll show you around this here city of the angels."

CHAPTER FOURTEEN

Is Someone Following Bonita?

B ryan and Hannah drove to the hospital to collect Bonita. She was making rapid progress and was being released to go to the Beverly Hilton to recuperate. Hannah had put pillows and a blanket in the backseat of the rental car and Bryan had purchased a dozen red roses to welcome his boss lady home. Javiar and Felice were anxiously awaiting her return in the Hilton suite and had prepared a light lunch for her to eat upon her arrival and before she rested for the afternoon.

Dr. Vyas rolled Bonita out as Bryan and Hannah exited from the private elevator to the sanctity of the eighth floor of the hospital. Only the very wealthy ever saw this floor of the hospital. The rooms had each been done by a different interior decorator and didn't resemble hospital rooms at all. They boasted ornate window treatments, canopied beds, overstuffed chairs, armoires, Louis XVI pieces or Queen Anne ones, Oriental carpets, Porthault sheets, down comforters, foam pillow tops on the beds, heated towel racks for the luxurious bath towels and washcloths, silk and/or terry robes for the occupants which they were allowed to keep, and twenty-four hour nursing care plus a gourmet kitchen to provide the finest in cuisine for those recuperating from all types of cosmetic surgery. The cost was $4000 per day per room and of course, all the rooms were private ones.

"Miz Bonita, how you feelin'?" Hannah asked.

"A little sore as if Bryan here had made me do a hard workout. Other than a little sore and a little stiff, I feel fine."

"These are for you, Sugarbritches," Bryan said and placed roses on her lap.

"Sugarbritches?" Dr Vyas said with raised eyebrows.

"Dr. Vyas, this is Bryan Wilcox, my personal trainer. He delights in calling me all sorts of names," Bonita said with a laugh.

Extending his hand, Dr. Vyas said, "I'm pleased to meet you, Mr. Wilcox. *Sugarbritches* is a new one on me."

"But I think it fits our dear Bonita perfectly, don't you, Doctor?"

"Well if it means she's going to look sweet in her britches, it's a perfect name. As soon as she heals, you're going to be amazed. Bonita's abs and thighs are going to look like those of a twenty-year old."

"Oh, marvy," said Bryan. "I can't wait to get her back to work."

"No exercise and no stairs for six weeks. Bonita, I want to see you back here in two weeks to remove the stitches and to check your progress. You have my number if you need to speak to me for any reason."

"I do, Dr. Vyas, and thank you so much."

Bryan took the wheelchair although Kamlash Vyas accompanied Bonita down to the main floor's back entrance and made sure she was securely deposited in the rental car. Hannah fussed with the pillows and blanket and got Bonita all tucked in on the back seat and the three waved good-by to the good doctor.

"Them nutritionists done fixed you a light, and I'm sure it's a light, lunch, Miz Bonita. I wanted to fix you something you liked, but they wouldn't let me."

"I can't wait to eat your good food again, but I've got to stick to the program right now especially with these surgeries. I can't gain an ounce while all this is going on, you know."

"I know what you say, but I worries about you never having nothing good to eat."

"Obviously, I've had plenty to eat in my lifetime or I wouldn't have been so heavy. Once I get myself together, I'll be able to eat your wonderful cooking again. Now tell me what's being on with all of you since I left."

By the time Hannah and Bryan caught her up on what they'd been doing, they were pulling into the parking garage. Bryan noticed two men at the entrance whom he had seen several times before when going or coming from the hotel.

"Sugarbritches, you don't think anyone would be following you, do you?"

"What do you mean following me?"

"You know like a private eye or something? Did you see those two men who were standing at the entrance to the parking garage talking?"

"I didn't notice."

"I noticed them and I've seen them before hanging around the entrance when we've left the hotel or returned. I've seen them enough times now that I know it's not a coincidence and they certainly don't work for the hotel," Bryan said.

Hannah said, "You talkin' 'bout them two men in slacks that was jest standin' there a minit ago?'

"They're the ones."

"It didn't really regster in my head 'til you said something, Bryan. I seen those two men in Spencer two or three times."

"You did, Hannah?" Bonita asked.

"I sure did. Matter a fact, one day I was walkin' out of Villagio to take a cab to go to the market when you was laid up, Miz Bonita, and when we come to the end of the driveway, one of them fellas was standin' by a car at the end of the driveway with a set of them binocular things in his hand. I told the cabbie to stop and I asked him what he was doin'. He said he was bird watching and that he had jest seen a yellow-bellied sapsucker or something like that and he was followin' it. I told him he was approachin' private property and he said he wouldn't go inside the gates so we went on to the store. I never thought 'bout it no more, but a few weeks later when I went to the market, I seen the bird watcher fella with that other fella that was outside jest now. They was in Spencer, Miz Bonita."

"If they were in Spencer, then I would surmise they are watching me. I don't think there's anyone else from Spencer here at the Beverly Hilton, but why would anyone have a private eye on me?"

"We're going to figure that out, aren't we, Sugarbritches? Maybe I'll go down and have a little talk with them," said Bryan.

"Do you think that's a good idea?" asked Bonita.

"They're not known for being the smartest people in the world. Most are excops. I might be able to find out who they're working for and what they're trying to find out or a clue towards one of those things anyway."

"What intrigue," Bonita laughed, "I can't imagine why anyone would have a private investigator following me."

Bryan helped Bonita into the elevator and up to the suite where Hannah ensconced her in Porthault sheets, a down comforter, fluffed pillows, her favorite soap opera and a glass of carrot juice that Javiar had at the ready.

CHAPTER FIFTEEN

New Gifts And New Girls

During Bonita's recovery period, Kim was making plans for a trip to Thailand to buy for her elegant Wilmington gift shop and to return some of her girls who were getting a little long in the tooth. Twenty-six was about the oldest any of Kim's girls reached before she retired them. Men weren't interested in paying for the favors of women who had wrinkles, sagging skin, or were beginning to show any effects of age. If they were in the company of a woman who possessed any of these undesirable characteristics, it tended to remind them of their own age.

Men, like women, have the same fears and regrets when facing old age, however, unlike women who often resort to plastic surgery and personal trainers, men prefer to cavort with younger women giving them the illusion that they are still young and virile. The plastic surgery and the personal trainer can fix the woman's face, neck, stomach, legs, buttocks, and arms and the personal trainer can tone all of those parts, but there are two parts of the female anatomy that no one has come up with a way to fix yet – those being the hands and the knees – sure telltales of one's true age. For the man with the younger paid escort, girlfriend, or trophy wife, his youth will most often rapidly deteriorate if he runs out of money. Now, all May-December romances aren't dollar-driven, but enough are to make a good statistical analysis. So, because of our youth-oriented culture, both males and females are chasing the ever-elusive world of youth, slimness, and beauty. As Kim was well aware of this, she was returning five of her girls to their homeland and their families and would be recruiting new lovelies while in Bangkok.

In Bangkok, Kim was acquainted with many owners of Houses of Ill Repute. After all, they were in the same line of work as she, the difference being that in Bangkok, sin capital of the world, Houses of Ill Repute are legal. Anything goes in Thailand's largest city. Wealthy American men travel there all the time to live out their sexual fantasies. Young girls are available, young men and young boys are available, ménage a trios is available, as well as group sex, sadism and masochism.

Once Kim had deposited her former employees at their homes, given them a large severance payment, and fondly told each of them good-bye, she journeyed to the home of her parents. It always made Kim so happy when she pulled her rented Mercedes up in front of her parents' home that she had purchased for them. Kim had been reared in a *Susie Wong* world of cardboard shacks, outdoor latrines, rats, malnutrition, filthy water, barely enough clothes to cover her body, hardly any money, and very few moments of happiness. Kim's ace in the hole had been her ethereal beauty. At the age of twelve, she was married to a man of fifty-five, who paid her family a huge dowry, and she went to live at a large estate on the outskirts of Bangkok as her husband's number four wife.

Although she hated every minute with the old fart and she despised having his hands rove over her body, she quickly learned what he liked in the bedroom and she honed those skills so that almost every night her husband was spending the evening and the remainder of the night with her – the lowliest of his wives. She fawned over him, teased him, cajoled him, and excited him no end. During the daytime hours when he was at work, she learned to cook so when he came to her quarters in the evening, she began to have a luscious meal prepared for him. Also during her free time, for she had no chores, as her wealthy husband employed servants for all the grunt work, she tried out different hairdos, different styles of make-up and went shopping for stylish clothes, as she had an unlimited budget. The one thing she was not allowed to do was to go to the shack city where her family lived. Her husband felt it was unsavory and unsafe. However, she did manage to get away from her husband's driver a few times and go to see her parents whom she gave money.

Nightly, in addition to a sumptuous feast she prepared for her husband, she was a *new* woman. Sometimes, she was a geisha, others she was a child of six or seven, sometimes she was a prostitute, sometimes a nurse, sometimes a maid, and other times a stranger who had lost her way and knocked on his door for assistance. Regardless of who she was or pretended to be, she screwed his brains out every night.

All of Kim's conscientiousness paid off, for when her husband Chou Jing dropped dead of a heart attack in her boudoir while on the up stroke, the other wives were outraged to learn that he had left the greater part of his fortune to his youngest bride. She was also the new owner of the house where she and the other three wives had resided with Chou Jing. Kim's first task after the funeral was to evict the other wives and move her parents into the large home. Kim continued to live at her home with her family and set about getting an education. She studied English and once she had mastered the language, she took numerous business courses and a practical nursing program. At twenty-one, Kim applied for and received a position as a stewardess for Pan American Airlines. Within months, she met Bart, a handsome co-pilot and became Mrs. Bartlett. After a few years, the couple moved to Wilmington and Kim started her import gift shop and catalogue business and then branched out into her barge/ restaurant/house of entertainment venture. She never told Bart about her previous marriage or that her family had been poorer than church mice and had lived in a shack.

After visiting with her parents for a few days and conducting no business, Kim told her mother that she would be going out to some of the surrounding area to look for items for her gift shop and that in the evening, she would be dining with some friends. Kim's mother told her again how proud she was of her "American daughter who do so well in the big business world and take such good care of old parents." Kim smiled at her mother, kissed her cheek, and they bowed to each other.

Kim drove out to the countryside and visited small shops, houses where she knew some craftsmen lived, and to the waterfront where the Thais did all kinds of beautiful things with shells. She bought and bought and bought. She told each of those with whom she did business that a truck would arrive on a particular day to pick up what she had ordered and then she went back to the city where she made arrangements for a container to hold her wares that would travel to Wilmington via freighter.

After a leisurely *hotsy* bath at the Bangkok Hilton spa, Kim showered and dressed in a native Thai outfit and went to the hotel's cocktail lounge where she ordered a cosmopolitan and waited for her friends to arrive. Within a few minutes, three gentlemen attired in Western suits, joined her at the bar. There was much hugging, kissing, and bowing, and then the four were shown to a table where they ordered an American dinner.

"So how's business in the North Carolina, Kim?" asked Mr. Bai.

The Chinese word *bai* means *white* in English – an interesting name for one in his profession. The Chinese surname comes first. Mr. Bai's full name was Bai Chi.

"Good. I brought five of my girls home and retired them, so I want you three to introduce me to some new young ladies. You know how our clients are? They prefer them young. Of course, I know there will be the usual finder's fee."

"And it's gone up, you know?" from Mr. Cheng.

Cheng is Chinese for *accomplished* and Mr. Cheng had definitely accomplished a great deal by selling young girls.

"Again? You gentlemen don't want me to make any money, do you?" Kim said with a smile.

"You're making plenty of money, Kim," said Mr. Cheng.

"We know about the men wanting younger and younger women," said Mr. Dong, "In fact, here in our *joy* houses, they prefer young girls under ten."

Dong is Chinese for *winter*, an apt name for the man who exuded no warmth or concern about the product he provided to the Houses of Ill Repute.

"It's illegal, but we pay off the authorities," answered Bai. "Another cost of doing business. At least you don't have that expense."

"Maybe not in the same way, but I do have to allow all of the North Carolina legislators to come whenever they wish and of course their meal and all other services are gratis. They then tell their friends or bring in some of the big boys from Washington and I have to do the same for them. It's pretty bad when all my reservations are made and then one of the North Carolina *boys* calls and wants ten girls for his friends that night."

"Do you let them come if you already have reservations?" asked Mr. Cheng.

"You bet. If I once didn't let them come whey they wanted to and on such short notice, they'd put me out of business."

"So you pay too, only in a different way?" said Bai.

"Right, so where are you going to get little girls?" Kim asked.

"Wherever we can. It seems the few human traffickers we get want an exorbitant amount of money for each girl," responded Dong.

"Human trafficking. I'm not into that," Kim replied.

"That's what we do, Kim. Call it anything you like, but we're in the business of selling human beings," said Cheng.

"I sell their services and their bodies for a specific period of time, but I don't buy and sell human beings. I take excellent care of my employees. Like I told you, I just brought five of them back to their native land and they were well remunerated for their time with me," Kim retorted.

"Think you would like to buy and sell human beings, Kim?" asked Bai.

"No, I would not!"

"It's could be very lucrative to you, Kim," Dong explained.

Just as those people who lived through the Great Depression often save and reuse aluminum foil, pinch pennies, reuse paper plates and hang paper towels to dry, those who have been desperately poor can sometimes never have enough money. While Kim was certainly well off from her inheritance from Chou Jing, her husband's airline salary, her gift shop and her barge extraordinaire, she was always interested in more money. She ascribed to the Duchess of Windsor's axiom, "One can never be too rich or too thin."

"But I come to you to get girls," Kim said.

"Yes, but obviously your clientele is interested in a different type girl than ours," explained Cheng. "I read about North Carolina on the Internet. You have a lot of Mexicans there, no?"

"I guess. There are many Mexicans coming into the United States now and many are legal, but the vast majority of them are illegal. I don't think we have too many illegals in Wilmington however. Anyway I'm not interested."

"You may change your mind when you hear the price we'll pay."

"Where am I supposed to find these girls?" Kim asked.

"From the illegals that come into your country," Bai answered.

"You want me to kidnap all the young girls?"

"You haven't heard our proposal," said Cheng.

"All right, let me hear it, so I can say no."

"We'll pay you $50,000 per for Mexican girls under age ten."

"$50,000 per girl? How am I supposed to get these girls? Kidnap them?" Kim asked.

"Buy them," Cheng answered.

"People who come in from Mexico don't sell their children," Kim almost screeched.

"Are you sure?" asked Cheng, who was handling the negotiations now while his cohorts remained silent.

"Well, no, but I don't think they would."

"All right, Kim, it was just an idea. Perhaps you will think about it and get back to us about it on your next visit, Mr. Cheng said patiently.

"I've thought about it and the answer is no. Now, let's get down to my business. Show me some photographs of girls for me to take back to America with me."

By the end of the evening, Kim made her deal with the three gentlemen. She selected five girls, paid the commission, and made arrangements to pick the girls up before her return to the United States. Once back at her parents' home, Kim called the airport for reservations for six passengers one week hence. The freighter with her container of gift shop purchases would arrive in North Carolina a fortnight after her return. All in all, it had been a fine trip plus she had been able to spend some quality time with her parents.

CHAPTER SIXTEEN

Bryan Checks Out The Bad Guys

*H*omosexual or not, Bryan was massively built. His body was quite muscular and he was strong, athletic and in excellent shape. Whenever Bryan left the hotel chauffeuring Bonita somewhere or on his own, he dressed in street clothes. As he entered Bonita's private elevator and hit the button to take him to the parking garage, he was dressed in jogging clothes with a sweatband around his head and Addidas on his feet. Once in the garage, he walked down the exit ramp until he came upon the two men in brown slacks sitting on a nearby bench smoking cigarettes. Bryan sauntered over toward them and said, "Hey, fellas, how's it going?"

"Not bad," one of them answered.

"You staying at the hotel?" Bryan asked.

"Nope," answered the other.

"I've seen you around here a couple of times. Keeping an eye on someone?"

The men exchanged glances and the first one said, "Why do you want to know?"

"I'm just curious. I guess I watch too much teevee. *LA Law* and such. I've noticed you both a few times when I've come out to take my afternoon run, so I thought maybe you were keeping someone in the hotel under surveillance. Am I right? By the way, my name is Bryan," and he extended his hand.

"Red," said number one as he extended his hand.

"Jim," said the other and he and Bryan shook hands.

"Maybe," answered Red.

"Cool! I bet it's really exciting work, isnt' it?" asked Bryan.

"Are you kidding?" asked Jim.

"No. On teevee, the guys watch and wait and then follow the *mark*. That's what you call the person you're following, right? Then they take pictures with those high-tech zoom cameras, sometimes get involved in a high-speed chase, and then get big bucks when they deliver the goods to whomever hired them."

"You have been watching too much teevee. Surveillance work is probably the most boring job in the world," Red responded.

"So you are watching someone?"

"Yep," said Jim, "But we don't want that information broadcast around."

"Working for a jealous husband?" Bryan asked.

"No, nothing like that," answered Red.

"Jealous wife?"

Both men shook their heads.

"Then who?"

"We can't tell you that. We've already told you to much by admitting that we're watching someone."

"Yeah, I guess. Well no harm done. I work at the hotel, help out with the gym and the spa, you know?"

"The gym and the spa, huh?' from Red.

"Yeah."

"Have you happened to run across a Mrs. Roberts? She might have come down to the gym or the spa."

"Mrs. Roberts? No, can't say that I have. Why, is that who you're following?"

"Could be."

"I'll keep my eye out for her and if she comes to the gym or the spa, I'll let you guys know, okay?"

"Sure, we'd appreciate anything you might be able to find out about her," said Red.

"So then I'd kind of be a private eye too, right?" Bryan asked excitedly.

"Yep, you'd be right in the loop, Bryan, providing information on the *mark*." Jim said as he winked at Red.

"You've got a deal. I have to take my run now, but when I get back, I'll start sleuthing right away. Will you be out here in the morning?"

The two men nodded.

"I'll come and report to you first thing tomorrow morning," Bryan said with a salute.

"Good job, Bryan, we'll see you tomorrow," said Jim and returned the salute.

Bryan took off running and thought to himself what major dimwits those two were and how they had given him far more information than he had ever expected to get out of them. Jim and Red shook their heads as Bryan moved away from them.

"What a nutcase!" said Red, "All excited about helping us with the *mark!*"

"Dumb as he is, he might prove to be of some help and besides, he's an employee of the hotel. Who's he going to tell? Certainly not Mrs. Roberts. He'll be so excited to be *sleuthing* he won't say anything to her. Come on, Red, let's bag it for today. The old broad hasn't left the hotel once since she checked in. She isn't going anywhere."

"I agree. A cold one would be real good about now."

"To the old watering hole it is then," and the two of them headed for their plain gray sedan and took off for their motel three blocks away.

CHAPTER SEVENTEEN

Keeping Bonita Under Wraps

*B*ryan began giving the *eyes* a tidbit about Bonita each and every day. He'd say she worked out at the gym, lunched in the tea room, bought something in the gift shop, sat out by the pool or that he hadn't seen her at all that day. Of course, none of that was the truth. The "Eyes" never thought to check to see if Bryan in fact was employed by the hotel. They had no reason to doubt his word.

Meanwhile, Bryan continued to drive Bonita when she went to Dr. Vyas; first for her check-up on the stomach and thigh surgery and then again when she had her buttocks raised, round two of her total makeover. he *Eyes* didn't think anything about Bryan's comings and goings as they assumed the car he drove was his own. Bonita was always safely tucked in a horizontal position on the back seat. With the rental car's tinted windows, Bryan drove right past the two of them and they could see nothing.

Javiar was enlisted to drive Felice on grocery shopping forays and because the "Dicks" had no reason to connect her to Bonita, everyone felt secure. Bonita arranged for Javiar to drive a second rental car, therefore, Red and Jim paid no attention to that car when it went out or came in. Hannah, however, had to lay low after she told Bonita and Bryan that she had seen those same men in Spencer, thus Hannah stayed in the penthouse twenty-four hours a day. She had become addicted to the soaps as she had little to do. The kitchen had been taken away from her and she couldn't go shopping and the hotel maids cleaned, so Hannah sat in front of the big-screen teevee and ate chocolates to her heart's content.

While Bonita had languished in her bed for those eight months, there had been a technological boon in the cell phone industry.

Upon Bonita's return to the real world, she had noticed Raven and then later Bryan with cell phones *glued* to their ears. The last time Bonita had seen a cell phone was when they were huge and shaped like a brick. She was amazed at the tiny, foldable little gadgets. Upon arriving in Los Angeles, she had procured cell phones for Javiar, Felice, and Hannah. She didn't order one for herself as with Raven and Bryan already owning one, all of her minions were now available by cell, therefore she didn't feel that she needed one herself.

Hannah had guffawed when Bonita presented her with a cell phone.

"What am I gonna use that thing for, Miz Bonita? Whenever you wants me you just ring your bell. I ain't got nobody that calls me."

"In these days and times, it's a good thing for you to have, Hannah. You keep it with you and if there's ever an emergency situation, you'll be able to summon help right away."

"Yes,m," Hannah replied and put the thing on its charger every night and kept it in her apron pocket everyday, but she had never once used it and the thing had never rung. Perhaps that was because the only people who had her cell phone number were the people she saw everyday anyway.

Sitting on the sofa watching the soaps, Hannah suddenly thought of her friend, Izonia. *I could use this to call my friend,* she thought. *It's mine. Miz Bonita said so.*

Hannah reached in her pocket and called the Jamison residence in Dorchester, South Carolina.

"Hello, Jamison residence," Izonia answered.

"Hey there, girlfriend," Hannah replied.

"As I live and breathe. I ain't heard from you for so long, gal, I was beginning to think you didn't care about your old friend Izonia anymore."

"Now you know that ain't true , Izonia. First, I was so worried about Miz Bonita. You know she stayed in that bed nigh on to nine months."

"You told me bout that some, but I think the last time I talked to you she had took to her bed for about six months. Is she up now?"

"My, yes. Remember, you can't breathe a word of what I'm gonna tell you."

"I know, Hannah. I ain't never told nobody a thing about where you and Miz Roberts is or anything else you told me. Well, 'cept for Anthony, that is," Izonia said with a laugh.

"How is the little fella?" Hannah asked.

"He's doing fine, just asittin' here with me while I make Mr. Jamison's favorite German chocolate pies."

"Well you tell him I said hello, but you know, Izonia, you have to be careful talking to Anthony. He told everything he knew about Miz Bonita."

"Hannah, that's only 'cause what he knew, Miz Celestine knew too. I ain't told her nothing and you know she the one who talks for Anthony."

"That's right. You know it's hard to remember that 'cause he seems so real."

"Ain't that the truth? I lives here with him all the time and half the time I think he can really talk, but now go ahead. Tell me what's happening."

"Well we're in Los Angeles in the Presidential Penthouse of the Beverley Hilton."

"It's real nice, but I don't have nothing to do all day

"And you complainin'? Some days I wish I didn't have nothing to do. Why don't you have nothin' to do?"

"When Miz Bonita was layin' in that bed not eatin' nothin', she lost so much weight. When she finally decided to get out that bed, she weighed 148 pounds, so now we in LA and she's getting all kinds of plastic surgery. She'd done had a tummy tuck, her thighs tightened and then she's doing a breast reduction and having her arms tightened and then a face lift and her neck and chest done. And we're moving again."

"My stars. I can't imagine Miz Bonita weighing 148 pounds. How do she look?"

"She got a lotta skin hanging off her body. That's what the plastic surgeon is fixing, but she's still a good-looking woman. Oh, and she ain't having her hair bleached either. It's dark brown. The reason I don't have nothin' to do is that she's hired a personal trainer and two nutritionists. They fix her the nastiest stuff to eat I ever seen, lots of nuts and berries and sprouts. It looks jest like what you'd feel to a pet rabbit, but she's thriving on it. Then they makes her these nasty shakes, they call them, with raw eggs in them. Nasty stuff."

Izonia laughed, "So you ain't cookin' and you ain't cleanin', you jest livin' the life of Riley."

"I am. I jest sits around this big suite all day and watches teevee. I's gotten hooked on *One Life to Live, General Hospital, The Young and the Reckless* and *The Bold and the Beautiful.* I can tell you everything 'bout any of them characters. I's beginnin' to feel like their lives are more real than mine. I can't go out of the suite neither."

"Why in the world not?" Izonia asked.

"Some private detectives are followin' Miz Bonita and they seen me back in Spencer, so they'd connect me to her so's I gotta stay here in the hotel."

"They followed her from Spencer to California?"

"They sure did. She don't know who's havin' her followed yet, but Bryan, the personal trainer, is trying to find out."

"Hannah, that's some job you got takin' care of Miz Bonita. All I does here is clean, cook, make pies and take care of Anthony, and of course, I goes to the grocery store once a week and to church for most of Sunday on my day off. It's real borin' compared to what you got goin' on."

"I'll be glad when we's finished out here in LA. I's getting real tired of jest sittin' around."

"I know what you mean. I say I'd like to have nothin' to do, but I'm sure it'd drive me nuts after a few days. Where you movin'?

"Don't know yet, but I know she's fixin' to move again after what happened in Spencer. I hope wherever it is that this time we can stay put for a while. After livin' out here for some thirty years, I don't much cotton to all this flittin' about," Hannah answered.

"You let me know as soon as you know where you's goin'. Maybe it'll be closer than Tennessee and we can get to see each other again," Izonia replied.

"I know it ain't gonna be in South Carolina. You know that chapter is closed too."

"Maybe it'll be in North Carolina. You know, Mr. And Miz Jamison got a summer place in Topsail Island?"

"No, I didn't know that. Well, I don't have no idea where it is yet and Miz Bonita ain't even said we're movin' yet, but I knows we will. I'll call you when I know. It's been so nice talkin' to you again, Izonia. I really miss you."

"I miss you too, Hannah, and I'm so glad you called. It's made my day hearin' your voice."

"I got my own cell phone now, so I'll call you more often and I'll let you know as soon as I find out where we'll be. I'll talk to you soon. Tell Anthony I sent my love."

"I will. I told him it was you on the phone and I swear I believe that doll smiled."

"Izonia, you's getting as bad as Miz Celestine."

"I know it, but I do love the little fella."

"I know you do, but remember he's a doll."

"I'll try," Izonia said with a laugh.

"Bye for now," Hannah said and hung up.

With Bryan reporting to them on a daily basis and because the hotel management didn't want Donnice's men hanging around inside the hotel, the detectives pretty much gave up their daily surveillance vigils and waited for Bryan's report. At the end of each week, one or the other of them called Donnice and gave her a report.

Donnice almost screamed over the phone after the reports, "She must go out of that hotel! What are you clowns doing over there? You haven't provided me with any decent information in over two months!"

"She doesn't leave the hotel. We're on it day and night and not once has she left the Beverly Hilton," explained Red.

"Then what is she doing out there?" Donnice hissed.

"We don't know yet. We're working on it. We have an informer on the inside and we'll let you know the instant we find out what she's doing here."

"You'd better find out something pretty damned quick. There are other agencies, you know? You can be replaced!"

"Yes'm."

Red didn't want to hear anything about being replaced. This a plush assignment – doing what he wanted all day and meeting Bryan each night at nine o'clock for the daily report. What Red's partner, Jim, didn't know was that Bryan had quickly discerned that Red was gay. Their daily meeting at the bar across the highway from the Beverley Hilton had developed into a torrid affair. Red had really fallen hard for Bryan. Occasionally, Jim would ask Red if he should go for the nightly meet in Red's place.

"I don't mind and besides that's the time you like to give your wife a call, isn't it? This is some plum duty, eh?"

Bryan had no feelings for Red other than to find out for whom he was working. He had hoped that a few romps in the sack would have provided Red with enough fun that he would spill his guts. Bryan decided he had to give Red something big and maybe he could learn the identity of his and Jim's employer.

"Sugarbritches, I haven't been able to find out who employing 'Frick' and "Frack.' I was wondering what you think about my giving Red something real. Then maybe he'd talk."

"Like what?" Bonita asked.

"I was thinking maybe I could tell him you were here for some surgery, but I don't know what kind."

"Hmmm. I guess that's innocuous enough as long as you don't tell him what kind."

"I won't. So it's okay if I tell him some kind of surgery?"

Bryan had filled Bonita in on what he was telling Red each day. She knew everything except about the recreational sex.

"All right, try it. I still can't imagine who would have me followed or why."

That night, Bryan met Red and while having a beer, Bryan told Red that Bonita had purchased a Versace dress and a pair of Dolce and Gabbanno shoes at the hotel dress shop that day.

"That Bonita is driving me nuts. My employer is so sick of my reports. She keeps asking me if Bonita ever leaves the hotel and when I tell her she doesn't she screeches. Bonita doesn't leave the hotel, does she, Bryan?"

"I don't know, but I think she may soon because of what I heard today."

"Yeah? What'd you hear?"

"You said *she*. Who's your employer, Red?"

"Why do you care? It's no one you would know."

"Oh, I know it's no one I would know. I just find it interesting that someone is tailing a fat, old woman."

"A fat, old, very rich woman," Red corrected him.

"Okay, but why?" asked Bryan.

"I don't know why."

"But you do know who?"

"Yep, I do."

"So tell."

"You first. Why do you think she'll be leaving the hotel soon?" Red asked insistently.

"You go first. I'm not getting anything out of this arrangement. I'm not charging you any money. Of course, I am getting to spend time with you and that's more than enough compensation," Bryan said as he flashed Red a million-dollar-smile with his mouth and made a silent grimace with his eyes.

"Okay, you win, but this is top secret info," said Red.

"And who would I tell?"

"True. We, Jim and I work for Eagle Eye Detective Agency out of New York City."

"Pretty slick, Red. Not that employer. Who's employing your agency?"

"Oh that employer?" Red smiled.

"Uh-huh."

"Another rich broad, but I've never seen her, so I don't know if she's old or fat."

"What's her name?"

"Donnice Maximillian. She's princess or a countess or some royalty."

"Where's she live?" Bryan asked.

"I'm not sure. Area code is Nassau County, New York, so I guess out in those ritzy Hamptons or someplace like that. Now it's your turn, Bryan Boy. Shoot!"

"Today when I saw Mrs. Roberts going into the dress shop, I was on a break, so I sauntered into the dress shop too. I'm friendly with one of the sales' girls there. Her name is Edyta. Isn't that a pretty name? I'd never heard it before I started watching *Dancing with the Stars* and then wham, I met a girl named Edyta."

"Bryan, get to the point."

"Well while I was talking to Edyta, I overheard Mrs. Roberts and another hotel guest talking and Mrs. Roberts said she was getting ready to go in for some surgery."

"What kind of surgery? When? Where? What hospital?" Red asked excitedly

"I don't know any of that. That's all she said. I don't know when, what, why or where, but I'll keep my eyes open and if she leaves the hotel, I'll tell you right away."

"How will you know with that private elevator to the penthouse suite?"

"I have another friend, Carmelita. She cleans the suite and she has promised to tell me if and when Mrs. Roberts leaves," Bryan said with a smile.

"Thanks, Bryan, you may have saved my job. Just be sure to let me know when she leaves that hotel. I think Jim and I better plan on staking out the Hilton again."

"That would probably be a good idea. Then I could call you on your cell and you could follow her," Bryan offered.

"What kind of car does Mrs. Roberts travel in?" Red asked.

"I don't know. She arrived at the hotel in a limo, but I'll find out tomorrow. I know the guy in the parking garage too."

"Great. Shall we get a room around the corner for a few hours?" Red asked suggestively.

"Love to, Red, but I can't tonight. There's a Japanese contingent at the hotel. They've been in meetings all day and want to use the Nautilus equipment tonight. I have to be there," Bryan said as he glanced at his watch. "In fact, I need to go now. They want to begin at ten thirty and it's a quarter after now. I'm really sorry, Red. You know how much I enjoy our time together. I'll see you tomorrow."

"Okay," Red said without hiding his disappointment. "I guess we'll be on stake-out in the morning."

"See you then," Bryan said as he rose to leave. What Red didn't know was that he had sampled Bryan's young flesh and rippling muscles for the last time. Bryan had finally learned what he wanted to know. The affair was over! And as far as Red was concerned, Bonita would never leave the hotel for surgery. Score one for the good guys!

CHAPTER EIGHTEEN

Crash And Change

Kim returned to the US with her new girls. She had thought several times about the proposal her Thai cohorts had made when she was in Bangkok. Her reaction was still one of disgust. The very thought of providing *babies* as she categorized young girls from ages six to fifteen for prostitution was repulsive to her regardless of how much the men wanted to pay her per girl.

It's said that everyone has his/her price. Kim was about to learn what hers was.

Kim's husband Bart was a fantastic *stick*. That's aviation talk for a good pilot. He had been exposed to a few close calls in his jumbo jet and had always responded according to the book with lightening quick reflexes thus avoiding what could have been serious consequences. He was popular with the flight crews, both those in the cockpit (a co-pilot and International Officer as captains cannot fly more than eight hours when flying internationally) and with the flight attendants, both male and female. He ran a tight ship, but he had a good sense of humor and was definitely well liked by everyone with whom he worked.

There were no incriminations or letters of complaint in his folder in the Chief Pilot's office. He had never been late for work, had never abused sick leave, had never misused his pass privileges, or done anything to cause anyone to think "Discrimination" or "Sexual harassment."

The only black spot on Bart's entire life had occurred only months before the proposal made to Kim in Thailand. Bart's flight from Bangkok had been diverted to Reagan National Airport because of weather. As Bart was illegal to fly the next morning when the passengers were flown to Raleigh and because he had slept in, he decided to rent a car and drive home. Everything would have been fine if he hadn't stopped for lunch at a little bar/restaurant on the Virginia/North Carolina line. There, he had run into some airline buddies and along with lunch had imbibed several martinis.

Now Bart had driven on many occasions, but had never flown, with three martinis under his belt and there had never been a problem. He bid good-bye to his friends, hopped in the rental car, and took off. He had hardly finished accelerating to the posted speed limit when he heard a siren and saw flashing blue lights in the rear view mirror. The state trooper had been staking out the eating and drinking establishment and insisted Bart take a breath-a-lizer test. Bart, of course, failed and was issued a ticket for driving while intoxicated. Fortunately, he was stopped in Virginia for had he been in North Carolina; the rental car would have been impounded. Bart was to appear in court in Emporia, Virginia, the following month.

Upon arriving in Wilmington and turning in the one-way rental car, Bart retained the best attorney in town to represent him. While a DUI is serious for any driver, it is doubly serious for an airline pilot. If that pilot is ever involved in any incident in a company aircraft, no matter how slight or seemingly insignificant, that DUI will jump right up and bite him in the ass and usually will result in termination.

The attorney did his best and pulled every trick out of his bag, but Bart lost the case, paid a healthy fine, and was placed on probation. The DUI became a matter of public record.

Four days after Kim's return to North Carolina, Bart landed at RDU Airport and to this day, no one is quite sure whether he landed long on the runway, didn't apply his speed brakes quickly enough, or didn't pull the power off quickly enough or sufficiently enough, but Bart dribbled off the end of the runway in a two-hundred-million-dollar jet. Several passengers were injured, the plane sustained expensive damage, and when Bart was called into the Chief Pilot's office the boss sat behind his desk with a copy of Bart's DUI conviction in his hand. Bart's two-hundred-and-fifty-thousand-dollar per year job was history. An entire career caput!

CHAPTER NINETEEN

How Can Bart Tell Kim?

*B*art went home to give Kim the news. While Kim was quite upset, the loss of Bart's salary wasn't going to change their life style, as the gift shop and the floating bordello were making money hand over fist. Kim was concerned about what Bart would do because flying was his life. She suggested he take over the barge operation.

"Might as well get involved in another illegal project. I've got a record and I'm on probation anyway. Kim, I think we need to get rid of the barge. We've been living in La-La Land long enough. Even though we know all the right people and have the Raleigh Legislature in our pockets. Eventually we're going to get caught, you know? And it's going to be jail time."

Kim had planned to continue her business for a few more years, but she could see the wisdom in Bart's words. They were involved in an illegal operation. The import business at the gift shop was bringing in well over half a million a year. They could certainly live comfortably on that and they could still run the barge as a restaurant and a spa as it was advertised.

"All right, Bart. I'll tell you what. I've just brought these new girls in. I'll run the barge for two more months and when it's time to rotate some of the girls back to Thailand then I'll give all of them a severance package and escort them home. We'll run the barge, as it appears to be, a restaurant and a spa. Besides, there are hundreds of people who have been dying to use the spa and we've never had a *vacancy*," she said with a smile.

"Good. The only thing I have to do is figure out what to do with my life. I don't want to dwell on "if only," but I will say this one time and one time only. If only I hadn't decided to drive down here, and if only I hadn't stopped at that bar, and if only some of my airline cronies hadn't been there, and if only I hadn't had those three martinis, and if only that trooper had left two minutes before I did, I'd still be employed. There, I've said it. Now, I have to get over it."

"What about looking for a job with a freighter or as a corporate pilot?" Kim asked.

"I wouldn't get hired as either, Kim. I've been terminated by a major airline. The only flying I'll be doing is in my own plane. In addition to losing my job, my commercial license has been revoked. My life as a pilot is a thing of the past. I'm never going to drink another martini as long as I live."

Kim was deeply in love with her husband and she knew there were going to be many difficult months ahead as the pilot searched for something to do. She also knew that he would probably never be truly happy again as he loved to fly maybe even more than he loved her. She asked Bart if he would assist her in tying up any loose ends at the barge and in closing up the operation. He agreed.

The next morning, Bart took the launch to the barge and begin going over the books. Two sets had been kept, obviously. One for the restaurant and one for the prostitution business on which he and Kim had paid taxes claiming the income was derived from a spa. He wondered if the IRS would have questions when the *new* spa business didn't bring in as much money as it had previously when the prostitution was halted, but he didn't think there would be an audit. If they could only get through these next two months, Bart vowed never to do anything illegal again.

Two days before Kim planned to leave with all her girls for their final flight to Thailand and with their handsome severance packages in their purses, the assistant at Kim's import shop called her and said she better get down there immediately. Kim jumped in her 560SL and roared downtown. She was met at the door by IRS agents who told her they were closing down her business for failure to pay withholding taxes on her employees.

"I've paid withholding taxes. Just let me inside and I can prove it. Every employee's withholding is documented and I can show you the checks I've sent to the IRS for the correct amounts," Kim stated confidently.

"Sorry. We have orders to lock and chain the doors," one of the agents replied.

"If you'll let me in, I have all the proof that I've paid," Kim said.

"Can't do that. We have our orders," and with that, the agent locked the door, chained it, and attached a large stick'um notice, which screamed in large black letters, "Closed Due to IRS Investigation."

Kim was devastated. That sign would frighten her customers away who of course could not get in anyway plus it would be a black mark on her reputation. In this business, she had done nothing untoward and they wouldn't let her in to get to her books to prove her innocence. She called Bart on her cell and he came down to talk to the agents to no avail. Once the agents left, Bart told Kim there was nothing to do but to hire a tax lawyer.

"Bart, the only way we have of making money is the restaurant and the new spa, which we haven't even gotten going yet. Maybe we should wait on taking the girls home."

"No. The IRS is looking into your import business. It won't be long before they start looking at the barge. We really have to shut the operation down now. You're leaving in two days and taking the girls home. Now, let's go down to Rodney's office and retain him. He's one of the best tax attorneys on the East Coast."

CHAPTER TWENTY

Bryan Hits Paydirt

*B*ryan couldn't wait to tell Bonita he had found out who was following her. As soon as he left Red, he sprinted across the highway to the Hilton, used his key to the private elevator, and tapped on her bedroom door.

Bonita was lying on her stomach, a most uncomfortable position for her, because she slept on her back, but couldn't at the moment because of her rear end lift. "Who is it?"

"Bryan."

"Come in."

"I'm sorry to barge in on you so late, Sugarbritches, but I found out who's having you followed."

"You did? That's wonderful, Bryan. Who is it?"

"Some rich bitch named Donnice Maximillian."

"O my god!"

"You know her?"

"No, I've never laid eyes on her, but she's my step-daughter - technically. She's Joshua's, my late husband's daughter, but we've never met. Now why in the world would she have me followed?"

"I don't have any idea, but she's quite upset with her boys here because they never have anything to report about your comings and goings and she doesn't know why you never leave the hotel. Apparently, because Hannah saw the private eyes in Spencer, she's been doing this for a long time."

"My heavens! Well, what can I do about it?"

"I guess nothing. At least you know who's got a tail on you. If I were you, I'd sure like to know why she's having me followed," Bryan said.

"I guess she's a vindictive little bitch. Joshua gave his ex-wife a nice settlement and I'm sure provided handsomely for his daughter, but he left the publishing company and the majority of his assets to me. If it's money she's after though, I can't figure out why having me followed makes her think she'll get any of it."

"Maybe she wants to know what you're doing," Bryan offered.

"Tailing me twenty-four hours a day is a very expensive way to salve her curiosity about what I'm doing," Bonita huffed.

"Red said she was rich."

"I'm sure she's well-off. Not only did Joshua leave her money, but she was married to some prince and I read in the Times' social notes that she took him to the cleaners and she retained her title as Princess, like that means a lot in the United States," Bonita seethed.

"I'm sure it means a lot to some people. Probably gets her invited to all the A-list parties."

"Oh, she's a socialite all right. I read about her in the papers every now and then. She's quite beautiful in the newspaper pictures. I just can't figure out why she's having me tailed. What does she think she'll gain by that?"

"You could call her and ask her," Bryan joked.

"Now, Bryan, that's not such a bad idea. Maybe, I will."

"I was kidding, Sugarbritches."

"I know, but sometimes when kidding, we make the most truthful statements or suggestions, don't we? I think I will give her a call first thing in the morning. That should give her something to think about, shouldn't it?"

"I guess so. You don't think she'll be able to put it together that Red told someone who she was, do you?"

"There is that to consider, but do you care about Red and what happens to him?" Bonita asked.

"Not one whit. Make your call in the morning. It's cool with me."

"I think I shall. Thank you, Bryan. I don't know what I'd do without you. There'll be a special envelope waiting for you in the morning."

"I don't want a special envelope, Sugarbritches. You're my best girl and I simply wanted to help you out. Besides, I love intrigue. All us gay boys do," Bryan said as he left Bonita's boudoir.

Bonita painfully arose and walked to the desk where she removed a hotel envelope. She took out her checkbook and wrote Bryan a check for $10,000 and placed it in the envelope and sealed it. She wrote his name on the outside and on the back, she wrote, "Thanks, Bryansie. Love, 'Sugarbritches.'"

Crossing back to the bed, she crawled on it with minor discomfort. She hoped the swelling and black and blue marks would go away soon as she was scheduled for her breast lift and arm liposuction in only ten days. The surgeries had been painful and she was miserable having to lie around all the time after the eight months she had lain in bed in Spencer, but she knew it was all going to be worth it. Her body was beginning to look fantastic and after the boob and arm surgery, she only had to undergo one more cutting and that would be the coup de grace when her face, chest and neck were made youthful once again. She calculated she had about four more months to go before she could check out of the Hilton and get on with her life.

Bonita had decided to move again. During her recovery, she had made use of her computer thanks to Raven by researching various small cities on the Internet. Bonita had made her decision and planned to move to Wilmington, North Carolina, a beautiful little seacoast town on the Cape Fear River. It had everything she liked and was without one thing she liked even more. The wealthy, society-conscious township had no debutante ball of its own. The daughters of the wealthy and the old Southern names made a yearly pilgrimage to Raleigh to come out at the Terpsichorean Ball held every year in September.

Perhaps she could persuade the locals that they should have their own ball named after the magnolia, of course, and that she, Bonita, could run the show only this time there would be no Anthony to wreck everything and no Ike to screw things up. Bonita had instructed Raven only the previous week to call Precious and to tell her to sell everything at Villagio except for one Picasso and one Renoir that she planned to keep.

Precious Woodson was a Spencer, Tennessee, native who had long ago squandered what was left of her family's *old money*, but as appearances had to be kept up, she had contacted Sotheby's in New York and had sold many of her family heirlooms. Her sale was so successful and Sotheby's was so impressed with the artifacts she had brought them that they had suggested she provide them with more items for auction. Precious, not having been born the previous day, realized that there must be others with no income, but with many treasures, who needed money to keep up their current life styles. She became a representative for Sotheby's and the soul of silence. Precious dropped a few hints here and there at teas, luncheons, and cocktail parties about what she was doing for Sotheby's and soon many genteel Southerners in Spencer and New Hanover County, Tennessee, were calling upon her for her services. Sotheby's was thrilled with Precious' finds; Precious was putting stacks of green in the Spencer Bank; and those who gave her their heirlooms to sell were able to pay their electric, heating, and water bills plus have a few intimate friends over occasionally for caviar and champagne. After all, in the South, appearances are of the utmost importance!

Bonita told Raven that the Louis XIV furniture, the sculptures, the Aubosson carpets, the antiques, the tapestries, and the objects d'arte were all to go. Bonita planned to retain her jewelry, several sets of china, several sets of silver and several sets of crystal, a few sentimental mementoes, and the new exercise equipment. Other than that, she wanted a clean slate. She also told Raven to donate all her *Omar-the-Tentmaker* haut couture clothing to Good Will although she would be keeping her shoes. Horribly and oddly enough, her size ten feet had not diminished with her drastic weight loss. Raven was also instructed to list Villagio with Hilda Bowen, the Realtor who had sold Bonita the estate, and to put a sales price on it of twelve million dollars.

Precious and Hilda were both ecstatic. Precious rushed right over to Villagio the next day to meet Raven to photograph and to videotape the items to be sold at auction at Sotheby's in New York. Following the reconnoitering, Precious booked herself on a flight to New York to present her latest acquisitions to the buyers at Sotheby's. Sotheby's executives were thrilled with Precious' latest find and began immediately putting together a catalogue for the *Sale of the Century.* Bonita's goodies promised to bring in more than had Jackie Kennedy's or the Duchess of Windsor's paintings and baubles.

Hilda Bowen arrived the same afternoon while Precious was there with a photographer in tow so she could begin preparations for the brochure to accurately show all the beauties and amenities Villagio had to offer. The estate was pricey, but worth every penny and Hilda knew the right buyer would come along. She hoped sooner than later. Her commission was going to be astronomical!

Bonita called Roberts' Publishing and instructed them to send a team to Wilmington, North Carolina, to find her either large acreage on which to build or an appropriate house. She further instructed the CEO of the Publishing House that no one at the corporation was to know about this bit of business other than he and the members of his team. She told him she was being followed, although not by whom, and she wanted all of her instructions to be kept under lock and key in case there was someone at Roberts' Publishing who was having her tailed.

"I cannot imagine that anyone here would be involved. After all, this is your company and if someone here were having you tailed, they would be using your money to have you followed," the CEO offered.

"Exactly, so I'm sure both of us hope it's not anyone there."

Bonita knew how to keep the boys at Roberts' Publishing on the straight and narrow. She was not only quite intelligent, but she was also a naturally suspicious person. Once she found out she was being tailed and even before she knew who was having her followed, she began to take precautions about her plans by making sure that each of her instructions was compartmentalized, so it would be very difficult for any one person to know what she was doing.

Back in bed, she began to mentally go over what she would say to the Princess Maximillian in the morning. She could hardly wait to put the screws to Joshua's daughter, the little bitch!

CHAPTER TWENTY-ONE

A Call To Donnice

Donnice, expecting the weekly report from Red, was pacing the floor. Those two incompetents were costing her a fortune and they had given her no new information since Bonita's arrival in Los Angeles. If Red hadn't come up with anything this morning, she was seriously thinking of dismissing them and finding another detective agency that could find out what was going on with Bonita Roberts.

The phone rang and Donnice went to pick it up. She saw in the receiver's window that the call was from the Beverley Hilton.

"Good. Maybe the jerks finally got inside the hotel and have something to tell me," she said aloud just before she said, "Hello."

"Good morning, Princess, and how are you?" A female voice questioned.

"Who is this?" Donnice asked.

"Why, this is your wicked step-mother, Donnice, Bonita Roberts."

Donnice was so shocked she couldn't speak.

"Hello?" Bonita said.

"Yes, I'm here."

"I've called to save you some money, Donnice."

"What are you talking about?"

"I'm talking about Red and Jim who work for the Eagle Eye Detective Agency out of New York City."

Donnice felt faint.

"It must be quite costly to have had them outside my estate in Spencer for almost two years and then to fly them to Los Angeles so they can hang out outside the parking garage for several months. What do you want to know, Donnice? Rather than spending that money, why don't you simply ask me about my comings and goings?"

"I've never spoken to you before this minute," Donnice sputtered.

"Maybe you should have rather than spend all that money."

"I don't know why you're so concerned about the money I spend."

"Actually, I'm not. I simply think you're quite immature and silly for spying on an old woman. What is it that you want to know?"

Regaining her composure somewhat, Donnice replied, "I have no idea what you're talking about. I don't know any Red or Jim or whatever their names are and I've never heard of the Eagle Eye Detective Agency in New York City."

"Oh, Donnice, let's not waste our time with denials. I know they work for you and I know they report to you on a weekly basis and I know that you are quite miffed that I haven't left the hotel since I've been here. I also know that you have threatened Red, that you're going to change agencies if he doesn't come up with some useful information. Need I go on?"

"How did you find all that out?" Donnice screeched.

"I think perhaps my detectives are better than yours," Bonita said with a laugh.

"You are a witch, a despicable old fat witch, a whore, someone my father paid to have sex with, and you somehow got him to marry you and you have the nerve to call me. I'm going to hang up."

"Without finding out what you want to know?"

"I don't want to know anything about you."

"For not wanting to know anything about me, you've certainly gone to great lengths and spent an incredible amount of money. If you don't want to know anything about me, why are you paying a detective agency?"

"I'm not."

"Donnice, you don't lie very well, do you?"

"I don't lie. I'm not like you, Bonita."

"And what have I ever lied to you about? Nothing. You said you'd never spoken to me before so how could I lie? Have you thought of seeking professional help, Donnice? I mean other than a detective agency. A good therapist might be where you should be spending your money."

"Shut up, you stupid bitch! I don't have to listen to you."

"No you don't. You can simply hang up, Donnice."

Silence.

"Oh, you don't want to hang up?" Bonita purred.

"I want you to leave me alone."

"I have left you alone. I've never met you, called you, written you, bothered you, or contacted you in anyway and now you want me to leave you alone?"

"Yes!"

"Then I suggest you call off your dogs and leave me alone too."

"I repeat I don't have any dogs."

"Call them off, Donnice."

"Or what?"

"Ah, an admission."

"I'm not admitting anything. Or what, Bonita?"

"Let's just say that the *or what* will not be a pretty sight," Bonita responded.

"Is that a threat, you old biddy?"

"No. I never threaten, dear."

"What does that mean?"

"I carry through, my dear. Ta-ta," and Bonita placed her receiver back on the cradle.

Donnice stood with the phone still to her ear in shock. *She threatened me! She threatened me! That old bag! Who does she think she is? She can't threaten me!* Donnice hurled the receiver through the huge plate glass window of her sitting room.

While she was still fuming, the doorbell rang and shortly after, there was a knock at her door. Donnice asked who was there and the maid announced herself.

"Come in," Donnice barked.

The maid opened the door. She held the receiver in her hand. "The gardener said this just came sailing from the second floor of the house. Oh my goodness, Your Highness, your window is broken!"

"So it is. Put the phone in the cradle and fix me a Bloody Mary with a double shot of vodka."

"Right away, Your Highness."

CHAPTER TWENTY-TWO

New "Eyes?"

*K*im was beside herself. The store was closed; Bart had no job; and now her main source of income, the bordello, was going to be a restaurant and spa because Bart insisted they had to stop breaking the law. Their lifestyle had escalated to the point where they needed close to a million a year to continue living, as they were accustomed. Almost on the hour, the proposition the three men had made to her in Thailand ran through her head and each time she rejected it.

Kim's maid was a legal immigrant from Mexico and for days she had been going on about her brother Manuelo who still lived there. According to her family members still there, Manuelo had been missing for almost a month. He had left his humble home on his way to his job at a local bodega in Tijuana, but he didn't report to work and no one had seen him since. Fabiola was hardly able to perform the simplest tasks as tears poured from her eyes constantly. Kim felt sorry for the girl, but she had no idea what to do to make her feel better.

Even though Kim and Bart were still quite wealthy, they both realized that they would not be able to continue living as they had unless something dramatic happened and happened quickly. Attempting to keep up appearances, they were still going to the club and attending various functions in Wilmington. Word of Bart's termination from the airline had not filtered down into the small town and he simply told everyone that he had taken early retirement. Some of his friends even commented, "Whoa! Not only do you have all the money from Kim's import business and the restaurant/spa, but now you've taken that huge lump sum in retirement money." Bart always replied with a tight smile. That lump sum retirement money was gone! He couldn't take advantage of that perk because of his dismissal, but no one else had to know that.

It was Friday night and the Heart Ball was starting at five-thirty that evening. Kim called to Fabiola and told her that she and Bart were leaving. Fabiola nodded her head as the tears continued to flow.

"Still no news about your brother, Fabiola?" Kim asked.

Fabiola shook her head.

"I'm so sorry. Why don't you take the rest of the evening off? The only thing I want you to do is to give Frisky her pill and then take her out for a short walk. She gets her pill at six o'clock. Just wrap it in a piece of cheese and she'll eat it and then be sure to put her on the leash and walk her around the block. All right?"

"Yes, Missy Bartlett."

Kim and Bart departed and Fabiola went into her room and lay on her bed for the next half hour. At a few minutes to six, she got up and called to Frisky, the Bartletts' seven-year-old Sheltie whom they absolutely adored. Frisky bounded around the corner and entered the kitchen.

"I make you nice piece of cheese, Frisky," Fabiola said through her tears as she put the dog's pill into the cheese and rounded it into a ball. Frisky gobbled the cheese and ingested her pill.

"Now, Fabiola take you for a walk."

"With that, Frisky began to bark raucously and to run in circles. Fabiola could hardly hear herself think. She liked the dog, but he was the barkingest *perro* she had ever heard. Kim had told Fabiola that the reason Shelties bark so loudly is that the breed began on the Shetland Islands and that dogs there are never more than one mile from the ocean so they bark loudly to be heard above the ocean's roar especially when they are herding the sheep.

"Frisky, you not in Shetland Islands anymore. You in North Carolina. You don't need bark so loud."

And Frisky continued to bark and run in circles. Kim said that Frisky was doing the dance of joy. Fabiola told Frisky to sit, snapped on the leash and took her outside. The two of them had only cleared the front gate when Frisky yanked on the leash. Fabiola realized immediately that she must not have snapped the leash in place with all of the dog's prancing around because Frisky had broken free. The dog dashed into the road.

"No. Frisky, come! Frisky!"

Before Frisky could turn around and come back to Fabiola, a car came seemingly out of nowhere and although the driver braked as soon as he could, he hit Frisky. Fabiola screamed. The driver got out of the car. Both of them ran to the bleeding dog. Frisky was alive, but she was bleeding from the mouth.

"Get in the car. We'll take her to the vet," said the driver.

Without a moment's hesitation, Fabiola gently picked Frisky up and got in the car with the total stranger.

"Where is her vet?"

"About two miles outside of town. Turn here."

The driver turned the car she's going to be all right. She just dashed out in the road."

"I know, Mister. She not my dog. She my lady's dog, the lady I work for. She love this dog so much. If anything bad happen to Frisky, I don't know what she do."

"We'll get there as fast as I can."

Within a few minutes, Fabiola was in the emergency room at the vet's office and Frisky had been taken away. The driver stayed with her for two hours. Finally, the vet came out and told them that he would be keeping Frisky overnight and that she was a very lucky animal. Because the car had not run over her, she had not sustained any internal injuries. The bleeding from the mouth had been caused because she bit her tongue, but other than a broken leg, which had been set, Frisky was going to be fine.

"Oh, gracias, Doctor."

"You're welcome. I know Mrs. Bartlett is going to be so relieved. I can't imagine her not bringing Frisky her herself."

"She not home, Doctor. She and Mr. Bartlett go to party at club. I was walking Frisky and she got away."

"I see."

"Doctor, my name is Gary Falkland. I hit Frisky and I want to pay all of her bills."

"Well, that's very kind of you. If you'll check with the receptionist, she can tell you what the charges are."

"I'll do that right now and then I'll take you home Fabiola."

"Gracias, Mister Falkland."

In the car, Fabiola and Mr. Falkland were on the way back to the house when they were overtaken by one of the New Hanover County school buses. Fabiola was glancing out the window as the bus passed.

"Mio Dio, mi hermano!" she screamed.

Gary Falkland slammed on brakes and said, "What? What's the matter, Fabiola? You scared me half to death."

"I see my brother on that school bus."

"Well that was quite a reaction."

"You no comprende. My brother live in Mexico. A month ago, he go to work and no get to work and no one seen him again. I know that him on the bus. He here in Wilmington. How can that be?"

"Are you absolutely certain it was your brother, Fabiola?"

"I know my brother. It was my brother. I'm sure."

"Well, that is a mystery."

Falkland took her home and gave her his card. "If there are any more expenses, please have Mrs. Bartlett contact me and I'll take care of everything. I hope you find out if that was your brother, Fabiola, and I'm really sorry about hitting Frisky."

"Gracias, Mr. Falkland. It was my brother, but thank you for paying the bill and taking Frisky to the vet. Mr. And Mrs. Bartlett be so happy Frisky going to be all right. Buenos noches."

Fabiola paced the floor until the Bartletts arrived home about midnight.

"Fabiola, what are you doing up? I told you to take the night off. Where is Frisky?"

Kim immediately knew Frisky wasn't there, as the dog always greeted her and/or her husband with great barking, wiggling, and circles.

"Oh, Missy Bartlett, Frisky get loose from her leash and run in the street and a car hit her, but she going to be all right. The man on this card hit her, but he take Frisky and me to the vet. Frisky only have broken leg. Vet already set it and Frisky going to come home manana. She fine."

"Bart, we have to go over there right now. I want to see Frisky."

"Kim, Fabiola says Frisky's going to be fine. Let's call the vet and see what he says."

Bart dialed the number and spoke with the vet for several minutes. When he hung up, he said, "Frisky is asleep. They had to sedate her to set the bone. It's a hairline fracture. She has on a cute red cast. She's fine and we can get her first thing in the morning."

"Are you sure, Bart?"

"Positive. What happened to her leash, Fabiola?"

"No se, Mister Bart. I put leash on her in house. We go down walk and out gate and Frisky pull like she do and suddenly she in street. I call her and just as she start to come back, Mr. Falkland hit her. He slam on his brake and no run over Frisky. That's why vet says she all right with nothing wrong inside her. I so sorry Missy Kim. I love Frisky too. Her leash not broken. I don't know what happened."

"All right, Fabiola. It's not your fault. We'll have to get a new leash and collar or maybe a harness. That's nothing to worry about as long as Frisky is all right."

"Missy Kim, something else happen on the way home."

"To Frisky?"

"No, Frisky stay at vet's. Mr. Falkland bring me home and just before we got into town, we pass school bus. I happen to be looking out window and I saw my brother Manuelo on that bus."

"I know you're so worried about your brother, but I don't think you saw him on a school bus here in Wilmington."

"Si, Missy Kim. I know Manuelo anywhere. He was on bus sitting next to window. Whole bunch of Mexican boys were on that bus. I saw them."

"Which direction was the bus headed?"

"It was headed into town just like us."

"What time was that?"

"About ten o'clock."

"What would a school bus be doing coming into town at ten o'clock at night?"

"No se, but I know Manuelo on that bus."

"Strange, Fabiola. We'll look into this whole thing tomorrow," said Bart.

"Gracias, Mister Bart. I know Manuelo on that bus."

They said goodnight to the maid and went to the master suite. As he undressed, Bart said, "Poor Fabiola, she's gotten herself so worked up that she thinks she saw Manuelo on a school bus."

"I wonder if she really did," Kim answered.

"What would her brother be doing on a school bus here?"

"I have no idea, but you told her you'd look into it tomorrow. What are you going to do?"

"I don't have a clue. I just wanted to say something to make her feel better."

"Oh," Kim said, her mind already working. Suppose Fabiola really had seen her brother on a school bus in Wilmington. Kim had an idea. She and Fabiola would stake out the highway the next night and Fabiola could look for the school bus and her brother again.

The next night and the next night for a week, Kim and Fabiola waited in several places along the main road into Wilmington where Fabiola had allegedly seen the bus and her brother, but neither got so much as a glimpse of one of the yellow buses.

"You think I loco," Fabiola said to Kim in tears.

"I don't think you're crazy, Fabiola. Sometimes, we want something so much we think we see things that we don't."

"I saw Manuelo. I know him anywhere. It was my brother."

"I believe you, Fabiola. If Manuelo is here in Wilmington, we'll find him, I promise."

CHAPTER TWENTY-THREE

Intrigue For Bryan

Bryan was pleased with himself for finding out who was having Bonita tailed. Bonita had relayed word for word her phone call to Donnice and Bryan had eaten up every word – he loved the entire drama.

"So why do you think she's having you tailed, Sugarbritches?"

"I suppose because she thinks I took her darling daddy away, but Joshua hadn't really loved his first wife for years. I don't think he and Donnice were particularly close either. I know he left her a great deal of money, so I don't think that's what she's after. Maybe she just gets off on knowing what her *wicked stepmother* is up to. You're sure those two buffoons never knew that I was here for surgery?"

"Absolutely. As far as those two knew, you never left the hotel. You occasionally went to the gift shop or the dress shop, but you didn't leave the Hilton," Bryan said with a wicked grin.

"Bryan, you are too much. I bet you had fun feeding Jim those stories about me and what I bought at the shops."

"Oh, I did, Sugarbritches, and your taste as always was impeccable."

"Well, tomorrow's the day. The final segment of the journey. Kamlash will be doing my face, neck and chest."

"Do you think it's going to hurt?"

"Nothing will ever hurt as much as that breast reduction. If I stood that pain, anything else he does to me will be minor. The body is yummy from the tips of my toes right up to my cleavage. Now the wrinkles and sagging skin will disappear from the rest of me – I can hardly wait."

"You look absolutely fantastic, Bonita, and you've been such a trooper through all of this. What are your plans after this final segment of the journey?"

"We'll be leaving California and we'll be moving to North Carolina. Raven is working on that now. My scouting team from the publishing company did their homework and Wilmington is the place for me. I've always thought it was a lovely town from pictures I've seen in magazines and travel brochures. My team found me land and I was thinking about building, but Raven emailed me today that a Realtor there contacted her about a "Tear-down" on a beautiful promontory overlooking the Cape Fear River. I asked Raven to catch a plane and to up there and look it over. She's getting back in touch with me by the end of the week, so after a few days of recovery, I'll talk to Raven and then I'll know even better what the future will hold."

"Splendid, and I suppose after your full recovery, you won't be needing my services any longer," Bryan said.

"What are you talking about, Bryan? I've got to keep this body once I've paid to get it. You'll be going with me as will Felice and Javiar unless you'd rather not."

"Heavens no! I adore working with you and I know we'll have a gym in the new house, right?"

"Definitely, but now I need to rest, Bryan. Big day tomorrow. Please call Hannah so she can help me with my bath."

"Right away, Sugarbritches, and I'll be up bright and early to drive you to Dr. Vyas' office."

"See you on the morrow then," Bonita said as Bryan gently closed her bedroom door.

CHAPTER TWENTY-FOUR

A House In Wilmington

*R*aven flew to Wilmington and Iva Talbot, one of the leading Realtors in the area, met her at the airport in a sporty, red Corvette. She whisked Raven out to the promontory, priced at three point seven million dollars, explaining all the way that the house was not worth saving, but the land was absolutely gorgeous. They approached the house from the rear as it faced the river. Raven loved the house the moment she saw it. It was gray clapboard with a wide porch across the back of it. Live oaks lined the driveway.

Iva threw the Corvette in park and jumped out, key in hand. "Right this way," she chirped as she started up the three steps to the porch and an entrance to the house. Inside, the two of them were in a foyer that opened into a two-story living room. A two-story fireplace separated the living room from the formal dining room. A balcony secured the hallway around the living room on the second floor with a beautiful curved staircase leading connecting the first floor to the second. Underneath the stairs, one entered a den with curved walls and lovely built-in walnut bookshelves. Across the huge living room from the entrance was a very large and well-equipped kitchen. It was a little dated, but definitely had possibilities. On the other side of the dining room was a sunroom facing the river with a fantastic view. The house was actually a huge two story square with a three-story square at each corner of it. At each corner of the second floor was a bedroom and a bath all with marvelous views. On the main floor, there was a powder room and a laundry room. Iva took Raven into the laundry room and down stairs into the basement where there was a living room, full kitchen, two bedrooms, two baths, and a den. The basement's sliding doors walked out to the swimming pool level. On the main floor, one walked out onto a deck and then down steps to the pool. Each second floor bedroom and the master suite had balconies.

"The house is a contemporary, but it's definitely a tear-down. I've already gotten estimates for you for the cost of tearing it down and carting it off. I have a list of builders ready for you too. Does your employer have house plans yet?"

"Only an idea, but this house is lovely. I'm sure my employer is going to fall in love with it. I don't think it's a tear-down at all."

"Oh, this house will cost a fortune to fix up. It needs a new roof, exterior paint, major fix-ups and modernization inside, a new kitchen, new bathrooms, new flooring, just to name a few things. I think your employer would be much happier to just tear this down and start fresh."

"We'll see. I'm going to describe it to my employer and if you don't mind, I'm going to take a few pictures," Raven responded.

"No, I don't mind, but I'm sure your employer won't want this house."

Raven snapped pictures and listened to Iva go on and on about how the house should be torn down. "It'll cost a fortune to fix this house up. It's so dated."

"It probably won't cost as much to fix this one up as it would cost to build a new house, do you think?"

"Probably more and we don't even know how the foundation is. You know, you start doing stuff in these old houses and you never know what you're going to find."

"How old is the house?"

"It was built in 1976."

"It's only thirty-two years old. That's not an old house."

"Sweetie, it's on the water. The saltwater ages everything three times as fast. Everyone here tears houses down and starts over."

"Then I think maybe my employer will be starting a new tradition."

Iva and Raven started back to the car and Iva thought Raven really was a stubborn one. She was dying to know who her employer was. Raven had not batted an eye when she mentioned the price of three point seven million and the employer was either going to build or redo that piece of junk that should be torn down. Remodeling it would cost a fortune. Neither of those facts seemed to bother the pretty young lady. *She must work for the Asterpoops,* Iva thought. *Whoever they were.* When she was little, her mother always talked about the Asterpoops and so Iva had always thought that the Asterpoops had all the money in the world but a quarter. Raven either worked for them or for one of their offspring. The Realtor was accustomed to big-ticket sales, but Raven had not asked if there were any negotiating room. It looked like this was going to be a full price sale and Iva was thinking about that commission – three-hundred-seventy-thousand-dollars in her little Coach purse. Sweet!

CHAPTER TWENTY-FIVE

Xandi And Hair Tdf

*T*hough there were several beauty salons in Wilmington, the salon of choice was HAIR tdf (to die for). Alexandra Westley, the proprietor, was known affectionately to all her clients as Xandi (pronounced Zandy). In addition to being a fantastic colorist, hair designer, and shearing genius, Xandi was also an accomplished singer. She had sung with local groups, performed in some musicals at the Wilmington Dinner Theatre, and often sang at weddings and funerals.

In her other life prior to moving to the quaint little city by the river, Xandi had performed as a backup singer with Gloria Estefan and the Miami Sound Machine. Now in her forties, Xandi was once again smelling the grease paint, seeing the klieg lights, and hearing the crowds' roar. She was calling on some of her old showbiz buddies and was planning a huge music fest on Wilmington's shores for the Fourth of July.

Everyone who was anyone in the Wilmington area had their "dos" done at HAIR tdf. Many of the town's most influential women made Xandi their confidante. She knew many secrets and one of the reasons was she didn't share them. Kim had to keep up appearances and so she went for her weekly appointment a few days after the failed bus-spotting episode with her maid Fabiola. As she sat in Xandi's chair, the stylist asked, "So what happened with the IRS? Can you open your store yet?"

"No," replied Kim, "It's costing me a fortune closed up."

"I can imagine. When do you think they'll let you reopen?"

"Who knows?"

"Well, the restaurant seems to be flourishing. We finally got a reservation there last week after trying to get one for about a million years."

"We've expanded, you know? We turned some of the spa rooms loose and now we have a larger seating capacity," Kim explained.

"It was really a nice evening riding the little launch over to the barge and the food was excellent."

"I'm glad you enjoyed it. Tell everyone you know."

"Oh, I have been. So what else is going on in your world? I heard your husband took early retirement. How is it having him home all the time?"

"It's okay," Kim answered.

"Not according to a lot of my clients. I have women who are climbing the walls now that hubby's around all day. One lady said now that her husband's retired, he wants to go everywhere with her, but since he's been out of the loop so long, he complains about the cost of everything he sees. He asks her 'Are you going to pay $9.99 a pound for a piece of meat?' Then he went to a boutique with her and about had a cow when she paid $400 for a simple dress. 'You can get a nice dress for $20,' he says. His wife tried to explain to him that it wasn't 1960 anymore and everything has gone up, but he just continues to bitch and moan."

Now Kim was laughing, "Xandi, you always make me feel better and you always make me laugh."

"Just part of the service we offer here at tdf, ma'am."

The shampoo girl Sue approached Kim and asked if she'd like coffee or a soft drink. Xandi also provided a variety of candy bars, Danish, cookies, and other treats for her clients.

"No, thank you," Kim responded to the girl and then to Xandi, "Well, Bart is not driving me crazy, but my maid is getting to me."

"Why?"

"Her brother disappeared in Mexico a couple of months ago and she's frantic. The other night when Bart and I were at the club, she took Frisky out for a walk. Frisky got away and got hit by a car."

"Oh, no! I'm so sorry. Is she all right?"

"Yes, she's fine. Fortunately, the car didn't run over her, but only hit her. The driver took Fabiola and Frisky to the vet and then the driver brought Fabiola back home. She saw one of the county school buses a few miles outside of town and she swears she saw her brother Manuelo on the school bus. She was so convinced that for the past three nights, we've been playing detective and sitting on the side of the road waiting and watching for a school bus, which has never materialized. She has not seen her brother again, but she's sure he was on that bus. It's all she talks about."

"What time was all this?"

"About ten at night."

"Well, maybe it's not as odd as it sounds. I've seen an occasional bus out on the roads late at night too."

"When?"

"Off and on. I figured it was a bus load of kids on their way back from an away game or something."

"Of course that's what it would be. The bus was coming back from an away game and Fabiola only thinks she saw her brother. It was on a Friday night and that's when the sports events are held."

"I guess she's so worried she's imagining things," Xandi commented.

"I hope it's over soon. She mopes around all day saying his name like

some kind of mantra."

"Why don't you take her out one more time? Call the school and find out if they have an away game this Friday night and then take Fabiola to wait for the bus and she'll see her brother wasn't on it."

"Good idea, Xandi. I feel much better. A few laughs, a good suggestion and a good do – what else can a gal want? Now tell me what's happening with the big music fest you're planning."

Xandi filled Kim in on her plans so far and told her on the qt some of the groups that would be performing.

CHAPTER TWENTY-SIX

Two Mexican Maids

As was the case with Hannah and Izonia, the Jamisons' maid, in Montiac, South Carolina; the maids in Wilmington fraternized too, mostly on their days off. One of Fabiola's best girlfriends was Delilah, Alexa's and Norman's maid. Delilah and Fabiola were from the same town in Mexico and had known each other since they were children. Fabiola placed a call to Delilah and told her about Frisky and about the school bus and that she saw Manuelo on the bus.

"Fabiola, no mira Manuelo en Wilmington."

"Si, en el autobus."

"You come see Delilah your day off. I ask Miss Alexa for day off too. We walk and talk, okay?"

"Okay."

Thursday, Kim delivered Fabiola to Alexa's door to visit Delilah. The two women had coffee in the kitchen and Fabiola told Delilah the whole story. After they finished the coffee, Delilah asked Fabiola if she wanted to take a walk. Delilah had gained quite a bit of weight and was trying to diet and walk off some of the excess poundage.

"Si, I like to walk.'

They went down the driveway and walked to the main road and back. When they were almost to the house, Fabiola said, "Do you ever walk on any of the other acreage? There's so much land here."

"Sometimes. There's a back road. I've walked down that a few times, but there's a gatekeeper at the back road. I don't know what he's there for."

"Let's go see."

They walked down the long, winding road behind La Reina de la Mar and eventually came within sight of a guardhouse and a huge locked gate. They veered off the road and starting walking in a meadow. They walked for a long time and then Delilah said, "Let's sit for a few minutes. I brought us a healthy snack." She opened a little kerchief she had carried along and had some celery and carrots in it and two bottles of designer water.

After sitting a little while, they were getting ready to return to the main house when they heard Spanish being spoken loudly in a male voice.

"Where's that coming from, Delilah?"

"No se, but it sound like it's coming from over the hill."

They started in the direction of the noise and when they came to the crest of the hill, they looked down on what looked like a barracks area that was as concealed as possible. There was camouflage netting over the whole area and the barracks were built into the hillside. Two men were sitting in front of one of the barracks. They obviously had been playing cards and now an argument had ensued. They had rifles lying next to them.

"What in the world is going on here, Delilah?"

"I have no idea. I've never been here before."

They were lying down on the hill's crest watching the two men. There didn't seem to be anyone else around.

"Let's go down the other side of the hill behind that building over there," Fabiola said, as she pointed.

"Do you think it's safe?"

"It's safe if they don't see us. We were pretty good at hiding when we were kids, remember?"

Delilah let out a soft giggle and they scampered down the hill they were on and around to another side of what appeared to be a barracks camp. Once they were behind a building, they slid down the hill. They were out of sight of the guards. They crawled along the building and peeked into the windows. There were rows of cots and a few clothes behind each cot on hooks.

"We need to get inside," Fabiola said to Delilah.

"I'm afraid, Fabiola. We need to go back to the house. Whatever is going on here, someone's trying to hide it. I don't think we should be here."

"No one knows we're here. Let's get inside for a peek and then we'll leave, I promise."

"You always could talk me into things I knew I shouldn't do," Delilah said with a slight smile.

They inched their way around to a door. Fabiola reached out and turned the knob. The door opened. They walked over the threshold and lights begin to flash and sirens went off.

"O mio Dio. Now look, we're going to get caught."

They heard the two men grumbling and then they heard them running.

"Come on," Fabiola said as she pulled Delilah into the building and shut the door. "Get under a cot and don't breathe."

They secreted themselves under cots just as the doors of the bunkhouse flew open. A voice came over a loudspeaker in the room, "What's going on down there?"

"Nada. There ain't nothing here. Probably a squirrel like the last time. There's nobody here."

"Have you searched completely?" asked the magnified voice.

"Si, si," the guards said as they gave a quick look see all the while shaking their heads and laughing silently. "All secure here."

"Make sure it stays that way," said the voice. Then there was static and the voice was gone.

"Make sure it stays that way," mimicked one of the guards and then turned to the other, "So you want to go lose some more of your money?"

"Should we look for the squirrel or whatever it was?"

"Nah, what's he going to do, just eat up some of the goons' fajitas."

The two men shut the door and left. Fabiola and Delilah waited several minutes and then Fabiola climbed out from under the bed. "Come on, Delilah. Let's check things out."

"Let's get out of here."

"This is a perfect time to look. They don't know we're here."

Fabiola started looking at the clothing on the hooks and then went to the back of the bunkhouse and found a hallway that was attached to an outdoor Joey. "Whoever lives here doesn't even have indoor plumbing."

Then she went through another doorway and saw all kinds of food on make shift tables. There was no refrigeration, no fans, and not really much ventilation. "Whoever stays here lives worse than a dog."

"Fabiola, we came through the door and set off some kind of alarm. How are we going to get out without setting it off again?"

"We'll go out a window."

"You think the windows aren't wired too?"

"Relax, they'll think it's the squirrel again. What's do you think is going on here?"

"Obviously, there are people living here, but they are living in squalor. I do not think this is something I can ask Senor y Senora Masterson about."

"I don't either, but there's definitely something fishy going on here."

Just then, they heard the rumble of some kind of truck or large piece of machinery heading towards them.

"We have to get out of here," Delilah said and grabbed Fabiola's arm. They headed for the closest window, opened it and jumped out. The lights and sirens started again. By the time they reached the top of the hill, the guards had arrived to once again find nothing and no one. The two women crouched at the top of the hill and peeked over the edge. What they saw completely confounded them. A yellow county school bus was pulling up in the concealed barracks area. They watched as a group of ragtag men filed off the bus and into the barracks. Fabiola had to put her hand over her mouth to stifle a scream. She recognized Manuelo. She wanted to call out to him. *What in the world was he doing here in Wilmington in this awful place?*

After all the men had filed into the barracks, the guard from the gate entered the concrete area and yelled at the two men who had been watching the barracks, "Well, what have you found? The alarm went off again."

"Nada, it's just squirrels, I think," one of them answered.

"Now, the gate guard was at the barracks. He walked around the building and yelled to the two barracks' guards again, "Come here, you two stupid idiots! Do you think a squirrel did this?" he said as he pointed to the broken window.

"I don't guess so," the other answered.

"Then find out what or who did! Now!" He yelled and the two men started up the hill where the two maids were crouching.

"We have to run!" Fabiola said.

"They'll catch us," Delilah whispered.

"Not if we run as fast as can," Fabiola said and hiked up her dress and took off.

Delilah was right behind her and they ran as fast as they could until they were back on winding road leading to the mansion. When they reached the road, they stopped running.

"Now, cool down, Delilah. We're two maids taking a walk."

A few minutes later, the gatehouse guard ran out of a wooded area and said, "Who are you and where are you going?"

"I am Delilah, Senora Masterson's maid. This is Fabiola. We're out taking a walk. Who are you?"

"I work for Senor Masterson."

"Doing what? Why do you have a gun?"

"I was hunting."

"For what?"

"Squirrels. They're such pests here. Senor Masterson hired me to kill them."

"I see," said Delilah, realizing that she had the upper hand. "Well, I'll be sure and tell Senor I saw you and you were doing your job. What is your name?"

"That doesn't matter. You ladies have a nice walk," the guard said and hurried back into the woods.

"That was a very close call, Fabiola."

"He backed off when you told him you worked for Senora Masterson, but what are we going to do? What is Manuelo doing here?"

"I don't know what any of those men are doing here and why they are living in that awful place."

"Manuelo is not here legally. I know that. He had no papers. One day, he simply disappeared. Is this something you can talk to Mrs. Masterson about?"

"I'm not sure. Mrs. Masterson and Mr. Masterson are not the closest couple. In fact, sometimes, she seems to despise him. I know she runs the show and he does what she says."

"Then do you think you can ask her about Manuelo?"

"Let me think about it, Fabiola. I want to help you, but I don't want to get into trouble."

"I know, Delilah. It's almost time for Mrs. Bartlett to come for me. Do you think I should talk to her about this?"

"As if I could stop you. Just be careful, Fabiola. And please don't get me involved if you don't have to."

"I won't, Delilah. I promise."

CHAPTER TWENTY-SEVEN

Transformation Continues

*B*onita was delighted when she received Raven's pictures and telephone call of and about the "Tear-down" contemporary she had located in Wilmington.

"It sounds perfect, Raven. What's happening with Precious? Has she contacted Sotheby?"

"Yes, they're putting the catalogue together now."

"Then I'll call the company and have them cut a check for the house. Buy it and can you stay there long enough to get the renovations started? I'll still be out here for a little while."

"I certainly can. My father's high school reunion was two weeks ago. He wasn't going, but I insisted. He went and his high school sweetheart was there. She's a widow and Daddy's acting like a teenager again. He's flying down to Palm Beach this weekend to see her. Suddenly, he's not too interested in what I'm doing or if I'm there to fix his meals. It's wonderful, Mrs. Roberts."

"It certainly is. I'm happy for him and for you, Raven. Maybe now you can get out and enjoy yourself sometimes."

"It hasn't bothered me. I've been so upset for him and how his heart was broken, but I think it's on the mend now."

"They always say the best thing for getting over a woman is another woman. Of course, that works for women too, doesn't it?"

"If you say so, Mrs. Roberts. I'll get started on the Wilmington house right away."

"And hire movers to take what's left in Spencer to Wilmington, please. I don't plan on going back to Tennessee anytime soon. When I leave here, I plan to go straight to Wilmington and a new life."

"Good for you. Not only a new life, but you're going to be even more beautiful than ever," Raven crossed her fingers for that last line because Bonita had certainly not been beautiful when she lived in Spencer.

"You always say the right thing, Raven. Talk to you soon."

"Bye, Mrs. Roberts."

A tap sounded on Bonita's door.

"Come in," Bonita trilled.

"My, you is lookin' fine, Miz Bonita. You looks jest about like you did the first time I seen you."

"I doubt that, Hannah. I was about sixteen when we met, but it surely is a colossal improvement, isn't it?" Bonita said as she looked at herself in the mirror.

Vyas had performed the final surgery, the face, neck, and chest lift, a week prior and although she still had stitches, Bonita was recovering nicely. She had hardly any bruises and just minor swelling. Hannah had hydrogen peroxide and Neosporin on a tray and said, "Are you ready for the cleanin' and de-germin'?

"Ready," Bonita answered as she moved to the vanity stool.

Twice a day, Hannah applied a mixture of half hydrogen peroxide and half water to all of Bonita's stitches. Once she had given it sufficient time to bubble and do its work, she used another long Q-tip to dry the area. When everything was dry, Hannah took a third Q-tip and dressed all the stitches and scars with Neosporin.

At night, for the third cleaning, Hannah accompanied Bonita into the oversized master bath at the Beverly Hilton, tilted her back toward the washbasin and shampooed her hair. That counted as one of the three daily-recommended cleanings. After the shampoo, Hannah applied more Neosporin, so Bonita's hair only looked clean immediately after the shampoo as the ointment seeped into her hair almost immediately.

The treatment over, Bonita said, "Hannah, Kamlash tells me that I should be as good as new in another month. Then I only have a few procedures left."

"What you gonna do next, chile? You done everythin' I can possibly think of to do to yourself."

"There are miles to go, Hannah. I'm going to have permanent make-up tattooed on."

"Do what? You gonna get tattoos on that new, beautiful body?"

"Not that kind of tattoo. I'm going to have black tattooed on my eyelids so they'll be lined permanently and then I'm going to have my lips tattooed a coral shade, so I'll always look as if I'm made up, even when I awaken in the morning. Think how much time that will save everyday. Then I'm going to have a full body tan spray, so I'll look healthy and like I've been in the sun. I'm so pasty after being in the hotel all this time. After that, a few days at the spa downstairs for a mud bath, herbal wrap, pedicure, manicure, facial and new hairstyle and then we're going home."

"To Villagio?"

"No. I've instructed Raven to sell Villagio, to get rid of everything in it except a few paintings I want to keep and the new exercise equipment. Raven has found a marvelous house for us and she's getting the renovations started immediately. You'll have your own apartment in the basement, Hannah, which opens onto the pool area plus we're going to have an elevator put in so you won't have to trudge up and down the stairs."

"Where is this new house?"

"Wilmington, North Carolina."

"When was you in Wilmington, North Carolina? When we lived in South Carolina?"

"No, I've never been there. I found it on the Internet and then had the team at the publishing company scout it out. Next, I sent Raven. She's found the perfect house. We're moving, Hannah, and we're starting a new life."

"Are *we* starting another Magnolia Ball too, Miz Bonita?"

"I'm not sure, Hannah, but we're not going to talk about that now. I'm thinking of going back to my old name too – Maria. What do you think?"

"I think you would get awful upset with me 'cause I's always called you Miz Bonita. I'm sure I'd forgit about seventy-two times a day and call you the wrong name."

"Then I'll hold that in abeyance right now, but think about it, Hannah. Maria Roberts. Then I'll have shed everything from my past that I can because I certainly can't let either you or Raven go."

"Well, I ain't planning to go nowhere, but Miss Raven ain't gonna be able to move to North Carolina, Miz Bonita. She takin' care of her daddy."

"She called me earlier. Her daddy went to a high school reunion and ran into his high school sweetheart. He's like a teenager again and flying to Palm Beach, Florida, to see her this weekend."

"Well, ain't that somethin'? Who woulda ever thought? He was so broke up about his wife runnin' off with Alfonso."

"Maybe he's getting over it now, Hannah. If so, he won't be clinging to Raven and she might be able to move with us."

"I likes that girl. She is so sweet and so pretty. I wonder why she don't have no boyfriends."

"I don't know, but maybe Mr. Right is in North Carolina."

"Who's Mr. Wright? That somebody you knows there?"

"I don't know him, but maybe he's there."

"What you talkin' 'bout, Miz Bonita?"

"I'm talking about the right man for Raven."

"Oh, I thought you was talkin' 'bout somebody named Mr. Wright."

"Hannah, I do love you so. You amuse me daily and you took such good care of me when I was so ill in Spencer."

"You my baby and Miz Bonita or Miz Maria or Miz Whoever you gonna be, I loves you like you was my own chile."

"And I love you, Hannah. Now, because you're the only one I trust to do this, I want you to fly to Spencer in a few weeks and pack up all the clothing that I can still use and my jewelry and don't forget to go to the bank and clean out the safe deposit box. I'll give you the key and write a permission slip for you. Several of my best pieces are in the box. Take one of my travel jewelry cases with you to the bank and put the jewelry in it and then pack it in a suitcase that you hand carry on the plane and fly those rocks to Wilmington."

"All right, Miz Bonita-Maria, whatever you says."

CHAPTER TWENTY-EIGHT

The Hunt

*A*s soon as Fabiola got in the car with Kim, she started talking a mile a minute half in broken English and half in Spanish.

"Fabiola, slow down. I can't understand what you're saying," Kim admonished as she started down the La Reina de la Mar drive.

"Mrs. Bartlett, my brother Manuelo is here at this place – La Reina de la Mar."

"I'm going to take you to the doctor. You're seeing your brother everywhere. We need to get your eyes checked."

"He here. Delilah and I took walk and we walk behind the mansion down a winding road. We see a gate that must be on another road that lead to mansion and there was a guard at a house with a machine gun. We duck off road and go up hill. When we get to top, we look down and see camp with houses like soldiers live in and guards with guns. Delilah and I go around to the back of that place and shinny down hill and go in house. People live there or being kept there with very little food, unsanitary conditions, no running water, and little cots. And then, guess what, Mrs. Bartlett, school bus come and a whole bunch of Mexican men get off it and one of them was Manuelo."

"Did you talk to him?"

"No, we run because we set off alarm and the men with the guns look for us. We run uphill and circle around and come back to house."

"Fabiola, do you know how ridiculous this all sounds?"

"Yes, but Mrs. Bartlett I swear on my grandmother grave, everything I say happen."

"I trust you, Fabiola, but this tale is just too wild. I want to see all of that for myself."

"Is there back road to La Reina de la Mar?"

"There's an old road that was closed several years ago that may go around the back of the estate, but I didn't think it was used anymore."

"There's guard at house there with high fence all around the estate and he has machine gun. Guard at the houses do too. They kidnap Manuelo."

"Who kidnapped Manuelo?"

"It must be Mr. Norman. The men live on his estate and ride school bus. I bet they work in Mr. Norman factory."

"Okay, Fabiola, I'm going with you and you're going to show me these houses, these men with machine guns and the school bus."

"I don't want to go back. Delilah and I almost caught today."

"You don't want to go back because you made this tale up, right?"

"No, I tell you truth. How we go back? The men be more on guard now."

"Tomorrow, call Delilah and find out when Alexa will be gone and then we'll go there and you can show all this to me."

"Do you think we talk to Mr. Bartlett first?" Fabiola asked.

"Absolutely not! You show this to me and let me put my eyes on your brother Manuelo and I'll get him back for you. I promise."

"All right. If I can get Manuelo out of horrible place, I do whatever you ask. I call Delilah when we home."

A week later, Delilah called Fabiola at the Bartletts' home. "Fabiola, I hope I don't lose job over this, but you my best friend and I know you want Manuelo free, so I call to tell you that Senor and Senora go to Raleigh tomorrow afternoon to dinner at Capital City Club and performance at Civic Auditorium and spend night at Sheraton. You and Mrs. Bartlett come tomorrow evening. I ask Mrs. Masterson if it all right you visit me tomorrow night. I'm sure she say okay and then she alert guard at front gate to let you in. No one get in without permission."

"Perfecto, Delilah. Thank you. I promise no get you in trouble. I see you tomorrow."

"All right, Fabiola, but I no go back there with you. I help you, but I can no do that."

"Okay, Delilah. Gracias."

Fabiola ran to find Kim and told her about Delilah's phone call. "All right, we'll go there about 4:30 tomorrow, Fabiola."

"We no take your car, Mrs. Bartlett. If your car stay, won't the guard think that's funny?"

"You're right. We'll take a cab. I'll wear a hat and sunglasses and you tell the guard I'm a friend of Delilah's too."

"I hope this work."

Alexa and Norman left and Delilah called Fabiola to tell her the coast was clear and that Mrs. Masterson had alerted the guard that she and a friend of hers were coming to visit. Kim called a cab and she and Fabiola set out for the Masterson mansion. They were waved through by the guard without his really looking in the car. Kim paid the cabbie and the taxi departed. Delilah met the two of them at the door and invited them in, but Fabiola said they were going to go down the back road. Delilah shut the door and prayed that they would not be caught.

As they walked down the road, Fabiola spied the place where the guard had accosted her and Delilah on her previous visit.

"Let's go in woods here. Guard come out right here after Delilah and I run away from compound. It must go straight to bunk houses. In woods, no one see us on road."

The two of them walked through the weeds and woods, and after about ten minutes came to a hill that had obviously been man-made in the flat North Carolina field. "I think it's right over this hill. We better get down flat and crawl the rest of the way."

They got to the edge of the hill and looked over and sure enough there was the compound. Kim gasped.

"See, I tell you, and those two men there. They got machine guns."

"AK-47's," said Kim.

"What?" Fabiola whispered "That's the kind of guns they are. Something serious is going on here, Fabiola. I don't know what it is, but something really bad is happening here."

Kim reached into her pocket and extracted a digital camera. She hit the zoom button and took about twenty shots.

"Evidence, Fabiola."

"The men prisoners, Mrs. Bartlett. I know it."

The women lay on their stomachs and watched the two guards playing cards, taking a few drinks out of a jug of wine, laughing and talking for over an hour. Just as the sun was setting, they heard an engine. Within minutes, they heard the electric gate at the back guardhouse slide open and a school bus appeared in the middle of the compound below them. Once it stopped, about forty Mexican men got out of the bus and headed for the two bunkhouses.

"There Manuelo. See that one with read bandanna? That my brother! That Manuelo!"

"And that's a New Hanover County school bus. What in the world are those men doing on a county school bus?"

"How we going to get Manuelo?"

"We're not."

"You promise, Mrs. Bartlett."

"I know I did, Fabiola, and we will get Manuelo, but we can't get him today."

"I think you mean today."

"I don't have on a Kevlar vest, do you? We can't get him with AK'47s down there. This is going to take some doing, but we'll get him out of there and soon. I promise, Fabiola. Now, let's get out of here before those guards start looking around."

"All right."

Mistress and maid slid down the hill and hurried back to the mansion through the woods with the final trek on the dirt road behind the house. Delilah was waiting for them on the rear veranda. "Is everything all right?"

"We're all right, Delilah," Kim answered, "But something that's going on here is certainly not all right."

"I know. I worried about those men. I don't know what to do about it. I no can tell it to Mr. Masterson and I don't know if Mrs. Masterson know about it."

"Could you call us a cab, Delilah?"

"Si. What you going do about those men, Mrs. Bartlett?"

"I haven't decided yet, Delilah, but I'll let you know as soon as I do," Kim answered, but she had already figured a few things out. Norman Masterson was sneaking hordes of illegal Mexicans into the USA along with the paltry number of legal Mexicans he was bringing into the country. He was housing them on his property, using county property to transport them, probably paying them next to nothing, and was keeping them little better than slaves. He had to have a network to collect the illegal Mexicans in Mexico and he had to have an *in* with someone at the docks to get them off the boats and into the buses to get them to the compound in the first place. And the only person that someone could be was Joey Scappaticcio, the dock master. Kim decided she would rise very early in the morning and stake out the entrance to the old closed road that must wind around the back of La Reina de la Mar.

It was still dark when Kim slipped out of bed the next morning and dressed in warm, dark clothing. She tiptoed down the stairs and into the garage where she started her Mercedes and drove out of Wilmington in the direction of La Reina de la Mar. She turned off the main road about a quarter mile before the entrance to the abandoned road and drove her car back into the woods so it could not be seen from the highway. Then with a flashlight, she set out on foot until she came to the abandoned road. Sure enough, the road was closed with a NCDOT barricade in front of it. Kim switched off the flashlight and went about six feet into the woods and sat down next to a tree. She didn't have to wait long before she heard the sound of an engine. Sitting very still, she had a direct view of the barricade when the school bus' lights shone on it. The bus stopped in front of the barricade and the driver got out and removed the middle of the barricade, as Kim took a picture, drove the bus through it, stopped the bus, and replaced the mid-section, as Kim's camera snapped again. Once the bus taillights were out of sight, Kim went to the barricade and shone her flashlight on it. The steel had been cut, probably by a welder, so it could be removed and replaced at will. She photographed the barricade and returned to her tree just in time to hear the bus engine again. The bus stopped at the barricade and the driver got out and removed the mid-section while an armed guard stood at the bus door. The driver got back in, drove through the barricade, replaced it and went out onto the main highway. Kim waited a few seconds and then sprinted to her car in the woods and took off after the bus, but not too closely. She followed the bus straight to Seafood World, where it drove through a garage door that must have been activated by the school bus driver. Kim caught the bus entering the building with her digital camera. As soon as the bus was inside the building, the garage door descended. Kim waited and shortly, the garage door opened and the bus backed out and started back the way it had come. Kim followed the bus again and the driver drove it to his house. Kim snapped a picture of the bus at the driver's home and then waited and in about an hour, the driver came out of his house and started on his morning run to pick up the children and take them to school. Kim photographed and followed him for his first two pick-ups and then returned to her house.

"What an operation!" Kim exclaimed aloud.

That afternoon, Kim drove to Seafood World in her SUV and waited for the school bus. Sure enough, the school bus arrived and did the garage door thing again and left headed in the direction of La Reina de la Mar. Kim followed at a discrete distance and when the bus stopped at the barricade, she drove on past knowing the rest of the routine, but not before she had gotten her evidence on the camera's memory stick.

When the Mastersons returned from Raleigh, Norman had a message at his office from Kim Bartlett requesting an appointment.

"Kim, Norman Masterson here. You don't need an appointment to come in to see me. What's on your mind?"

"I'd prefer to discuss it in private, not on the phone. When is a convenient time for you, Norman?"

"I'm at your service."

"Then I'll be there in half an hour

Kim walked in to Norman's office and he immediately rose from his desk, Southern gentleman that he was. "Kim, it's so nice to see you. How are you? How's Bart? Lucky stiff. I wish I could retire early, but with Alexa's spending habits, I guess I'll be working until they take me out of here on a stretcher," Norman said pleasantly.

"Hello," Kim said as she sat in front of his desk. "Before I tell you why I'm here, I want you to know that I have become privy to certain information and that I have written it all down, supplied photographs of all we're going to discuss, and sealed it. The letter and the pictures are in the hands of my attorney and several people have sealed copies, so keep that in mind as we talk."

"Sounds very serious, Kim. Are you ill?" Norman was completely at ease. He had not so much as looked at another woman since Alexa had caught him with her daughter Jill and he had never gone on Kim's barge so he knew he had nothing to fear. *Pictures of what? Not of him.*

"Not at all. I've never felt better."

"Then what is all this cloak and dagger stuff?"

"How large is this plant of yours – I mean, really, how large is it?"

"You've had a tour of the plant, Kim."

"I've seen what you show people, but I think your plant must be larger than what is visible to the naked eye, Norman."

"I don't know what you're talking about or what you're getting at," said Norman and his chivalrous ways were quickly fading.

"What I've seen of your plant hardly warrants another forty or so workers in addition to those I've already seen."

"You've lost me, Kim."

"And why would those extra workers be riding a county school bus, Norman?"

"Come again."

"I've seen the school bus coming here and going to the back road to La Reina de la Mar."

"You know very well why the school bus comes here, Kim. I give the county the gas to un the buses."

"And are your gas storage tanks inside the building?"

"Of course not."

"Then why does the bus go inside the building and why does the bus driver have a garage door opener? And why does the school bus go to your home on a barricaded, closed back road and why does the driver remove the barricade that's obviously been tampered with and when he returns and removes the barricade, why is there an armed guard with an AK-47 on the bus?"

"Again, Kim, you've lost me."

"Then I'll simply lay everything out on the table, Norman, and remember those sealed envelopes with pictures I told you about earlier. I know that you're keeping illegal Mexicans on your estate. I know they have no plumbing, no running water, eat rancid food, live in unsanitary conditions in bunkhouses with guards surrounding them with AK-47's and that they are transported back and forth to Seafood World by county school buses. There are a whole lot of things going on here that I think several different branches of the legal system would find quite interesting."

"Kim, I know you're under a lot of strain because of your shop being closed, but I assure you, I have no idea what you're talking about."

"I'm sure you do, Norman. You're bringing illegal Mexicans in to work in your plant with the few legals you bring in and someone at the docks is helping you. Joey Scappaticcio, I imagine. Now, I want to show you a set of these pictures I printed up just for you."

With that, Kim spread the pictures on Norman's desk. Norman looked at them and then at her and said, "All right, what do you want?"

"A piece of the action."

"What are you talking about?"

"I suppose you already have a network to collect these illegal Mexicans and bring them into the country. I want some illegals brought here too, but I don't want them to get off the boat, so whoever has to be talked to at the docks has to be in on it. Once your human trafficking takes place at the docks, I want my cargo containers which will be outfitted with toilets, comfy beds and plenty of food, unlike those bunk houses of yours, to continue on to Thailand."

"Why do you want to send illegal Mexican laborers to Thailand?"

"I didn't say anything about laborers, did I?" Kim answered.

"Then who?"

"Young girls."

"Kim, no, I won't be involved in anything like that. You're going to sell those young girls."

"I didn't say that, but I'll pay $10,000 a girl. You and Joey or whoever you deal with can split it, throw it in the river, or shove it up your ass – your choice, but you will do this or I will expose you and when they put you in the big house, they will throw away the key. Now who do we talk to and when do I get my first shipment?"

"I've heard about you Asians being hard core, but you really take the cake."

"Oh, I intend to take the cake, Norman, and I plan to eat it too. Oh, and one more thing, I want Manuelo Ortiz released from that bunk house prison this afternoon."

"Who is Manuelo Ortiz?"

"My maid's brother and he's been missing from his parents' house for two months. Fabiola has been beside herself. I want him this afternoon."

"I have no idea who he is."

"Then I seriously suggest you go back into the bowels of this plant and yell his name. I guess he'll respond."

"I hope you choke on that cake, Kim."

"Ortiz, now," Kim said, as she gathered up the pictures. "Would you like me to leave this set of prints with you, Norman?"

"No, thank you."

"I'll wait for you call and now if you would get Mr. Ortiz, I'll take him with me to see his sister. Oh, yes, I almost forgot, Norman. Do whatever you have to do to get Manuelo legal – he's staying in this country and working for me."

"You can't do that, Kim. Suppose he talks."

"He won't and neither will my maid. I know how to handle these people."

"I guess you've had experience with your girls, haven't you?"

"They were legal and well taken care of in addition to being well paid. Let's not have any pots calling kettles black, shall we?"

"I'll go find Ortiz."

"I think I'll just walk along with you," Kim said with a smile. She then sealed the deal as Norman walked her into the hidden factory underground. Kim had him for sure now.

CHAPTER TWENTY-NINE

Precious And Miss Twyla

*W*ithin the month, Raven had a crew working on Bonita's *teardown* contemporary readying it for her imminent arrival, Bonita had been tattooed, sprayed, wrapped, herbed, massaged and was ready to leave Beverly Hills and Precious was in New York ready to attend the auction where Bonita's treasures were to be sold. These days when Precious went to New York, she tended strictly to business. She no longer dabbled with young boys. Besides she definitely was getting a little long in the tooth now.

As a treat, Precious would eat at the Russian Tea Room as often as she could. She was waiting to be seated when she saw a woman that looked familiar to her although it must have been sixty years since she'd seen her. Precious signaled to the host and asked if he knew the lady's name. "Oh, that's Miss Twyla, one of our regulars."

"I knew it," Precious gushed. "We went to college together."

"Shall I see if you may join her?" the host asked.

"Please."

The host spoke to Miss Twyla who turned and looked at Precious with a questioning look.

"It's Precious, Twyla," Precious whispered.

"My goodness, Precious. Well, come right over here and sit."

Precious crossed to the table. Miss Twyla rose to give her a hug and they exchanged air kisses.

"How did you know who I was?" Miss Twyla asked.

"You're hardly changed at all, Twyla, same hair color, same gorgeous figure, so slim, same stylish clothing. I'd have known you anywhere and I know why you didn't recognize me. Many face lifts, but not necessarily with the same physiognomy as before, new hair color, some enhancement here and there and some lifts of those parts of the body that gravity seems to love to pull upon," Precious said deprecatingly.

"You look marvelous!" Miss Twyla trilled.

The college friends ordered champagne to celebrate and reminisced and caught each other up to date. When Precious said that she was in New York to sell the estate of Bonita Roberts, Miss Twyla almost choked.

"Has Bonita Roberts passed away?"

"Oh, no, dear. She's moving and she's getting rid of everything in her Spencer estate Villagio."

Miss Twyla had told Precious she worked for a major publishing company but had not disclosed the name of the corporation.

"Not that it makes any difference to me as I don't know the lady, but where is she moving?"

"I don't know. She's very secretive about it, but wherever it is, she's going to start over. You should see the things she's putting up for auction at Sotheby's – Faberge eggs, paintings by all the masters, Louis XIV furniture, exquisite pieces, Oriental antiques, Marie Antoinette's fan which is authenticated, tapestries from India and Turkey, gorgeous Aubusson carpets, French pieces to die for, everything really except her clothing, jewelry, two paintings and her exercise equipment."

"She's quite heavy," Miss Twyla said.

"Then you do know her?"

"Oh, no, but I think I remember seeing a picture of her in the Times. Wasn't she married to Joshua Roberts?"

"Yes. Oh, I see. Roberts' Publishing and you're in publishing, but you didn't say for whom."

"Oh, didn't I? I work for Houghton Mifflin," Miss Twyla said and crossed her fingers in her lap.

Miss Twyla could hardly remain civil to Precious, so anxious was she to get to her telephone and call Donnice with this latest information. The woman who had stolen her Joshua from her was on the move again and Miss Twyla wanted to let Donnice know right away. Maybe her lover's child could bring that uppity *whore* down.

CHAPTER THIRTY

Tying Up Loose Ends

*B*onita dispatched Hannah and Felice to Wilmington, North Carolina. Bryan drove them to the airport.

"Guess you're accustomed to moving around, huh, Hannah?"

"Lately, but for the first thirty years, Miz Bonita and I stayed in one place. Ever since she married Mr. Roberts, we been on the move. First, New York City, then Montiac, South Carolina, Spencer, Tennessee, and now I reckon we'll be calling Wilmington, North Carolina, home."

"What are you going to do there?" Bryan asked.

"Miss Raven's already there. You gonna love her, Bryan. She's so pretty and I reckon you'll be friends with her. You too, Felice. She's handling the remodeling of the house Miz Bonita bought. Felice and I are sposed to design the kitchen and I gotta tell the carpenters about Miz Bonita's requirements for the owner's suite."

"Where will you stay?" he asked.

Felice answered, "We're booked at the Wilmington Hilton for a month."

"Who knows?" from Hannah. "If North Carolina's like South Carolina and Tennessee, they promise everything on time and deliver whenever they's good and ready."

"I guess Mrs. Roberts, Javiar, and I will be arriving in about a month too," Bryan mused.

"Once Miz Bonita gets to North Carolina, she'll get everything going so if thing ain't done when she gets there, they will be soon," Hannah said with a chuckle.

"Here's the airport. I'll pull over here and get your bags out. We'll check'em curbside so y'all won't have to lug'em everywhere." Bryan said.

"Thanks," said Hannah.

Bryan hugged the two women and they went into the terminal. Bryan returned to the Hilton.

Bonita talked with Precious and then hung up. Precious was ecstatic. Bonita's items had brought in ninety-five-million-dollars at Sotheby's auction. It was Precious' largest commission ever. She got five per cent, as did Sotheby's. Precious was four-and-three-quarter-million-dollars wealthier after handling Bonita's goods.

Precious had told Bonita what her estate had brought and Bonita had told her to have the money wired to her Spencer account. She also thanked Precious for all her help.

"It was my pleasure, Bonita. I'm so sorry you're leaving Spencer, but I understand. I still feel responsible for your problems here after I introduced you to that horrible Isaac Kahn."

"Stop! The whole thing was quite unfortunate, but I'm a big girl and now, I'm to start a new life, so thanks again," Bonita said before she replaced the phone in the cradle and began a list of the other items to which she had to attend.

The permanent make-up was done and she now had permanently lined, not quite Cleopatra eyes, permanent rose lipstick that was quite a change from the fluorescent pink she had worn in her fat days, and a slight brownish tint to her upper lids. She was definitely over the blue eye shadow days. Bonita had also invested in permanently implanted individual eyelashes. She had a hint of permanent peach blush on her cheeks. Her hair had returned to its natural color, dark brown with a few streaks of gray, but Bonita had employed Mr. Kenneth, hairdresser to the stars, to dye her hair a warm brown with reverse frosting and golden tips. The natural curl of her hair was allowed to flourish and Bonita's hair was shiny, full-bodied, and beautiful. With her naturally dark brows, she was once again a gorgeous woman!

When Bonita awakened in the morning, all she had to do was run a brush through her hair and she was ready for the day. Her last visit had been to a cosmetic dentist where she had Lumineers placed on her teeth – her smile was now dazzling white.

Bonita, five feet eight inches in height, now weighed 135 pounds. Her muscles were toned, her entire body was tan as she had been sprayed, her make-up was permanent, her hair the kind women dream of having, and she had a body that was picture perfect. Her pendulous bosoms now measured thirty-eight-inches and she was a "D" cup. Her waist was twenty-eight-inches and her hips were thirty-eight. The surgical scars had pretty much faded and the tan spray helped to cover them.

Physically, Bonita was ready to start her new life. Left to do, she needed to select an entirely new wardrobe. That would entail a trip to NY to the houses of couture. Bank accounts had to be opened in Wilmington and money transferred there. She'd have a representative from Jimmy Chu or perhaps Jimmy himself would come to her hotel to outfit here with shoes and handbags. She preferred Jimmy to all the other designers for her footwear and purses. She needed new luggage having grown tired of the pedestrian Louis Vuitton seven piece set. Maybe she'd try Gucci this time.

Once her wardrobe was complete, Bonita planned to leave for Wilmington. There, she'd start her search for new furniture, artwork, and accent pieces. She knew Hannah would take care of her suite to her satisfaction, as Hannah knew her requirements down to the minutest detail. Hannah knew about the mirrors she wanted, the kind of tub, the soft pink palette for the painters, the way the closet and dressing area were to be arranged and Hannah would make sure there were a sufficient number of shoe racks built into the closet area. She knew that Hannah would also make sure there were lingerie drawers, and hanging space with shelves above and below for matching purses, hats, and other accessories to complement each and every outfit.

Bonita chuckled to herself when she thought about Hannah and Felice trying to design a kitchen together that would please both of them. Hannah would demand oversized double ovens, a separate island for rolling dough to make biscuits, pie shells, and her mouthwatering rolls while Felice would demand a Ronson station to attach the blender, the food processor, and the mixer for the frosties and shakes she make. Felice would also want several spice drawers for her array of spices that she used in Bonita's prepared food to replace salt and yet made the dishes delectable.

Bonita guessed they would agree on an appliance garage, a commercial gas cook top, trash compactor, and a microwave. Bonita had instructed them that she did not want granite in the kitchen, but quartzite, as it was not only heat and scratch proof, but was also stain proof.

The colors would probably cause another bone of contention between Hannah and Felice. Hannah liked bold jewel tones as Bonita herself did while Felice preferred soft, muted hues. Hannah would need large areas in which to prepare for Bonita's large and lavish parties while Felice would opt for a smaller space as all she really cared about was what went into Bonita's digestive system. There were probably going to be several arguments at the new house, but Bonita knew she could rest easy with Raven there to smooth everything out between the two women. She made a mental note to give Raven a giant raise in pay.

She heard Bryan return and called to him, "Bryansie, come in here please. I'm leaving tomorrow for New York. I'm going shopping."

"Are you going to get some fab clothes to go with that fab face and body?"

"I plan to and when I come back in a week or so, I'll restart my exercise routine and do my shoe and handbag purchasing. My last appointment with Kamlash is coming up. I'll make a few trips to the spa and then, we'll depart for our new home."

"Sounds like a plan," Bryan replied.

Bonita called Roberts' Publishing Co. and spoke to the CEO. She told him she wanted the private jet at LAX to collect her the following morning.

"It'll be there, Mrs. Roberts."

"Thank you," Bonita said with a smile. She hung up the phone and turned out the light.

CHAPTER THIRTY-ONE

Kim's Proposal

*K*im had Norman by the short hairs. She knew everything about his operation; the illegal aliens, where he housed them, and that his plant had a colossal underground facility of which the inspectors and the IRS were unaware. His choices were to play her game or to have her terminated. As he wasn't into hiring hit men, although he did consider it for a few seconds, Norman told Kim he would set up a meeting for her with someone she needed to know.

Kim was relatively certain that someone was Joey Scappaticcio, the dock master. Norman told her to meet him at Seafood World's office the following evening at eight-o'clock.

"We've got trouble, Joey," Norman said on his office phone.

"What kind of trouble?" Joey asked.

"Kim Bartlett's maid saw her brother Manuelo on one of the school buses. Her maid and Alexa's maid are friends. Kim's maid came to visit our maid and they went on a walk and discovered the compound. The bitches went right down the hill and into one of the barracks."

"What were your hired guards doing?" Joey asked.

"Oh, they were there, but there's never been an intrusion – only a few squirrels – so they weren't too concerned. They checked it out and didn't see anything. Then when they discovered a window broken, they searched the area. My head guard came upon two women walking and when Delilah told him she was Alexa's maid he couldn't do anything to them. How could he? Anyway, to make a long story short, Fabiola went to Kim and Kim went out to La Reina de la Mar with her and checked out the compound. They didn't go down the hill so no alarms were set off."

"What's Kim going to do? Turn you in?" Joey queried.

"No. She wants a piece of the action. She wants to bring in young girls illegally."

"Oh my God! For the barge?"

"She closed that part of the barge operation. Apparently, young girls are quite the thing in Bangkok," Norman explained.

"I'm not getting involved in white slavery, Norman."

"Then we're both going down. We don't play her game, she'll turn me in and it'll only be a matter of time before they find you, Joey."

"Then they'll have to find me. I won't do it!" Joey was adamant.

"Your choice. She'll be here tomorrow night at eight p.m. I'd advise you to think about it. We're talking prison time here, Joey."

"No young girls, Norman!" and Joey hung up.

Norman put the receiver down, rubbed his eyes, and wondered what he was going to do. If Joey wouldn't go along with Kim's plan, then her plan was kaput and she'd expose Norman.

As Norman sat there thinking, the phone rang.

"Yeah?"

"Norman, it's Joey. I still have contacts in New York. I can arrange an accident for Kim."

"And I won't be involved in having someone bumped off, Joey."

"You won't be involved. I'll handle it."

"Then you should have handled it and not mentioned it to me. Once I know, I'm an accessory. It's no good, Joey. Listen to reason. You're not going to have to do anything. You're simply going to have to look the other way – same as you're doing now."

"I'm a Catholic, Norman. It's not only those things we do, but also those things we fail to do."

"All of a sudden, you're religious? I'm sure she's going to pay you a shit pot of money for your poor eyesight."

"No way. I won't play!"

"Think about it, Joey."

Norman gathered some items together, shoved them into his briefcase, locked his office, and climbed into his Mercedes to drive home, but he knew he would find no solace there.

Joey left the docks and went home for dinner.

"Joey, have you heard about the contemporary house that's been sitting there empty for three years? Some wealthy lady has bought it and is renovating it. Whoever it is paid 3.8 million and she's all but tearing it down to redo it. I wish we could redo this place or get a new house. This one's so dated! Everyone has granite or quartzite in their kitchens now, not this old laminate and our bathrooms need to be larger with sunken tubs," Nina whined.

Every night there was something else she wanted. Joey loved his wife, but he felt that he only meant one thing to her – he was her personal cash cow.

"By the way, I'm so excited! I've been asked to chair the annual heart ball this year. I accepted, of course, and made a pledge of fifty-thousand-dollars."

"Fifty-thousand-dollars? Nina, I'm not made of money!"

"Joey, I had to pledge at least that. Last year's chair, D'Lancey Simpson gave one- hundred-thousand."

"Her husband can afford it. I don't have an extra 50K lying around."

"I don't understand, Joey. You have the trucking company and you run the docks. Why can't we afford what all our friends have?"

"Because you spend money like it's growing on a tree outside the back door."

"As chairperson you know I'm going to be going to lots of meetings and I'll need a different outfit for each, a designer gown for the ball itself, and you'll need a new tux. Yours is starting to look seedy."

"It's two years old, Nina."

"Exactly! You'll need a new one. After the ball, I want to have all the committee members to a catered breakfast. I guess we'll have to do that at the club. I can't invite those people to this old house."

"Nina, Nina, Nina, stop it! Is your whole life about what you have and how much you can spend?"

"You're a Yankee. You don't understand. I'm from a good, solid Southern family. I don't want to be one of the genteel poor. I have the maiden name. I want the money and the status to go with it. That's what matters in the South."

"A little shallow, don't you think?" Joey asked.

"Shallow? Of course not! One's social position and wealth are what makes the world go round in the Confederacy."

"The Confederacy doesn't exist anymore. Your boys in gray were defeated over a hundred years ago."

"Joey, the Confederates may have lost, but we haven't lost our way of life, our values, and our sense of what matters."

"And those things are your good name, money, clothes, big houses, modern conveniences, big cars, and chairing charity balls?"

"Oh, Joey, you do understand."

"No, I don't. I was being facetious."

At that point, Nina, whom Joey adored and was in fact obsessed with, burst into tears. Joey could not stand to see her cry.

"You're so mean. You knew all those things were important to me when we married. I wish my family had old money, but they lost everything they had in the war. It's not my fault. I still run around with my friends from boarding school and finishing school and they have all those things. You know how hard it is for me around them married to a Yankee. For a long time, they considered me a traitor. Now that I've been asked to chair the heart ball, I'm accepted again. I'm back in the fold. I have to be dressed perfectly, pledge fifty-thousand-dollars, entertain the committee for a catered breakfast, and I really would like to fix this house up. A new one would be even better. You see, Joey, old is good if it's very old, but our house is not the family manse. It's just a house built in the forties that happens to be in the historic district of town. It has nothing to make it special and I need to live in a special house. Why can't you see how important all this is? It's not only important to me. It's important to every female friend I have in Wilmington, in North Carolina, and in the South."

Her wailing and explanations continued for over an hour. Nothing Joey did would stop her crying. She was approaching hysteria.

"Nina, please stop. I'll figure it out. I love you so much, Kitten. We'll get the house, the clothes, a new tux, whatever you want, just please stop crying. I'm so happy for you and so proud that you've been asked to chair the heart ball. Everything will be all right," Joey said as he held his lovely wife in his arms.

Nina stopped crying immediately. Her mood swing was faster than a quarter horse scooting to a stop in a reigning contest.

"Oh, Joey, thank you," Nina cooed and sat in Joey's lap and gave him a big wet kiss.

Joey knew he'd be in Norman's office tomorrow night and he knew whether it was little girls, pygmies or munchkins, he's be in on Kim's deal. Why had he fallen in love with such a needy little girl?

CHAPTER THIRTY-TWO

Twyla Gets The Goods

*M*iss Twyla slammed her door, gave a cursory hello to the kitties and ran for her phone.

"Donnice, it's Twyla."

"Hello, Twyla. You sound out of breath."

"I am. I practically ran from the car to get to the phone. I had dinner at the Russian Tea Room this evening."

"That's nice," Donnice said. She knew she'd have to wait for Twyla's roudabout way to get any information. Twyla would not be hurried, but Donnice knew too that when Twyla called, it was about Bonita. She never called simply to chat – and for that, Donnice was truly thankful.

"It was good. I had steak tartar. The Tea Room is the only place I'd ever order it. I *know* their meat is good. One has to be so careful now eating rare or raw meat with that nasty E-coli virus thing running all over the place, not to mention Mad Cow disease."

"You're right about the Tea Room, Twyla. I'm sure their meat is good there."

"Yes. So, as I was beginning my entrée, someone called to me. I glanced over and didn't recognize the person. It turned out to be a girl I went to college with from Spencer, Tennessee."

Pay dirt! Donnice thought. *Here it comes!*

"Her name is Precious Woodson."

"Her name is Precious or is that just what people call her?" Donnice asked.

"No, no. Her name is Precious. They have the craziest names you've ever heard down there in *dear* ole Dixie!"

"I agree."

"Anyway, Precious is an agent now for Sotheby, Parke, Bernet. She was here in the city for a giant sale at Sotheby's. And you'll never guess whose articles Sotheby's was selling."

"I might have an idea, but I don't think it would be Bonita."

"Oh, but you're wrong, Donnice. Bonita's sold all of her furniture, almost all of her artwork, all of the china, silver, crystal, and practically everything from her mansion *Villagio* in Spencer, Tennessee."

"Why?"

"She's moving!"

"Where?" Donnice asked excitedly.

"Precious didn't know."

"Oh she must have."

"She didn't. I asked several different ways. She didn't know. She simply said that Bonita has no intention of returning to Spencer again. Someone in her employ named Raven is taking care of everything at *Villagio* and the estate is for sale."

"That's quite interesting news, Twyla, and very helpful. You'll be receiving a something in the mail from me post haste."

"You don't need to send money, Donnice. It's my pleasure to help you. That woman is so despicable! I know how heartbroken you were when your father left your mother to marry that harlot!"

"I was and I know you were too, Twyla. Thank you so much and I hope you're doing well."

"Same old, same old. My life doesn't change much. I go to the office everyday and of course, I have my darling kitties, but I miss the old days."

"Don't we all, Twyla? Don't we all? I'll mail you a check in the morning."

"If you feel you must, Donnice. Please give your mother my regards."

"I will. Good-by for now, Twyla."

Miss Twyla smiled with satisfaction, removed her jacket, and turned her attention to the mewing felines while Donnice placed a call to her good friend Glenn Close, the movie actress, and asked for a recommendation for a good detective agency in LA.

"We're not checking up on the ex-husband are we?" Glenn asked.

"Hardly. I could care less what he's doing. No, I'm checking up on my father's harlot widow."

"Why do you care what she does?'

"Because I'm a vindictive bitch, Glenn. You know that."

"Call the Eye on U Agency. They're the one all the big attorneys use out here."

"Thanks. I'll call right now," Donnice responded.

"When are you coming west again, Donnice? I'd love to see you."

"Maybe sooner than I think. I'll let you know."

Donnice called the agency and asked to speak to the owner.

"I'm sorry. He's not available. May I direct your call to someone else?" said the agency's receptionist.

"This is Princess Maximillian and I wish to speak to the owner."

"Just a moment, please."

"Hello," said a male voice.

"Are you the owner of Eye on U Detective Agency?" Donnice asked.

"Yeah. Can I help you?"

"I'm Princess Maximillian. I wish to hire you to shadow someone in LA."

"Fine. I have a number of agents here," he responded.

"You don't understand. I want to hire you."

"I don't do private eye work anymore, Lady. I'm too old."

"I want your very best dicks on the job. I want to know every move Bonita Roberts makes. She's staying at the Beverley Hilton."

"That's going to be tough. The Hilton won't let my guys hang out in the lobby and they don't release any info about their guests," he explained.

"What is your name, sir?"

"Buddy Holmes."

"Mr. Holmes, your agency came highly recommended to me. I'm sure you can figure out a way to tail Mrs. Roberts."

"Maybe so, but it's going to cost you plenty. I'm going to have to get someone inside the hotel, like working there, to help with this."

"I don't care what it costs and I want the surveillance to begin today."

"I'll need a picture of this Bonita woman."

"I only have pictures from newspaper articles, but I'll scan them and email them to you. She was huge, over three hundred pounds with bleached blonde hair, but I think she may have lost a great deal of weight now," Donnice explained.

"Send the pix and we'll get right on it."

"I want daily reports. I understand she's getting ready to move and I want to know where. She doesn't live in LA. She's been there for about five months doing I don't know what," Donnice said.

"We'll get on it and we'll give you daily reports," Buddy replied.

"Good," Donnice said and hung up to go scan and email pictures of Bonita to the agency.

Buddy called Housekeeping at the Beverley Hilton. The woman in charge was one of his old flames.

"Millie, this is Buddy. I need a favor."

"And why should I do anything for you, you old renegade?" Millie answered.

"For old time's sake?"

"What do you want?"

"I've got a job shadowing one of your guests. I want to send over one of my girls and have you put her on as a maid."

"I can't do that, Buddy. The guests' anonymity is of utmost importance here."

"It would mean a lot to me, Millie."

"Who's the mark?"

"Some broad named Bonita Roberts."

"It wouldn't do any good to send anyone over anyway. The Roberts' woman has the presidential suite and her own staff. Housekeeping doesn't take care of her suite except to do the laundry. Her staff does everything."

"Do you ever see her coming and going?"

"I've never laid eyes on her. There's a private elevator in her suite and that goes straight to the parking garage."

"So she has a car there?"

"I presume so."

"Okay, thanks, Millie."

Buddy would have to get one of his people in the valet department. He dispatched one of his youngest private eyes to the

Hilton to apply for a position in the parking garage. As luck would have it, the garage was short-handed that day and Chas Christian was hired on the spot. He wasted no time in talking with his fellow employees and getting the lowdown on the cars and the people who owned or rented. Within two hours, Chas had learned that the black Mercedes with the darkly tinted windows was driven by Bryan, Bonita Roberts' personal trainer. The car went in and out of the garage on a regular basis.

Chas called Buddy.

"Rick'll be there in ten minutes with a transistor. Can you get it attched under her car?" Buddy asked Chas.

"Sure can."

"Okay. I'll get a van set up across the street and we'll follow that car everywhere it goes."

"Right."

Rick delivered the transistor and Chas placed it under the car. Bonita's rental car could now be tracked wherever it went. Not to arouse suspicion, Chas finished the workday, but called in the following morning to tell the supervisor of the garage that he'd found a better position.

Buddy reported to Donnice that Bonita's rental car had been identified and now had a transistor on it and it could be tracked. Donnice was delighted!

Men were dispatched and the electronics van was set up. Two men were on surveillance in the van all night. They were rewarded in the early morning when the blip on the radar screen began to move. A radio message was sent from the van to the chase vehicle that was to follow Bonita's car. The chase car followed Bonita's rental car to General Aviation at Los Angeles International Airport. The private eyes watched Bryan get out of the car and assist a slender dark-haired lady to a private jet. Bryan came back to the car and got bags out of the trunk and carried them onto the plane.

Harry, one of the private eyes, called Buddy reporting what he'd seen. "The woman sure doesn't look like the pictures of the Roberts' woman."

"No, that can't be her. How much would you say she weighed?" Buddy asked.

"135, maybe 140 pounds."

"False alarm," Buddy said, "Follow the car and report again when anything happens."

Buddy called Donnice and said his men had followed Bonita's rental car to General Aviation at LAX and that a slender, dark-haired woman had gotten into a private jet, but that it wasn't Bonita Roberts.

"Was there writing or a logo on the jet?" Donnice asked.

"No, it was solid white – no markings except the ID number, but my men were too far away to read that."

"That's the Roberts' Publishing Company's corporate jet."

"How do you know that if it doesn't have any writing on it?"

"I know because the Roberts' corporate jet is white and has no markings," Donnice answered emphatically.

"There are a gajillion plain white private and corporate jets," Buddy said.

"I know it's from Roberts. Check it out!" Donnice directed.

Buddy got on the phone to General Aviation and asked if the Roberts' Publishing Company's corporate jet had landed there in the last twenty-four hours and taken off from there that morning.

"That's affirmative," was the answer.

"Where'd it go?"

"Let me get the flight plan. Says here it's headed for La Guardia Airport in New York City."

"Thanks." Buddy hit the button and punched in Donnice's number.

"It's Roberts' plane and it's expected to land at La Guardia at approximately 12:30, but the passenger is definitely not the mark. She's slender and has dark hair."

"That plane's flying Bonita Roberts. Follow that passenger when she lands."

"You got it."

Buddy called a New York City agency he had worked with in the past and gave them the information so the passenger would be tailed in New York.

Bryan had warned Bonita that Donnice may still have her followed and he had worked out a plan for her arrival in New York. When Bonita spoke to the CEO about sending the plane, she had requested Sheila as the flight attendant. Sheila was slender, about five-feet-seven-inches tall, and had dark hair.

When the corporate jet landed in New York, the private eyes were waiting. A limousine pulled up to the plane and a slender dark-haired woman disembarked and got into the car. The luggage was placed in the trunk of the limousine by the driver and the car took off. The agents tailed the car to Roberts' Publishing Company. They sat there waiting for the mark until the end of the day when some five hundred people filed out after work. They couldn't identify the mark in the crowd.

Meanwhile, Bonita remained on the plane for an hour and then had the pilot call a cab that took her to the Waldorf Astoria. The limousine had delivered her luggage there hours before. Bonita's reservations had been made in her maiden name of Maria Gomez.

Buddy called Donnice. The Princess exploded when he told her the guys in New York had lost the mark. Donnice called Miss Twyla. She offered no greeting. When Miss Twyla answered the phone, Donnice screeched, "Did Bonita come to the office today?"

"Why, no."

"Someone did who had flown in from LA on the corporate jet. Who was it?"

"I have no idea, Donnice."

"I want to know who was on that jet. Can you find out tomorrow, Twyla?"

"Of course, Donnice. I'll call you as soon as I find out," Miss Twyla answered. She had never known Donnice to be so rude. She must really be upset.

"Good!" and Donnice slammed the phone down. The harlot was giving her more trouble than those damned red complicated pictures where one tries to find Waldo.

Bonita checked into her suite. She knew the executive director of the Waldorf quite well and he had personally made Bonita's reservation in the name of Maria Gomez. He assigned a maid to her and by the time Bonita arrived and was whisked to her suite on a private elevator, her bags were unpacked. There was a massive bowl of fresh fruit, two-dozen red roses, chilled Evian, and a chilled bottle of Krystal champagne, her favorite, waiting for her.

Yolanda, the maid, took Bonita's full-length mink and asked if she would like a bath drawn.

"That would be nice," Bonita answered.

After a long, relaxing soak, Bonita dismissed Yolanda until morning. Then she made some phone calls to set up her couture appointments. She called room service and ordered dinner. While she was tempted to order steak and/or lobster, her favorites, she abstained and ordered a salad with oil and vinegar on the side, a broiled filet of sole and steamed veggies. Her one indulgence was a single glass of champagne.

The next morning, Bonita went to Oscar de la Renta's salon where Oscar himself selected the originals for her approval. He was amazed by Bonita's new body and face. Oscar couldn't believe this was the same woman he had made tents for only a few years prior.

Bonita made selections and told Oscar to have them delivered to Maria Gomez at the Waldorf.

"Traveling incognito, Bonita?"

"For the moment," she laughed.

She returned to the Waldorf exhausted after selecting over $100,000 in outfits at Oscar's and she had only begun!

Calvin met with her the following day where she spent the day at his salon. When she left, Klein was $75,000 wealthier.

"Her forays continued two more days until Bonita felt she had enough clothing for a minimal wardrobe. She had spent close to half a million dollars and was now ready to return to LA. She called the CEO on his private line and told him to have the Roberts' jet ready to take her back to LAX the next morning.

"You haven't mentioned my flight to anyone other than the pilots and Sheila, have you?" Bonita asked him.

"Absolutely not, Mrs. Roberts. Do you want Sheila on your flight tomorrow?"

"I do. Deliver her to the airport in a limousine. I'll need to keep her in LA for about two hours before the jet returns."

"That will be fine. I'll have the plane ready for you at ten in the morning. Is that suitable?"

"Let's see. That will put me in LA at five in the evening. Have the plane there at nine please. Sheila should arrive at 9:45 a.m. and we'll take off at ten. Thank you."

"My pleasure, Mrs. Roberts."

"And remember, hush-hush."

"You have my word," said Roberts' Publishing Company's number one man.

Miss Twyla tried everything she could to find out about the Roberts' jet and its trip to LA and then back to New York, but she could find out nothing. She didn't know the pilots and the girls who served as flight attendants on the corporate flights were rarely at headquarters. Miss Twyla really wanted to get the information for Donnice, her beloved's daughter. She was on her way to lunch in the executive dining room when she saw the CEO enter. Twyla quickly detoured to his office and there in the outer office sat his secretary.

"Hello, Caroline," said Miss Twyla.

"Hello, Miss Twyla, what may I do for you?"

"Not a thing. I was wondering if he's in."

"He just went to lunch. You can catch him in the executive dining room."

"All right, thank you." Twyla turned to head for the dining room when she caught a movement out of the corner of her eye. Caroline was leaving her post headed for the ladies' room. Miss Twyla whirled around and marched right into the CEO's office. She glanced down at his desk and there on a notepad was everything she wanted to know. " Jet at LGA General Aviation at 9 a.m., Sheila to arrive by limo at 9:45 a.m., take-off at 10 per Mrs. Roberts."

Miss Twyla scurried out to make it to the dining room before Caroline had gotten her panty hose down in the executive ladies' room. After placing her lunch order, Miss Twyla hurried to her desk and called Donnice.

"She's leaving on the Roberts' jet tomorrow at ten in the morning."

"Headed for where?" Donnice asked.

"I don't know."

"Where's she being picked up?"

"I don't know that either. I don't think she's using a company limousine though."

"Why?"

"Because the plane is to be at LGA at nine a.m. Sheila, the flight attendant is to arrive by limo at 9:45 a.m. and the plane is to take off at ten."

"So Bonita is somewhere in the city?"

"I would presume so," answered Twyla.

"Thanks, Twyla. You're great. Look for a check in a few days."

"It's my pleasure, Donnice."

Donnice clicked off and called Buddy.

"She's in NYC. Call every hotel until you find her. Start with the Waldorf, the Ritz, theFour Seasons, all the top hotels. She won't be staying in a Motel 6. Bonita always travels in style and she's leaving on the plain white Roberts' jet at ten in the morning from La Guardia. Be on it!"

"Right," Buddy responded.

He set his secretary to calling the major hotels in New York to speak with Mrs. Bonita or Mrs. Joshua Roberts and then alerted the New York agents to be at the airport the next morning at 9:30 a.m. to take pix of the woman boarding the plane. He told the agents to fax the picture to him immediately.

The next morning Bonita left the Waldorf by taxi at 8:30 a.m. and was safely ensconced in the Roberts' jet by 9:15 a.m. The chief pilot Richard served her orange juice and coffee. Precisely at 9:45 a.m., Sheila arrived by limousine and proceeded to prepare a full breakfast for Bonita. The jet lifted off at exactly 10:00 a.m.

The New York detectives had their pictures and faxed them to Buddy. He promptly gave them to his two best men and told them the Roberts' jet would land at approximately 5:00 p.m. at LAX General Aviation.

"This broad will get off. Follow her. Do not lose her under any circumstances and report to me where she goes. Stay there in case she leaves until you get the word from me that your replacements have arrived."

In flight, Bonita called Bryan and explained how she had stuck to his plan.

"Okay, Sugarbritches. When you land, a limousine will be waiting for Sheila. It'll take her to a La Quinta Inn on Sunset Boulevard. Tell her to go in the motel and have the driver bring your luggage behind her. She's to walk right through the lobby to the back entrance where there'll be a taxi waiting for her. The cab driver will take her back to the airport and then deliver your luggage here. You wait half an hour and then there'll be a cab at the airport to get you."

"Bryan, you're brilliant!"

"I bet Donnice will have an ulcer after all this," Bryan said with a laugh.

"Oh, I'm sure of it."

"I think she's interested in what you're doing, Sugarbritches."

"I can't imagine why," Bonita answered.

"You took away her daddy!"

"She was grown and married herself when Joshua and I married, Bryan."

"My parents got a divorce when I was twenty-three. They've both remarried, but I pray each day that they'll get back together."

"Joshua's dead. Donnice isn't praying for him to get back with her mother, "His death took away her hope, so now she wants to do something bad to you."

"Well maybe you're right, but I hope not!"

"You can't be too careful, Sugarbritches. See you soon."

"All right, Bryan, and thank you."

"You are so welcome and besides, I'm having fun!"

Everything went according to plan. Buddy's men called and said the plane landed, the woman got off, and they followed her to a La Quinta Inn on Sunset.

"Is she checked in there?"

"We'll see."

The men reported that there was no Bonita Roberts registered there.

"Find out what name she used and report back."

Buddy reported to Donnice.

"Bonita is not at a La Quinta," Donnice screamed. "I cannot believe your men are so incompetent!"

Buddy didn't think he could take any more abuse from this woman regardless of how much she was paying his agency.

"Princess, I'll tell you what. I'm off this case. Find another agency. I'll send you my final bill."

"I didn't fire you," Donnice screeched.

"Don't waste your breath firing me. I quit! No amount of money could make me work for you one minute longer, Lady!" Buddy said and he hung up on the Princess.

Donnice called the Beverley Hilton.

"Bonita Roberts, please."

"I'm sorry. We've been instructed not to put any calls through to Mrs. Roberts' suite."

"Then she's there?"

"She's registered here."

"Has she gotten back from New York?" Donnice asked.

"Excuse me?"

"Mrs. Roberts has returned from New York. Is that correct?"

"Mrs. Roberts has been here for nearly six months. I don't know anything about New York," responded the receptionist at the front desk.

"You mean she didn't leave your hotel last week?"

"Not that I'm aware," he answered.

"Connect me with the concierge," Donnice demanded.

"Right away."

Donnice continued her interrogation, but the concierge gave her no new information. She could not remember when she had been so angry. She knew Bonita had flown to New York and was now back in LA, but that's all she knew and it was driving her crazy. The Princess couldn't understand why the detective agencies were so incompetent or how the fat bitch could travel across the country and no one seemed to know about it!

CHAPTER THIRTY-THREE

The Meeting

*K*im had dressed careful to look totally professional. She maneuvered her 560SL into the parking lot at Seafood World three minutes before eight o'clock and walked into Norman's office precisely at eight. Norman was behind his desk, but there was no one with him.

"I thought someone else was going to be here," Kim stated.

"He won't go along with your proposal, Kim. I'm sorry."

"You better believe you're sorry. No matter. I'll get twenty-five-percent when I turn you in to the IRS."

"I'm sure we can work something out, Kim. Why don't you have a seat?"

"No thanks. We have nothing more to discuss," and Kim started for the door as it opened.

Joey Scappticcio entered, "Hello Norman, Kim."

"Hello, Joey. I didn't expect to see you," from Norman.

"I'm in," said Joey with downcast eyes.

"That was easy. Do you know about my proposal?" Kim asked.

"Smuggling young girls from Mexico and transporting them to Bangkok," Joey stated.

"That's right," Kim said.

"Don't you think Wilmington is a little out of the way? You'll be shipping them in the opposite direction from Bangkok and then doubling back to get them to Thailand," Joey explained.

"I'm up on geography. I want the girls brought here so I can personally check them over, restock the containers, and make sure the numbers are correct. It makes more sense than my being in Mexico each time there's a shipment. Suspicion may arise if I go to Mexico every couple of months. Having the girls come through Wilmington makes the most sense."

"Whatever you say. It'll be ten-thousand per girl for me *not* to check your containers."

"That's a little steep. How many containers do you check now?" Kim asked.

"That's the price. Deal or no deal? I didn't come here to be questioned by you about how I run the docks," Joey said angrily.

"Okay, okay, deal! Ten-thousand per girl," Kim acquiesced.

"And I'll be needing a piece of the action too," Norman interjected.

"I don't think so, Norman. My silence is your cut," Kim answered.

"Once you start, I can turn in," Norman retorted.

"You could, but you won't. You have too much to lose."

Joey asked, "How often will these shipments be coming in?"

"I'd say about six a year, so every couple of months, but I don't have all the details worked out yet. My plan is to bring in one hundred girls six times a year on ten containers each trip."

Kim had calculated this would bring her about thirty million a year. Of course there would be expenses. Joey's six million, the cost of passage on the ship, the price for the girls, a salary to her procurer in Mexico, the container cost plus the expense of fitting them with beds, food and water supplies, chemical toilets, and then the pay offs to the dock master in Mexico and his counterpart in Bangkok. She was also going to pay a trusted adult to travel in each container with the young girls. Kim figured she'd clear about twenty million the first year and much more after that without having the expense of outfitting the containers.

"Joey replied, "I'll have to know the ship's arrival date and how long it'll be in port. Are those girls going to be traveling in any kind of comfort?

"I'm having the containers specially constructed with air vents, bunk beds, a water supply, plenty of food, chemical toilets and an adult in each container with them."

"I'll have to go in and take a head count each time they come into port," Joey demanded.

"I think that is not a good idea. I'll be going in to check them over and I think they need to be isolated from anyone but my people from Mexico to Bangkok. You'll have to trust me on the numbers. Each container will hold ten girls. You'll be able to take your count from the number of containers."

"Fine. I'd rather not see them anyway. I can't believe I'm getting involved in something so despicable."

"I'll have to put on new supplies here too," Kim said.

"This is becoming very complicated," from Joey.

"It'll work. I'll hire some of Norman's illegals to supply the containers," answered Kim.

Joey realized that she had him two ways. She knew about the illegals Norman brought in and of course, Joey was a part of that operation too.

"Whatever. I hope you know what you're doing. If we get caught in this deal, they'll throw away the key," Joey said.

Norman had thought about what Joey said and he spoke up, "I don't want a piece of the action, Kim. I really don't want any part of this."

"Fine, Norman. Your only part will be providing me with men to resupply the container. Oh, and I want you to get Manuelo his papers and release him to me."

"All right," Norman said resignedly.

"Fabiola will be thrilled," Kim said with a smile.

"And what guarantee do I have that Fabiola and Manuelo will keep their mouths shut?" Norman asked.

"I'll take care of that. You have nothing to fear, Norman. We all have something on each other, n'est pas?"

"If this is settled, I'm going home," Joey said as he stood.

"Give Nina my love, Joey, and congratulate her for chairing the heart ball," Kim said sweetly.

"Yeah," Joey said and he was out the door.

"A good meeting, Norman. It's been a pleasure doing business with you."

"I wish I could say the same."

Kim awakened the following morning to a pounding on her front door and Fabiola's yelling, " Just minute. I'm coming. I'm coming."

Kim got up, put on a robe and started for her bedroom door.

"What's going on?" Bart asked

"I don't know, but someone's pounding on the door."

Kim reached the door as Fabiola opened it to two IRS agents. They flashed their credentials at Kim and said she was to get dressed and they would be accompanying her to her store for a field audit.

"Good and you'll find that I don't owe the IRS any money. I'll be out in a few minutes," and Kim shut the door. "You no invite senors inside?" asked Fabiola.

"No, let them cool their heels on the sidewalk."

By the time Kim got back to the bedroom, Bart was dressed. He asked, "Who was it?"

"IRS agents. They want me to go with them to the store for a field audit."

"Do you want me to go with you?" Bart asked.

"No, Sweetie, you had nothing to do with those books. I'll handle it. Just take care of the restaurant, okay?"

"Okay. I'll eat breakfast and head over there right away."

Kim showered, put on a jumpsuit and heels, applied her make-up, blew her hair dry, grabbed a purse and headed out the door. The IRS agents had waited fifty-five minutes for her and they were not amused.

For the next five days, the men pored over Kim's books. Finally, they presented her with a bill for thirty-thousand-dollars.

"You've closed my store for over a month for 30K. You people are totally incompetent!" Kim sneered.

"The agency thought you owned a lot more," responded the taller of the two agents.

"I told them I didn't. What about the bad publicity of those IRS stickers slapped all over my door and my display windows? What about that big chain and padlock? What about my lost income?" Kim demanded.

"We're sorry," the other agent said.

"Sorry? That's it?" Kim asked.

"I'm afraid so. We got down here for the field audit as soon as we could."

"Remove that chain and padlock and those stickers now," Kim ordered.

"We'll take the chain and padlock, but we're not paid to remove stickers. How do you want to make the payment?"

"I'll write you a check now, but I want a receipt and as soon as you're back in whatever cave you crawled out of, I want a letter from your superiors that this false accusation has been cleared up. An apology would be nice also."

The men left with Kim's check. She called her assistant at home and told her they were back in business. The IRS agents couldn't have arrived at a better time. Kim advised her assistant that she was going to expand into imports from Mexico and that she would be leaving within a few days to do the buying.

Kim flew to Mexico City and bought exquisite leather and wooden pieces for the Wilmington store. She next worked with the merchants, kept her ear to the ground and soon made contact with a potential procurer of what she really wanted – the young girls.

The woman she hired, Consuelo Souto, was a retired prostitute who had run her own successful brothel for years. Consuelo had no qualms about supplying Kim with young girls for prostitution in Bangkok. She wanted five-thousand-dollars per girl. Kim agreed.

Through Consuelo, Kim found carpenters to outfit the containers with no questions asked. After a month of planning, buying, building, and pay-offs, Kim was ready to head back to North Carolina and Consuelo was ready to begin collecting Kim's cargo.

Kim flew out on a Wednesday morning and Consuelo went into the poorest sections of the city shortly after with ten-thousand-dollars of Kim's money in her purse. She knocked on doors and offered Mexican families five-hundred-dollars a piece for their daughters between the ages of six and eleven. Consuelo told the families the children would be adopted by families in America and would grow up in the lap of luxury.

Five-hundred-dollars was more than most Mexican families earned in a year and as many of them had six or more children, Consuelo's job was easy. The family would have money and their child would have a good life away from the poverty of the ghetto.

As Consuelo recorded the name and address of each family who agreed, she had the head of the household sign a contract, usually with an "X", and she told them she would contact them within a few weeks as to when she would collect the child and they would receive their money in cash. Within a month's time, Consuelo called Kim and told her she was ready to send *one hundred sacks of sugar and spice* on a ship that would be arriving in Wilmington the first of the following month. Kim notified Joey Scappaticcio of the first shipment and the white slavery trade headquartered in Wilmington, North Carolina, began.

CHAPTER THIRTY-FOUR

Magnolia Ball In Wilmington?

*B*ryan carted carload after carload of luggage to UPS and shipped Bonita's acquisitions to the new address in Wilmington. He called the Wilmington Hilton and booked Bonita a suite and made all the arrangements for checking out of the Hilton in Beverley Hills. Finally, Javiar, Bryan, and Bonita descended in the private elevator and left for the airport. No one followed them as Buddy and the Eye on U agency had quit their surveillance job for Donnice. Chas had gone back to the parking garage and removed the transistor from the rental car the same day Buddy terminated with the Princess.

Raven, Felice, and Hannah were all atwitter awaiting Bonita's arrival. Raven had arranged for a limousine and the three of them met Bonita when she and the two men landed in Wilmington. There was much hugging and kissing.

"Now, I want to go straight to my new home," announced Bonita.

Raven, Felice and Hannah could not believe how fantastic their employer looked.

"Miz Bonita, you looks like you did forty years ago," Hannah crooned.

"I wouldn't go that far, Hannah, but it is a definite improvement, I would say."

Raven couldn't fathom that this svelte, attractive woman was the same Bonita Roberts for whom she had worked in Spencer, Tennessee.

Bonita adored the new house. She couldn't compliment Raven's taste enough. She loved all the modifications Raven had ordered. Bonita only wanted to make a few more changes.

"I'll have to decide on the furniture style I want and then we're in business," Bonita proclaimed.

The entourage left the mini-estate for the local Hilton and dinner after which Bonita decided she was going to furnish the house with massive Mexican furniture, paintings by Mexican and Spanish masters, large tapestries, bright-colored floor coverings, and a massive carved front door. It was hardly a return to her roots, but at least she was perhaps ready to acknowledge her heritage.

"There's a darling import boutique in town and they're going to carry a line of Mexican furniture and accent pieces beginning the first of the month. There was a large advertisement in the local paper today," Raven told Bonita.

"I'll take a look, but I think I'll be going to Mexico to shop some myself. Hannah, you and Bryan will accompany me."

"What are we going to do?" Javiar asked as he pointed to himself and to Felice.

"Take a few weeks off, with pay of course, and then when we return, you can start whipping up those shakes again," Bonita said with a chuckle.

"Deal!" said Javiar and he and Felice exchanged a high five.

"Raven, I'd love to take you, but I think you need to stay here to take care of the remainder of the renovations."

"I agree," said Raven, "They've gotten pretty accustomed to taking orders from me."

"And she don't give'em any slack neither, Miz Bonita," chimed Hannah.

"I had an excellent teacher," said Raven and everyone laughed.

Bonita, Hannah, and Bryan were in Mexico City exactly two weeks while Bonita bought, and bought, and bought. When she finished, she arranged for two containers to be put on the next ship for Wilmington. Her shipment was due to arrive the first of the following month.

The threesome returned to Wilmington and everyday, they went to the new house. Neighbors from surrounding estates came by to meet the new owner and soon Bonita was attending luncheons, dinners, and receiving invitations for cocktails, dinner parties, to join various clubs, and for shopping excursions with the well-to-do matrons of Wilmington. Interestingly, Bonita was a favorite of the late thirties, early forties set. No one would have believed she was pushing sixty.

While lunching on the barge one afternoon with Kim, Nia, Alexa, Luzanne, and several other wealthy matrons, one of them named Betty Lou said, "I think we should have our own debutante ball here in Wilmington. Why should we truck our daughters over to Raleigh every year?"

Bonita couldn't believe her ears. She had vowed to herself to keep her lips tightly sealed about debutantes, balls, debutante parties, ball gowns, white gloves, red roses, or anything and everything to do with debutantes.

"Betty Lou, going to Raleigh to deb at the Terpsichorean Ball is a big honor and a tradition. Who'd want to debut in lil old Wilmington?" asked Alexa.

"Lots of girls would, I think. We could have the ball right here on the barge. Wouldn't that be wonderful, Kim" asked Betty Lou.

"Definitely," Kim answered. "I think it's a wonderful idea."

Sandra Lee, another of the matrons added, "It would be fabulous! With each girl having her own party and a big ball on the barge – we'd put Wilmington on the map."

"I love it," said Nina. "Girls could still bow in Raleigh if they wished."

"What do you think, Bonita?" Luzanne politely inquired of the newest member of the group.

"It sounds like a splendid idea to me."

"I think we should start planning. Those of us sitting right here could form the committee," said Betty Lou taking charge.

"What will we call our ball?" asked Alexa.

"The River Ball?" suggested Sandra Lee.

"The Barge Ball doesn't sound very good," from Kim and everyone laughed.

"The Spanish Moss ball," said another. More laughter

"What about the Magnolia Ball?" suggested Bonita. She simply couldn't help herself.

"The Magnolia Ball. I love it!" cooed Betty Lou.

"Doesn't some town in South Carolina have a Magnolia Ball?" Alexa asked.

"They did. In fact, it was one of the longest running debutante balls continually held in the South, but there was some big scandal several years ago and they don't hold it anymore," Betty Lou explained.

"The Magnolia Ball it will be," said Kim. "Let's get started!"

CHAPTER THIRTY-FIVE

All The Ships Come In

*B*onita's new house was completely finished the day before the ship was to arrive with her two containers of furniture from Mexico. Raven had hired four men and two trucks to empty the containers and to move the furniture to Bonita's new digs. Bonita insisted on accompanying them to the docks. The ship put into port at five in the morning carrying Bonita's cargo and one hundred girls for Kim.

Bonita was up at four and ready to leave by ten of five that morning. She, Raven, Bryan, Javiar, and Felice headed for the docks. They met Kim on the pier.

"What are you doing here, Bonita?" Kim asked in surprise

"My furniture from Mexico for the house is on that ship. I suppose your new shipment for your store is aboard."

"It is indeed," Kim responded.

Men arrived with trucks to move Bonita's purchases and shortly her containers were located. Joey Scappaticcio directed the crane to remove them from the slip. Unloading began. Bonita watched as the men hoisted massive piece after massive piece into the trucks. She noticed when the crane lifted off two other containers and Kim's trucks arrived to collect her items.

Bonita moved closer to the ship and was in awe of all the containers on it. It didn't appear that any more were going to be off-loaded in Wilmington. Once the crane shut down, Bonita thought she heard voices. They sounded like the voices of children. They were crying and saying "Help me" in Spanish. Bonita listened carefully. She was sure she could hear children crying for help and the voices seemed to be coming from several containers. Just then, the crane revved up again and the voices were drowned out. Bonita hurried to the dock master's office.

"Hello, my name is Bonita Roberts," Bonita said to Joey.

"How do you do? I'm Joseph Scappaticcio, Nina's husband. She told me she had met you."

"Mr. Scappaticcio, it's my pleasure to meet you," Bonita said as she extended her hand.

"Joey, please."

"I hate to trouble you, but I believe I heard voices coming from some of the containers on the ship. They sounded like crying children calling for help in Spanish."

"You must be mistaken, Mrs. Roberts. That ship is all cargo. There are not passengers aboard, just the crew," John patiently explained.

"Please call me Bonita, however I distinctly hear voices and call for help. Children's voices, Joey."

"It must have been one of the stevedore's radio, Bonita."

"I don't think so. I'd really appreciate it if you would check it out."

"I'll do that right now," Joey said and started out of the office headed for the ship.

Bonita watched him and saw him stop and speak to Kim. He seemed angry. Kim nodded and Joey walked on. He stayed aboard the ship for approximately forty-five minutes. When he returned, he assured Bonita that the ship carried only cargo. The docks were alive now and very noisy. Bonita went back to the spot on the pier where she had heard the voices, but there was too much other noise for her to distinguish any definitive sounds.

"I must have imagined it," Bonita said aloud.

"Imagined what?" Raven asked as he moved closer to Bonita.

"I thought I heard crying and children calling for help in Spanish. It was coming from the containers."

"Oh, people couldn't stay alive in those containers, Mrs. Roberts. You've seen how they're constructed."

"Of course, you're right. Are our trucks loaded?"

"They are. The furniture is gorgeous. Ready to go home and have the men place it?" asked Raven.

"Yes, let's!" Bonita answered.

She waved to Kim who was still supervising the unpacking of her containers.

The huge circular sectional leather and cherry sofa was placed in front of the two-story fireplace with a red, black, and gold rug in front of it. Large cherry end tables were set at each end of the sofa and a circular dining room sized coffee table was moved into the center of the brilliant rug. Two Diego Rivera masterpieces were hung in the two-story gallery above the living room along with a painting by Sergio Ladron de Guerara, two by Jose Baray and a miniature oil painting by Pedro Coronel. Occasional leather chairs and the dining room furniture consisting of a huge hand-carved mahogany table that could seat sixteen with matching hand-carved chairs were situated on a dramatic black and gold hand woven Mexican carpet that had set Bonita back thirty-five-thousand-dollars. Magnificent ornate candelabra that beautifully complimented the sterling silver chandelier were set upon the gigantic table.

Raven was astonished that Bonita had bought furniture and accent pieces to furnish every room including traditional furniture for Hannah's basement apartment. The only thing lacking in the house by the end of the day were linens, crystal, china, flatware, pots, pans, and cooking utensils.

"We'll stay tonight at the Hilton. Tomorrow, Raven, you take care of the linens, one-thousand count sheets for all the beds, down comforters and pillows, mattress pads, towels, bath sheets, and washcloths, all color-coordinated please. Buy what you can here in Wilmington for temporary use and then we'll order the permanent linens from Porthault. Hannah, you and Felice take care of the kitchen and get a set of china, flatware, and glasses until I decide on the crystal, china, and silverware. All right?" Bonita instructed.

Everyone agreed.

The following night Bonita en crew moved into the new house and ate from plastic plates. Bryan insisted on taking pictures of Bonita as she sat at the head of the seventy-five-thousand-dollar dining room table eating from a plastic plate with mundane flatware and drinking wine from a Dollar Tree wine glass.

In days, the Baccarat crystal, Limoge china, and the Rose Point by Wallace sterling silver had also arrived along with several tablecloth and napkin sets of the finest lace Bonita had purchased while in Mexico. One final foray to Kim's shop for accent pieces and the house was complete, although Bonita knew she would be purchasing more artwork in the future. For the moment, however, Bonita was ready to entertain. She called Betty Lou and told her she would love to host the first meeting of the Magnolia Ball Committee at her new home.

When Bonita replaced the phone in its cradle, Hannah asked, "What did you jest say?"

"I'm going to host the first meeting of the Magnolia Ball Committee here."

"I thought we won't doing that no more," said Hannah.

"It wasn't my idea, Hannah. I was asked to serve on the committee."

"And they jest happened to call it the Magnolia Ball, I reckon?"

"That part was *my* idea," Bonita relented.

"Chile, I ain't never told you what to do, but them last two Magnolia Balls ain't brought you nothing but pain and misery. They jest 'bout been the death of you."

"It'll be different this time. I didn't initiate anything. You could have knocked me over with a feather when Betty Lou Morris suggested having a debutante ball here in Wilmington."

"And you never said nothing to start that?" Hannah persisted.

"I didn't. I swear."

"Humph! I jest hope it don't come to no good," Hannah grumbled.

"It'll be wonderful, Hannah!"

"I hopes so, Chile," Hannah harrumphed as she headed for the elevator to descend to her basement apartment.

Bonita was invited to join the Wilmington Country Club, which of course she did. Although she wasn't sure when she'd be able to take advantage of the amenities there as she was so busy! Her mornings started with one of Felice's veggie shakes followed by a two-hour workout with Bryan in her private gym. Decorators from New York were flying in and out on an almost daily basis to take care of window treatments, bed coverings, and small accent rugs. The landscapers had ripped out the lawn and were starting on the landscape architectural plan Bonita had selected. A backhoe was digging in the backyard for the swimming pool. Carpenters were on site to build a guesthouse for Raven, another for Bryan, a gazebo, and a cabana. Bryan had convinced Bonita to have a labyrinth designed so she could walk it while she meditated, another regimen he was teaching her.

With the ongoing projects, Bonita spent the rest of the day making executive decisions and attempting to have a social life of some sort.

Javiar had soon tired of the small town life and had given Bonita his two-week notice. Felice told Bonita she was going to stay for a few more months to make sure Hannah had Bonita's nutritional program down pat and then she would be moving on too. Bryan, however, was planning to stay as long as Bonita felt she needed him and Raven was to become a permanent resident as her father was marrying his high school sweetheart in two months.

Bonita had managed to get through another day of meetings, decisions, color swatches, and plant selections and was soaking in her oversized pink tub prior to dressing for dinner at Elijah's Restaurant in downtown Wilmington with Norman and Alexa and Kim and Joey.

Hannah came into the room and said, "Get outta that tub fore you shrivels up. I got your clothes ready."

"Oh, this has been so relaxing, Hannah," Bonita said as she stood and Hannah wrapped her in an oversized plush bath sheet.

Once dry, Bonita walked into the bedroom where Hannah had laid out black hose, a Dior black jumpsuit with a plunging neckline and little black Jimmy Chu pumps. Bonita had sneaked away for an hour during the day and Xandi had slicked her hair straight back and attached a faux chignon at the nape of her neck. When Bonita brushed on a little powder, applied bright red lipstick, and clipped on her diamond earrings, she looked like a million dollars. A splash of Vera Wang perfume and she was ready to go.

"You looks fantabulous, Miz Bonita! Insegrevious even!"

"Thank you," Bonita beamed and knew that she did. Bonita was well aware of Hannah's highest compliments even though they were words Hannah made up.

"I can't get over it. You looks like you's in your thirties."

"Kam is a genius, isn't he, Hannah?"

"He shore nuff done good."

Bryan was serving as Bonita's chauffeur these days and he waited under the Porte cochere for Bonita in the new white Rolls she had purchased to replace the old maroon one Raven had sold in Spencer.

"You look smashing, Sugarbritches!" Bryan said as he held the door for his boss.

Bonita walked into Elijah's and there were audible gasps. She really was gorgeous! The hostess showed her to her table and her friends complimented her. Graciously, Bonita thanked everyone and ordered a Perrier with a dash of Rose's lime juice.

About five minutes later, Alexa said, "Kim, look! There's that couple with the doll."

Bonita glanced in the direction Alexa indicated and there were Jamison and Celestine Piersall. Celestine was holding Anthony who was decked out in a navy blue suit and matching tie. Bonita almost choked on her drink.

Alexa looked at Bonita and said, "I've seen that couple several times and the woman always had that doll with her. I wonder what that's all about."

"I have no idea," Bonita responded.

She seemed to recall the Piersalls had a summer home in North Carolina on some island. It must be somewhere near Wilmington. She tried to avert her face, but she couldn't very well dive under the table or keep her back to her new friends. At last, it dawned on her that the Piersalls probably wouldn't recognize her. Celestine looked her right in the face and showed no sign of recognition.

Jamison stated his name and told the hostess he had reservations.

"Yes sir, right here. That's two?"

"Three," answered Celestine.

The hostess smiled and said, "Right this way."

Later Bonita and Kim went to the ladies room and Celestine was powdering her nose. Once again, there was no sign of recognition, but Bonita was on edge. She wondered how often she would run into the couple because, eventually, someone might call her name and then she would be found out. Celestine left the rest room and gave Bonita a polite smile as she passed by her.

While going through her numerous bouts of surgery and recovery in LA, Bonita had researched a number of original paintings in which she was interested. Several galleries had brought paintings or pictures of them to her suite and she had purchased a few of them. While in New York to purchase her wardrobe, she had checked out some galleries and had bought a few more originals.

The curator of the Museum of Modern Art, whose taste and expertise Bonita trusted implicitly had also made some purchases for her plus she had the paintings that had arrived on the ship and had already been hung. She decreed the day before the first meeting of the Magnolia Ball Committee that the following morning would be the day for handing the remainder of the artwork in the gallery. Raven made arrangements to have handymen available with extension ladders.

At Bonita's instruction, Raven had seen that the electricians who had rewired the house had placed over one hundred pin lights in the ceiling of the two-story gallery. Once the paintings were hung to Bonita's satisfaction, scaffolding had to be assembled so the pin lights could be aimed to show every masterpiece to its best advantage.

Bonita instructed Hannah that she wanted a platter of hors d'oeuvres and a platter of dainty desserts for the meeting. She would be serving red and white wines and champagne.

"You should run the hors d'oeuvres by Felice so she doesn't have a fit, Hannah," Bonita said with a smile.

"Miz Bonita, she ain't gonna let me fix nothin' good."

"Of course she will. Fix a few things she wants you to make and then you make the rest of what you want."

"All right, but I needs Bryan to take me to the store," Hannah said.

"That shouldn't be a problem. Is it, Bryan?"

"I'm right here," Bryan answered.

"Are you able to take Hannah to the Fresh Market?"

"Sure can. Hannah, I'm at your service," Bryan said as he made a deep bow.

"I'll be ready in twenty minutes. I gotta talk to Felice first."

Hannah and Felice consulted and decided to serve tiny cucumber and no fat cream cheese crust less sandwiches, tuna strawberries, and asparagus pinwheels.

"I'm gonna fix some little pecan tarts, some miniature Napoleons, and my triple fudge brownies," Hannah announced.

"Fine, but don't pass that tray to Mrs. Roberts," Felice chastised.

"She won't touch it, you can count on that, Felice. She's sticking your diet like black on night."

"I hope she continues to after all the money she spent on surgery. She can't afford to gain any weight – that'll undo everything!"

"I'm going to Fresh Market. You want anything?" Hannah asked her.

"Yes. I need celery, eggs, tofu, and miso soup mix."

"The usual then?" Hannah answered with a big grin.

"Right, Hannah, the usual."

At the market, Hannah was inspecting each cucumber as if she were a physician giving it a physical when someone behind her said "Girl, you gonna pet those cukes all day?"

Hannah whirled around and there was Izonia.

"My heavens, Izonia. How in the world did you get here? What you doin' in Wilmington?" Hannah cried with tears running down her face. She was so glad to see her friend she was blubbering.

"Mr. and Mrs. Piersall got a summer home at Topsail Island. I told you that," Izonia explained.

"Is it close?"

"Shore is."

"I had no idea," Hannah said as she hugged Izonia again. It was at that point that Hannah spied Anthony sitting in the basket of Izonia's cart. He was done up in red Bermudas, socks, red sneakers, and a T-shirt that read, "My parents went to Panama and all they brought me was this lousy T-shirt!"

"Anthony-sitting, Izonia?"

"I am. Miss Celestine is even more Anthony-crazed than she was when you was in Montiac. Anthony can't be left alone no more. Mr. Piersall was playing golf today and Miss Celestine was going to the beauty parlor, so she told me to take Anthony with me to the store. She said he don't like all them smells at the beauty shop. Two nights ago on my night off, they went out to dinner and they took Anthony. I told Miss Celestine the next day she coulda left him with me, but she say, 'Oh, no, Izonia, I don't want you taking care of Anthony on your night off. I know what a little beast he can be.'"

"Uh-oh, she fallen off the deep end, huh?" Hannah asked.

"I reckon so," Izonia said with a sigh.

"Well, hi there, Anthony. You're looking pretty sharp today. You remember me? Hannah? I knew you when I lived in South Carolina," Hannah said to the doll.

A young couple putting apples in a plastic bag looked at Hannah like she'd lost her mind. Hannah smiled at them and they quickly moved on.

"Course he remembers you, Hannah, and I tells him everything you say when you call on the phone. But Anthony's promised to be good and not tell," Izonia said with a smile.

"You better not tell, Anthony," Hannah berated as she wagged a finger at him.

A stock boy gave her a strange look as he passed by. Both Izonia and Hannah convulsed into giggles.

"So we need to work out a way to spend some time together. We ain't gonna be able to see each other at Miz Bonita's or Miss Celestine's, Izonia."

"No we ain't. Let me think about it. You don't drive, does you?"

"No."

"I do. Think up somethin' on your day off and I'll meet you and we'll drive someplace for the day," Izonia suggested.

"I'm off Friday. I'll get Bryan to bring me to town and say I wants to spend the day looking around the town. I'll tell him I'll call him when I want to come home," Hannah gushed.

"Perfect!"

"I'll call you Thursday, Izonia. You a cell?"

"Course. Here's the number," and she handed Hannah a slip of paper.

"It'll be so good to spend a day together. Oh, I forgot, can you get off Friday?" Hannah asked.

"Shore can, but I'll probly have to bring his lordship."

"Good. I'll see you both on Friday then," and she hugged Izonia and then gave Anthony a hug too

CHAPTER THIRTY-SIX

Norman Frets

*M*r. Bai, Mr. Cheng, and Mr. Dong, the Asians in Thailand, were extremely pleased with Kim's acquisitions. The houses to which they had sold the young Mexican girls were happy with their purchases and soon, the men were pressing Kim for more girls as their tentacles spread to more and more brothels in Bangkok and surrounding areas.

Kim, ever on the lookout for another buck, raised her price to seventy-five-thousand-dollars per girl. The Thai contingent didn't balk. As fast as Kim could make arrangements with Consuelo, purchase more containers and have them outfitted and book on more ships, the population of Mexico City's young girls, aged six to eleven, would begin to rapidly shrink.

Norman, who continued to bring in more and more illegal aliens to enslave at Seafood World, saw that Kim was bringing in more and more girls and that Joey, the dock master, was spending more and more money. Joey's wife Nina was traveling to New York and Paris frequently to shop at the couture houses while renting suites of rooms at the Waldorf in New York and at the Georges Cinq in Paris. On her last two trips, she had flown her personal maid with her.

Norman had gotten Manuelo's papers. The legal Mexican was now working for Bart on the barge. Fabiola was relieved and happy to have her brother close by and they were both sending money home to their family.

Meanwhile, Zarot, the school superintendent, was demanding larger payments for the use of the school buses; Alexa was hardly civil to him and her spending habits had reached even greater heights; and he was making nothing on Kim's enterprise. Norman was not a happy camper.

While he didn't need any more money, it grated on him that Kim had discovered his secret and had gotten the better of him. He certainly didn't approve of what Kim was doing, after all she was trafficking in white slavery and in children at that, but he had no guarantee that she, Fabiola, or Manuelo wouldn't squeal on him. From experience Norman knew that when more than one person knew something; it was only a matter of time until a secret would surface. He lived in constant fear of the day when he would be exposed.

CHAPTER THIRTY-SEVEN

The Committee Meets

*B*onita garbed herself in a black, classic Dolce and Gabbano suit with a pink Hermes scarf at her neck. She wore black Christian Loubritin shoes with a small, discrete pink bow encapsulated in the Lucite heel of each shoe. Christian had designed the shoes especially for Bonita – there was not another pair like them on the face of the earth. Her make-up was muted and expertly applied. As she had the permanent make-up tattoos, she merely added a hint of brown shadow, a touch of mascara, and lightly brushed on a translucent powder. Her only accessories were a single diamond pendant and matching earrings about the size of headlights.

Hannah had removed the top rind of a wheel of Brie and replaced it with pear preserves, butter, and brown sugar and baked it in the oven to be served with small wedges of homemade French bread. She had carefully wrapped thin slices of prosciutto around cornishons and placed a party pick in each and she had cored one hundred cherry tomatoes and painstakingly filled each one with an herbal cheese mixture. After the guests arrived, she planned to pass a sterling silver salver containing crab stuffed mushroom caps. Hannah prepared the asparagus pinwheels, tuna strawberries, and *no fat* cream cheese and cucumber sandwiches she and Felice had agreed upon earlier.

Bryan had set up the bar and would be serving at the bartender for the evening. A carload of fresh flowers had been brought in from Raleigh and arranged by the florist in several large vases in the foyer, great room, and on the sun porch. Everything was ready for the meeting to discuss the Ball in Wilmington. The best part was that Bonita had not precipitated the subject, but had been *asked* to participate. She, Kim, Alexa, Kim, and Luzanne would be the charter members of the committee; however tonight there would be several other ladies present whom the others had invited.

Nina arrived in a lovely Kelly green Vera Wang dress simply cut with a matching macramé sweater, green Prada pumps and matching Prada purse. The elegant ensemble was enhanced by a huge emerald slide on a gold chain around her neck, an emerald tennis bracelet, emerald earrings and an emerald ring the size of a hen egg on the ring finger of her right hand.

"Good evening, Bonita. Isn't this exciting? Oh, my, your home is exquisite!"

"Thank you. Won't you come in and have a seat? I'll take everyone on a tour later if they'd like. Tell Bryan what you'd like to drink."

"Nothing at the moment, thank you. I've long thought we needed a deb ball here rather than everyone traipsing over to Raleigh although I'm sure most of the girls will still do the Terp Ball. I debbed there in '87. Where did you come out, Bonita?"

Fortunately, Bonita was saved from answering Nina's question by the doorbell. She excused herself and opened the door to Kim who wore a red Thai silk dress shot with silver threads, a mandarin collar, and slits on each side. It was absolutely gorgeous and fit her lovely figure like a glove. Sterling silver jewelry accented with jade, pewter-colored pumps and a diminutive purse the size of a pack of cigarettes completed her attire. Greetings were exchanged and once again the doorbell chimed and Alexa made her entrance accompanied by two older ladies.

"Bonita, I'd like you to meet Madeline Winthrop and Penelope Simpson. They're real Wilmingtonians from way back as in *natives*."

The ladies greeted each other while Alexa, who looked positively ravishing, said hello to Nina and Kim. Alexa wore a winter white skirt and a white angora sweater trimmed in white fox. Her dime-sized pearl necklace was the perfect shade with the winter white attire as were the winter white leather boots. Bonita's trained eye estimated that Alexa's clothing, not counting the full-length coyote coat Bryan had taken from her when she entered, had set Norman back close to 10K.

Madeline, whom Bonita had previously met at a country club luncheon, was in her fifties. A native Wilmingtonian, her family had lived in the town since whale-hunting days. A little stout, she was nicely dressed in a gray coatdress, a Dior original that was a few years old, but still stunning, with matching gray accessories and lapis lazuli jewelry. The blue stone was an excellent choice to complement the gray. Penelope, whom Bonita had also briefly met, was loaded with old Southern money, but she was not too much of a dresser. She wore black Lubello slacks, black ostrich skin cowboy boots, a black cashmere sweater and a very expensive butter soft black leather jacket trimmed in gold. A gold piece of costume jewelry in the shape of a lion graced her neck and she threw her Louis Vuitton purse down on the leather sofa and plopped beside it.

Luzanne was the last of the original group to arrive as she had been delayed taking George's teenage daughter Mindy to a halfway house before heading for Bonita's. Luzanne had convinced George that Mindy was a threat to her and had hit her on several occasions, but that's another story. Luzanne had with her two more members of Wilmington society, twin spinster sisters named Gladys Pearl and Beulah Carol Rochambeau. (Their father was French, but mama was obviously a Southern belle judging by the first and middle names of the *girls*.) Luzanne sported a bright yellow Escada dress with canary diamonds at her neck, wrist and ears. She wore Little Edie yellow pumps and a Robert Cavelli jacket. The twins, well into their sixties, were dressed identically in bright blue Bottega Venita suits and sapphires.

Sarafina Mathison, a native and friend of Nina's, and Grayson DeWitt finished up the group. A petite little thing, Sarafina was in a pale blue suit trimmed in dark mink, lizard pumps and carried a purse that looked like a Beagle. It sold in local gift shops for $14.99.

Bryan looked around the room and calculated that the cost of the clothing in the room, sans the Beagle purse, could feed the starving children in Biafra for months on end.

After greetings were exchanged all around the room, Sarafina showed off her purse.

"Isn't this the just the cutest thing you've ever seen? I got it at The Dragonfly today. It looks exactly like my Butchie. I know it doesn't go with a thing I have on, but I couldn't pass up this chance to show it to all of you gals."

Sarafina was obsessed with Butchie, so everyone made appropriate comments. The purse and Sarafina were comical as she held it in one hand and then the other, both of which were graced with at least $100,000 worth of rubies and diamonds. Sarafina had driven to Bonita's home with Grayson DeWitt, one of those fortunate Southern belles who had been blessed with momma's maiden name as her first. Grayson sported an Oscar de la Renta candy-apple red jumpsuit, red, patent leather shoe boots, matching purse, and a ring on every finger and on both thumbs, one diamond larger than the other.

Alexa commented, "Your home is marvelous, Bonita."

"It is. I can't believe what you've done with it. Please give us a tour," added Nina.

"I'd love to. I'd planned on doing it after the meeting, but right now is fine. Let's all get a glass of bubbly and then I'll take you through," Bonita agreed.

The ladies were duly impressed with Bonita's taste, her decorating techniques, the original artwork, the bronzes she had acquired, the French and Italian antiques interspersed with the massive Mexican furniture placed in conversational groupings, the touches of whimsy throughout the house with a few masks gracing the walls, movie posters in the home theatre, a giant golden lion at the entrance to her private gym, the pink boudoir, the statue of Michelangelo's David urinating in the pool that was under construction, the mosaic labyrinth, and the brightly painted turn style that separated the kitchen from the dining room.

"What is the significance of the turn style and where on earth did you get it?" asked Sarafina.

"I bought it when Grand Central Station was remodeled. Art students at Parsons' School of Design painted it for me and the significance of it is at the time, I was quite heavy, so I placed it between the dining room and kitchen as a constant reminder not to overeat," Bonita explained with a chuckle.

"I can't imagine your being heavy," Madeline said, "You have such a lovely figure."

As the tour concluded, the ladies returned to the great room dominated by a priceless French Medieval tapestry that must have taken years to weave. It depicted knights and maidens at rest after a picnic, a moment in time that had survived to cross into the twenty-first century. The guests could not begin to imagine what Bonita must have paid for it. Once everyone was seated in the great room, Bonita pointed to gold Cross pens arranged on the large, circular coffee table and told the ladies that they, along with the Irish linen notepads enclosed in gold cases, were gifts from her.

"Shall we begin? You can use the gifts to take notes," Bonita suggested.

The intent of the meeting was informally explained by Betty Lou and everyone was in agreement that a debutante ball in Wilmington was a splendid idea. The group then got down to brass tacks.

"The Terp's Ball in Raleigh isn't *really* a ball anyway. Last year, 230 girls were presented. Every year, parents spend thousands of dollars on the girls' gowns and the poor things sit for hours on those monogrammed stools waiting for their turn to be presented and then each girl goes and stands with her escort, her parents behind her, while all the other debs are presented. It's the same thing over and over every year, 'Miss Avery Cunningham Ronquist Miller presented by her father Mr. Avery Cunningham Ronquist Miller,'" from Sarafina.

The ladies laughed at Sarafina's cleverness.

"A real ball would be more fun for the debs, I think, with parties of their own preceding it," Penelope chimed in.

By the time the meeting came to a close, it had been decided the Wilmington Magnolia Ball would be held three months hence on December 28 on Kim's barge. Xandi's band would be asked to provide the music.

"That should please the young people. Xandi can sing anything from old swing songs to sixties music to what's popular today. My goodness, she can even do that horrid rap stuff," Kim said.

The Saturday after Thanksgiving, the young ladies to be selected at the next meeting, would be invited to a tea at the Wilmington Country Club. Each girl could give an individual or group party although Bonita suggested that no more than three girls could go together for one party. The parties would be held during the Christmas holidays culminating with the Magnolia Ball.

Kim invited them to *Thai Suite* for the selection meeting two weeks hence. Taking a note from Ike's book in Spencer, Bonita suggested setting up a charitable foundation to receive the proceeds from the Ball. This idea was immediately approved. Alexa said she knew Norman would be happy to make a large grant. The other women followed suit. Bonita wrote a check on the spot. With her check and the pledges made, the yet unnamed foundation was already destined to receive $400,000 and the group hadn't yet decided which charities were to benefit from their largess.

The icing on the cake occurred when Kim suggested that as Bonita really didn't know many of the local young ladies yet and as she had such a lovely voice, perhaps she would agree to serve as the emcee of the event and announce the presentation of each debutante. Bonita gracefully accepted.

Champagne was poured and the ladies nibbled on Hannah's treats. By 10:30 p.m., everyone was leaving and as Bonita stood in the foyer waving farewell, she thought how she had plotted and schemed to initiate a Magnolia Ball in Tennessee and here in North Carolina, it had fallen into her lap. Life was good!

CHAPTER THIRTY-EIGHT

Hannah And Izonia Meet

*H*annah and Izonia met in Wilmington as they had prearranged and Izonia, with Anthony in tow in a car seat no less, drove them to a small restaurant on the outskirts of Topsail Island. Anthony wore a maroon jogging suit, tiny tennis shoes and matching maroon socks.

"Anthony, you look cute as a bug!" Hannah exclaimed when she saw him.

"We had to order him some more clothes. We don't usually stay this long at the beach and Miss Celestine was worried to death Anthony'd catch a cold," Izonia explained.

"I guess he would have if he only brought swimming suits and shorts for summer wear," said Hannah.

And then she caught herself, "Izonia, he wouldn't catch a cold. He's a doll!"

"I know that, Hannah, but you fell right into the trap, didn't you?" Izonia said with a laugh.

"I did. I swear half the time I think he's real too," Hannah joined her laughter.

The two women selected a booth and Izonia asked for a high chair for Anthony that the host provided as he attempted to hide his smirk and rolling eyes. The maids ordered lunch and caught up on two years as it had been that long since they're they'd really been face to face long enough to talk. Hannah told Izonia all about Bonita's languishment in bed for eight months, the gym, Bryan, who *calls Miz Bonita 'Sugarbritches' and she lets him',* Javiar, Felice, the health food, Kamlash, the surgeries and tanning, the permanent make-up, Raven's coming to buy and to fix up the house in Wilmington,

Alfonso's marriage to Raven's mother, the arrest of Bonita in Spencer, the women in Wilmington who wanted to start a debutante ball and their asking Bonita to join the committee and to emcee at the ball, the meeting at Bonita's house a few nights before, the private eye following Bonita in LA and that she had found out the person having her followed was Donnice, Joshua Roberts' daughter, who was a princess, and everything else that had happened in the Roberts' household since Alfonso had driven Bonita and Hannah out of Montiac.

Izonia filled Hannah in on the doings at the Piersalls, their travels, Miss Celestine's increasing dementia in her belief that Anthony was her son, and Jamison's growing resignation to the situation shown by his talking to Anthony all the time now too and including him in almost everything the couple did.

The women had a delightful time with each other and enjoyed a delicious lunch that neither of them had to prepare. They each ordered the steamer bucket and devoured oysters, clams, crab legs, corn on the cob, baby potatoes, and sausages and washed it down with that Southern tradition, frosty glasses of sweet tea garnished with slices of lemon and sprigs of mint. They finished off their luncheon with ample slices of lemon meringue pie made with sweetened condensed milk, the only way true Southerners make it.

"I guess it's about time for me to try to waddle out of here," Hannah said.

"Me too, but it's been so good to see you again. We're leaving for Montiac next week. Can you get free one more time before then?" Izonia asked.

"Absolutely. I'm so glad we're near each other again, even if it's only for a short time," Hannah said with a sigh.

"Next Wednesday then. It's a date. I'll meet you at the same place?' Izonia asked.

"Shore thing."

Izonia drove back to Wilmington and as Hannah exited the car, she said, "Bye, Anthony. You be a good boy, you hear? And remember, you don't never tell nothing me and Izonia discusses, right?" and she ruffled Anthony's red woolen curls.

CHAPTER THIRTY-NINE

Hank Makes His Move

*H*ank couldn't believe his good fortune. Word had already reached him about the extremely wealthy *young* widow who had bought the riverfront teardown contemporary and had turned it into a palatial mansion when he first laid eyes on Bonita. The bon vivant was immediately intrigued with her. The woman was gorgeous, slender, toned, with high cheek bones, full lips, beautiful brown eyes and hair, and clothing, and shoes, purses, and jewelry that must have set her back a small fortune for each outfit.

Bonita was meeting the Smythes, her next door, although several acres away, neighbors. She walked into the dining room and Hank did a double take. He turned to his luncheon companion and asked her name.

"She's the widow that bought the contemporary on the riverfront and renovated it."

"I bet that cost a pretty penny," commented Hank.

"I'm sure it did, but I understand she's quite well off. She's the widow of Joshua Roberts, owner of Roberts' Publishing Company in New York."

"Have you met her?" Hank queried.

"No, not personally, but I've handled some funds for her through her personal assistant, Raven. Mrs. Roberts was here Saturday evening for dinner and my wife pointed her out to me. She's a very attractive lady."

"A very attractive lady," Hank agreed as he took a sip of his lemon drop martini.

"Do I detect stars in your eyes, Hank?"

"Could be. She's really quite lovely," Hank answered.

Bonita spotted her host and hostess and joined them. She was not oblivious to the stir she caused when she entered the room. How sweet it was to be an attractive woman again.

Hank's eyes followed Bonita across the room and he stole surreptitious glances at her throughout lunch. When he and his friend Langston had finished their repast, Hank went over to the Smythes' table to speak to them, but actually he wanted an introduction to Bonita.

"Hello Hank," Dex Smythe said as Hank approached his table.

"Dex, how are you?" Hank replied as he took Dex's outstretched hand.

"Fine, Hank."

"Hello Cynthia, you look lovely today," our new neighbor, Bonita Roberts." Hank said to Dex's wife as he made a slight bow.

Cynthia extended her hand. As Hank took it, she said, "Hank, I'd like you to meet

"Enchante," Hank said.

When Bonita offered her hand, Hank kissed her fingertips. She felt a shudder run through her right to her toes. The feeling shocked her, as she had been sexually neutral for years. In fact when she thought about it for a second, she realized she had been sexually dead.

"Good afternoon," Bonita offered.

"It's getting better by the minute now that I've met one of the loveliest ladies in the room," Hank said as he looked directly into Bonita's eyes.

"Have a seat, Hank. Join us for an after luncheon liqueur," invited Dex.

"Oh, do, Hank," chimed Cynthia.

"Do you mind, Mrs. Roberts?' Hank asked as he inclined his head.

"Not at all and please call me Bonita."

"Only if you promise to call me Hank."

"I shall. . .Hank," Bonita purred

"Early and often," Hank continued and Bonita laughed.

The foursome had several liqueurs and Bonita definitely enjoyed Hank's company, his devoted attention to her, and his compliments. By the end of the luncheon engagement, Bonita was smitten.

"May I escort you to your car, Bonita?" Hank inquired.

"Thank you, Hank. My driver is coming for me, but I'd love you to escort me to the main entrance."

They walked out together and heads turned at the sight of the handsome couple. When Bryan pulled up with the car, Hank signaled with his hand that he would open Bonita's door. Once she was in, Hank said, "I really enjoyed meeting you, Bonita. I'd love to see you again. Are you free for lunch tomorrow?"

"I think so, but I'm still quite busy with decorators. Could I check my book?" Bonita asked.

"Of course. May I ring you in the morning?"

Bonita gave him her card. Hank called the next morning. Bonita had checked her book and had already canceled her 11:30 a.m. and her 1:00 p.m. appointments. She accepted Hank's invitation. They drove to an intimate little seafood restaurant in Ocean Isle, North Carolina, and a smoldering romance began.

Bonita loved her new home, Wilmington, the whole Magnolia Ball concept, that she had not *had* to introduce it to her new friends and acquaintances, the fact that she was going to emcee the event, her new body, her new face, *and* she loved Hank! Life was not only good – it was getting better every second!

Within a few months, Hank proposed and Bonita accepted. Their marriage was to take place the following spring.

CHAPTER FORTY

Bonita To The Rescue

*B*onita was busy every minute of the day with her continuing renovations, her exercise program, her work on the Magnolia Ball Committee, and now her exciting social life with Hank. She dashed out of the house for her weekly standing appointment with Xandi to have her hair shampooed and dried with a diffuser. She had allowed her natural curl to return, so after she was dried she only needed a few whisks of Xandi's magic brush and she was out the door. Xandi welcomed Bonita and sent her back to the shampoo girl who handed Bonita a smock. Bonita went into the ladies room, removed her blouse, and donned the smock. When she returned to the shampoo room, Alexa was being ushered in to have the rinse segment of her permanent.

"Hello Alexa. How are you?" Bonita asked.

"I'm fine, but my maid is driving me crazy."

"And why is that?" Bonita asked.

"Delilah, that's my maid, has a twin sister who's still in Mexico. Her sister has six children and she and her husband are very poor. Delilah sends them money weekly, but feeding six children takes more than she can send. She received a letter from her sister last week and she told Delilah how a woman had come to see them and offered them money for their eight-year-old daughter. The woman told them she would pay $500 for the child and that the little girl would be taken to America where she would be adopted by wealthy Americans and would be brought up in the lap of luxury, so Delilah's sister and her husband sold the child."

"My heavens! I can't imagine someone selling a child," responded Bonita.

"Me either, but I guess we've never been extremely poor, have we?"

Bonita didn't respond as her youth rushed back and she realized if a woman had come to her parents' door when she was growing up, they may well have sold one of their children in a heartbeat for $500.

"Anyway," said Alexa, continuing, "The woman told Delilah that the child would be boarding a boat going to Wilmington, North Carolina, where she would be adopted. Delilah is practically insisting that I take her to every house in the area to see if she can find her niece. I've told her that is impossible and that if, in fact, her niece has been adopted, I wouldn't be able to get her back anyway."

"That's interesting that the woman told Delilah's sister where her child would be adopted. Was 'the woman' affiliated with a particular agency?"

"I have no idea. It doesn't sound like any adoption agency I've heard about anyway where they buy children."

"No, it doesn't. You're right about that," Bonita agreed.

The shampoo girl's bell rang. "All right, Mrs. Masterson. Now we're going to take the rollers out and rinse once more."

The second shampoo girl said, "And you're all done, Mrs. Roberts. Xandi is waiting for you at her chair."

"Well, I hope for your maid's sake, she finds out something soon, Alexa," Bonita said as she rose to head for her blow dry.

"Thank you, Bonita. I do too. Delilah cries all day long."

"So sad," Bonita said.

As Xandi dried her hair, Bonita thought back to the day her furniture had arrived and she distinctly hear children's voices and cries for help in Spanish. She realized that she should have pursued those cries because she knew she'd really heard them, but after Joey Scappaticcio had assured her that there was only cargo on the ship, in the excitement of getting the furniture to her new home, she had forgotten about what she heard.

Bonita left Hair tdf and crossed the street to get a low cal latte as a little energy boost before she returned home. It was a beautiful day and once she had the latte in hand, she sat at one of the small tables in front of the coffee shop. Two Mexican women were at a nearby table and Bonita overheard their conversation that was in Spanish, which of course she spoke fluently.

"Fabiola, no se what to do. Mi hermana say the child going to be adopted in Wilmington. How I find her?"

"No se, Delilah. I feel so lucky to get mi hermano Manuelo papers after he kidnapped and brought here, but no se how you can find your niece."

"Mi hermana and su exposo don't have much money. I send them as much as I can, but I send some to parents too. If only they had let me know what they were doing, I maybe could borrow $500 from Mrs. Masterson and then work it off so niece could have stay with family."

"If she adopted by rich family though, maybe she better off."

"If she is, but it sound fishy to me."

"Si. I wonder where they take your niece."

"No se, but I think not good place."

Bonita finished her latte, returned home and called to Felice. "Felice, you speak Spanish, don't you?"

"Si."

"I need you to do something and there'll be extra money in your paycheck. I want you to pretend to be my maid and I want you to find out where the Mexican maids gather and I particularly want you to meet Delilah, Alexa Masterson's maid."

Bonita explained to Felice what Alexa had told her and what she had overheard in the restaurant.

"I want to know where the sister lives, if she knows the name of the woman who bought the child for $500, the name of the ship, and anything else you can find out. Can you do that?

"Of course, but how do I start?"

"If you leave right now, Fabiola, Kim Bartlett's maid, and Delilah are sitting in front of the coffee shop. Go on up there and buy a latte and see if you can make an initial contact today and then try to set up a meeting with them until you can get Delilah to take you into her confidence. Alexa Masterson is getting a perm, so Delilah may be at the coffee shop for a while."

"I'll leave right away."

CHAPTER FORTY-ONE

Another Story

*L*uzanne had quickly tired of playing mommy to Ralph's four children by his first wife. She became so overwrought that she started seeing a psychiatrist. She convinced the psychiatrist through her twice weekly visits that Ralph's children had severe emotional problems and that one of them had made threats toward her and had ended up hitting her. What had actually occurred was that Luzanne had invited Leslie, Ralph's second child, to hit her when Leslie was upset with her. She egged her on until Leslie threw a punch at her. No one was around to witness what occurred; however Leslie's punch connected and Luzanne suffered a black eye. The next day, she called Dr. Turner for an emergency appointment to show him her injury. Dr. Turner said he would like to see Leslie.

Luzanne carted the teenager over to Dr. Turner. Leslie hated Luzanne. She did nothing for Leslie and her siblings. Everything was done for Philippe, her natural child. Leslie told the doctor how much she hated Luzanne and how Luzanne had made her brother Phillip change his name to Night because her son's name was Philippe. Leslie swore that Luzanne had provoked her into hitting her.

After the appointment, Dr. Turner spoke with Luzanne and told her that Leslie was filled with rage and was so unhappy and upset that it was possible she may do harm to others or to herself. Luzanne said that she did not feel safe with Leslie in the house and that Ralph worked all the time. She needed a solution, as she feared for herself and her son, Philippe. Dr. Turner recommended that Leslie be sent to a halfway house where she would receive therapy and anger management in a family setting until her deep-seated rage could be controlled or reversed. Luzanne told the doctor that he would have to tell Ralph what his recommendation was because Ralph would never accept it from her.

That night, Luzanne told Ralph that Leslie had hit her.

"Leslie? I can't believe that. She's the gentlest of children."

"Ralph, look at my eye? I didn't walk into a door. I told my psychiatrist what had happened and he asked to see Leslie. I took her to the doctor today. . ."

"You took my daughter to a shrink?"

"I took your daughter to a doctor, Ralph. He had an hour session with her and says she has deep-seated rage. He has some recommendations for treatment. He'd like for you to come to his office with me tomorrow."

"Luzanne, tomorrow is Thursday. It's a work day."

"All seven days of the week are work days for you, Ralph. Surely, you can leave your precious office for one hour to meet with the doctor about the mental health of your only daughter."

"What time and where?"

"I made the appointment for 9:00 a.m. so you don't have to go to the office and then leave. You can just go in a little late."

"Well, all right, but I have to call my secretary and tell her that I won't be there until 9:30."

"Ralph, I can't guarantee that you'll be finished in time to be in your office by 9:30. Can't you tell your secretary that you'll be there when you get there? You are the boss!"

"All right, all right, but I hope this is not more of your nonsense, Luzanne, after last week when those Buddhist monks were here for three days kowtowing to Philippe and telling you he's the next Dahli Lama. What a pile of horseshit! Or like that guru you hired who comes here smelling like a sewer telling you all about your karma and your yoga instructor and your aromatherapy therapist and your reflexology therapist and every other damned therapist you can think of – do you realize how much money you spend on stupidity every week?"

"Everything comes down to money with you, doesn't it, Ralph? You're never here. I have to find something to do with my time."

"I'll tell what to do with your time. Why don't you try being a mother to my four children and your own? Why don't you do a little housework? You don't even boil water. You have a maid, a cook, a gardener, a personal secretary, a personal trainer and you even have the veterinarian come to walk that damned horse you call a German shepherd. The rest of the day you keep the dog locked up in the powder room. When you do decide to let him out, usually right when we're about to sit down to dinner, he's a wild animal. The kids hate him! Why the hell do you want a dog? And I think there may be a law in Wilmington against having chickens in the back yard. What are you going to do go into the butter and egg business?"

"Ralph, everyone I know in Wilmington has servants. I don't know why you want to deprive me of the same thing all our friends have. As far as the dog, it's good for children to have a dog. He's wild when I let him out because the children never pay any attention to him. They never play with him or feed him. I have to do everything for him, but I can't walk him. The time for his walk is the same time I'm working with my personal trainer."

"Then change your time with your personal trainer to another time, Luzanne. You don't even make sense half the time."

"I want the chickens so the children can have animals to care for. Nurturing animals is "Trust with a chicken. Luzanne, you are a lunatic!"

"Now I'm a lunatic, but you want me to mother your children and put on a housedress and do housework and cook. Why would you want a lunatic to mother your children and why would such a successful businessman as yourself have married a lunatic, Ralph? Why, I ask you, WHYYYYYYYYYYY?"

"I have work to do. I'm not going to continue this ridiculous conversation. You're irrational. When you think you can discuss this in an unemotional manner, than I'll talk with you. Meanwhile, I'm calling my secretary and then I'm going to my study. I'll go to the appointment at 9:00. Good night."

Ralph wouldn't see her again until morning, because shortly after she and Philippe moved into the house, Luzanne had told Ralph how difficult it was for Philippe to adjust to his 'new' family and to the house and his new room, so she was going to be sleeping in the room with him for a few nights. The few nights had turned into months and the twin beds in Philippe's room had been replaced with a king-sized bed. Luzanne slept nightly with her ten-year-old son.

Dr. Turner compassionately explained to Ralph that his daughter Leslie had severe emotional problems and made his recommendation that she be sent to a home where she could receive the proper mental therapy without the problems she was encountering in her own home.

"You talked to my daughter for one hour and you have determined that she should be removed from my home and placed in some juvenile detention facility?" Ralph yelled.

"No, no, no, not a juvenile detention facility, Ralph, a home situation where she will receive therapy and anger management sessions. After a few months, she should be able to return home with a much better attitude and outlook."

Ralph argued, but when he finally glanced at his watch and saw that it was almost 10:00 a.m., he gave in. *He had to get to work!*

"You're the doctor, Dr. Turner. I'm not sure I agree with this, but if it'll only be for a few months, I do want the best for Leslie."

"I'll make the arrangements so Leslie can go today," the doctor said with a smile.

"I have to go to the office now. Could you make arrangements for her to go this evening so I can see her before she leaves?" Ralph asked.

"Certainly."

"Luzanne, I have to go. Can you stay with Dr. Turner and get all the information?"

"Of course, Ralph, and I know this is the right thing for *our* daughter."

Ralph harrumphed and left. Luzanne looked at Dr. Turner with a beatific smile, "See, I told you, Dr. Turner, work, work, work, that's all he thinks about."

"You have my sympathy, my dear. Now let me call and make arrangements for poor Leslie."

That evening Luzanne waited for Ralph to come home until one hour before her meeting at Bonita's house for the Magnolia Ball Committee. Leslie was supposed to report to Children's Garden home by 6:00 p.m., information that Luzanne had passed on to Ralph via his secretary that afternoon. The secretary had called her back and told her that Ralph would be home no later than 4:30 p.m. to meet with his daughter. At 6:15 p.m., Ralph was still not home.

Luzanne called him at the office and he told her he couldn't get away right then. One of his biggest clients was having a flaming fit.

"Call the doctor and tell him we'll take Leslie tomorrow."

"The reservation has been made. She's already late tonight. I'll just take her now. You can go and visit her on Sunday."

"All right. Thank you, Luzanne."

"Think nothing of it, Ralph

Luzanne bundled Leslie up, grabbed the suitcase she had packed for the child earlier and drove her to Children's Garden kicking and screaming. Once Leslie was inside, Luzanne looked in the rearview mirror, arranged her hair, put on a little more lipstick, and started for Bonita's.

The main thought in her head was *one down and three to go.*

Once Luzanne was rid of Leslie, she complained to Dr. Turner about *Night,* Ralph's son Phillip, whom Luzanne had insisted change his name. "I think he may a manic-depressive, Doctor. He goes through these periods where he's hyper and then sinks into the worst depressions. You know their mother is an alky and a drug addict. I really worry about Ralph's children's mental health."

Luzanne was an extremely pretty woman and very convincing. She was able to wheedle a lithium prescription out of Dr. Turner and she began medicating Night in his food until he was little more than a zombie. After several weeks, Luzanne called Ralph's attention to his number one son's demeanor.

"Something is definitely wrong with Night, Ralph. Look at him. He walks like Frankenstein's monster, he hardly speaks, and he's even drooling."

"Make an appointment with Dr. Miller and see what's wrong with him."

"Dr. Miller is a medical doctor, Ralph. Night isn't suffering from anything physical. There's something mentally wrong with him."

"No, Luzanne. You take Phillip. . ."

"You mean Night," said Luzanne.

"All right, Night. You take Night to Dr. Miller."

"I will make an appointment in the morning."

Luzanne kept her word and took Night to Dr. Miller who could find nothing physically wrong with him.

"I'd like to run some tests, Luzanne. I can't see anything physically wrong with Phillip, but I think he may be having a reaction to a drug."

"He's not on drugs, Doctor."

"Parents don't always know when children are on drugs, Luzanne."

"No tests. I think he has a mental problem."

"That may be, but I'd like to run some tests to see if there are any drugs in his system."

"I don't think that's necessary, Dr. Miller. I'm going to make an appointment with Dr. Turner."

"Of course, that's your prerogative, but if I were you, I'd want to rule out drugs or a reaction to a drug. It could be something as simple as a reaction to cough syrup or a vitamin supplement."

"He doesn't take any vitamins and he hasn't had a cold. I'm taking him to Dr. Turner."

"Very well. He's a minor so I have to have your permission to okay the tests. If you won't give it, my hands are tied," the doctor said resignedly.

"Thank you for seeing him and I'll keep you posted, Doctor."

Luzanne took Night and went straight to Dr. Turner's. After Dr. Turner met with Night, he asked Luzanne how much lithium she as giving him each day.

"Exactly what you prescribed, Doctor."

"We need to cut that dosage back. He's obviously overmedicated on the lithium. The zombie-like movements and the slow speech plus the drooling are all indications of overmedication on lithium plus he told me he's gained fifteen pounds in three weeks. That's exactly how long he's been on the lithium. This is not a drug to mess around with, Luzanne. I want to see him again in three days. If he hasn't drastically improved, you are to stop the lithium altogether. It could be poisoning his system."

One could only hope, thought Luzanne.

CHAPTER FORTY-TWO

Mexico Bound

*F*elice made contact with Delilah at the coffee shop. She sat at a table and overheard the two maids talking. She walked over to them and spoke in Spanish with them and soon the three were chatting away. After a half hour, Delilah told Felice what she and Fabiola had been discussing. Felice told the two women that she had heard of another family who had sold their child for $500 to a woman, but she couldn't remember the woman's name. The women conversed in Spanish.

"The woman who got my niece is named Consuelo."

"That's right. Consuelo. I wonder what her game is?" Felice asked.

"I'm afraid it might be white slavery," Fabiola said and Delilah began to cry. "I'm sorry, Delilah, but the adoption story just doesn't seem right to me."

"I know, Fabiola, and I've been thinking the same thing. I just didn't want to say it. Once it's said out loud, I really have to consider it, but I don't know what to do."

"Where does your sister live, Delilah?" Felice asked in a very concerned voice.

"Mexico City. She lives in a very poor section. My sister said that several of the families there have sold their children so they can have a better life."

"Children? Have any boys been sold?" Felice asked.

"I don't know. My sister only said other children."

"It would be interesting to know if any boys have been sold. If it's about adoption, I'm sure there are families that would want to adopt boys."

"I'll write her tonight, Felice. She doesn't have a telephone, so I'll have to wait for her answer."

"Here's my number. Let me know as soon as you hear."

"Can you do something, Felice?"

"No, but I think I know someone who can."

"I would be forever grateful to you if you could help me find her, Felice."

"I'll do what I can, Delilah."

Felice reported everything to Bonita.

"Thank you, Felice. That was excellent work."

Consuelo? Could it be the same Consuelo I knew at the Beverley Wiltshire? She was Mexican and as I recall she was from Mexico City. She'd be about sixty-two now. What was her last name? Consuelo Rodriguez! That's it! But Consuelo is such a common Mexican name. Hmmmm!

A few weeks passed and Delilah called the number Felice had given her.

"Roberts' residence," Hannah said as she answered the phone.

"May I please speak to Felice?" asked Delilah.

"Jest a minute. Felice, the phone is for you!" Hannah called.

Felice came to the phone.

"Hello. . .oh, hola."

Felice listened and then she began to speak in rapid Spanish. In a few minutes, she hung up. She raced up the stairs to find Bonita.

"Mrs. Roberts, Delilah just called. She received a letter from her sister today. The sister has been to all the other homes where she knew children had been sold to Consuelo. Not a single family had sold a boy. The children were all girls and were between the ages of six and eleven."

"Thank you, Felice. I think we know what's going on, don't we? Those young girls are not being adopted. There's something sinister happening. I'm going to Mexico City."

"What are you going to do there, Mrs. Roberts?"

"I'm not sure yet, but I want you to get Delilah's sister's address for me."

"She lives in a terrible part of the city. It's not someplace you should go and you certainly shouldn't go there by yourself."

"I'm a big girl and whether you believe it or not, I can take care of myself. I've probably been to worse places than a Mexico City slum."

At dinner that night, Bonita told Hank she would be leaving in a few days for an extended stay in Mexico City.

"I have some business to take care of down there, Hank."

"Would you like me to accompany you, my sweet?"

"I can think of nothing I'd like better, but not this time. I'll be busy almost all of the time I'm there."

"The evenings too?"

"Especially then, but I can't explain now. I'll miss you terribly."

"And I you, but if you must, you must. I'll amuse myself with golf, eating alone, and reading books at night until your return," he said with a little pout.

"Poor Hank," Bonita said, but she hoped what he said was true and that he would miss her terribly.

In the morning, Bonita gathered her employees in the breakfast room and told them that she was leaving for Mexico City. She related what she had been told by Alexa, what she had overheard from Fabiola and Delilah, what Felice had been able to find out and finally about her knowing she had heard children's voices crying and calling for help in Spanish the day her furniture arrived.

"I'm convinced this Consuelo woman is involved in white slavery trade and I'm particularly curious as she apparently told Delilah's sister that her child would be going on a ship to Wilmington, North Carolina, where she would be adopted by a wealthy family.

"What you gone do down there, Chile?" Hannah asked.

"Keep my eyes and ears open and try to find this Consuelo woman."

"Mrs. Roberts, Mexico City is colossal. There are over twenty million people there and half of the women are named Consuelo. How do you plan to find her? You don't even know her last name," Raven asked.

"I'm not sure, Raven, but I just have a hunch that I'm needed to find out what's going on down there."

"You're not planning on going alone, are you?" Bryan asked.

"Yes."

"Miz Bonita, you can't go down there by yoself doing detective work. I be worried to death," Hannah said, her voice cracking.

"Hannah, you're a love. I can take care of myself."

"You may think you can, Sugarbritches, but if you're going to be going into the bad sections of Mexico City, then I'm going with you," Bryan stated.

"Bryan, may I remind you that I'm your employer and I'm not asking or expecting you to go with me."

"Fine, then fire me and I'll follow you down there. You're not going by yourself," Bryan blurted.

"How sweet, Bryan. If it'll make all of you feel better, I'll take Bryan with me, but remember once we're down there, Bryan, I am the boss. If I say I'm going someplace, then I'm *going!*"

"Fair enough, but I'm *going* with you!" Bryan replied.

"Felice, were you able to get Delilah's sister's address in Mexico City?"

"I have it. Delilah called this morning. She was quite suspicious about my wanting her sister's address, but I reminded her that I might know someone who could help her. She insisted that the person I thought could help should be looking here in Wilmington, not in Mexico City, but she gave it to me. She's a wreck worrying about her niece."

"I'm sure," Bonita replied. "Now everyone, the official word as to why I've gone to Mexico City is to purchase some more art work. It happens that there's to be an auction while I'm there of works by Rodolfo Morales and Ruben Ortiz Torres, so I'm sure I'll be bringing back some lovely paintings. Not a word about what we know is going on down in Mexico City. Do you understand?"

Raven, Felice, and Hannah all vowed that their lips were sealed.

"How long you gone be down there, Miz Bonita?" Hannah asked.

"I'm not sure, Hannah. I guess as long as it takes."

"I still don't know what you's gone do or how you think you gone find that woman," Hannah almost wailed.

"I don't either, but I have a plan. Bryan, we'll leave tomorrow afternoon on the 1:00 p.m. flight. Call and make your reservation, first class. I already have mine. Also, Raven, would you please call the hotel and change my accommodations to a two bedroom suite as my shadow insists on going with me," Bonita said with a kindly smile at Bryan.

Later, Raven tapped on Bonita's door and told her she had reserved the Presidente Suite at the Inter-Continental Presidente Hotel, the most luxurious hotel in Mexico City. There were two large bedrooms, separate dressing rooms and baths, a wet bar, a living room with balcony, a separate dining room and a kitchenette.

"Splendid, Raven. Thank you."

"Please be careful down there, Mrs. Roberts," Raven said softly "I will, my dear. I promise."

After Raven left, Bonita thought about her employees' loyalty. Hannah had always loved her, but now Felice, Raven, and Bryan were all concerned about her welfare. In the old days she would have simply thought they didn't want to lose their meal ticket, but Bryan had really touched her when he said she could fire him and he was still going to Mexico City to protect her. Bonita decided she liked being liked. She supposed she hadn't been very well liked in Montiac. *Face it, Bonita. Everyone hated you and with good reason. You thought you were the Queen of Dorchester County and you acted that way, selecting those girls you wanted, dismissing those you didn't, using the committee to settle any little disputes you had or anything anyone had done to you or said to you that you didn't like. You were definitely a witch! That poor little Sandy committed suicide because she wasn't selected to make her debut and it was all because you had found out about her mother's past. But you got paid back, didn't you? That pitiful Celestine told everyone about your past through her surrogate Anthony and you were disgraced. Serves you right!*

And did you learn a lesson from that? No, because you weren't much better in Spencer ramming the Magnolia Ball down everyone's throat and elevating yourself to the head poobah of the entire operation. Got bitten again too, only that time you weren't guilty, but no matter. Everyone in Spencer hates you too!

But now you have a chance, old gal. Everyone thinks I'm younger and I didn't bring up the Ball, although I did slip in the suggestion for it to be called The Magnolia Bal. I didn't set myself up to run the show. The committee asked me to emcee. And then Hank came into my life. Good things are happening to me at last. I've realized that even with all of Joshua's money and all of my possessions I wasn't happy. Look how easy it was for me to give all of it up. I had Raven sell everything while I was in LA. I don't even remember most of the things I owned at Villagio. Material things are lovely and fun, but they certainly haven't been keeping me warm at night, inside or outside, have they?

Maybe I can do something for someone else for a change, something really good. I'll do all I can to rescue these young girls who've been purchased from the parents in Mexico and shipped off to God knows where. I'll do it to honor all those girls I blackballed who should have debuted and in memory of Sandy and in thanksgiving that even though I ended up a prostitute I met Marvin Hamblin on the road and he took me to Hollywood. At least I escaped the poverty of my family and my thirty years at the Beverley Wiltshire weren't so bad. I had beautiful clothes, good food, Hannah to take care of me, and some of the men I met were actually very nice. After all, I met Joshua and Kamlash and both of them did me huge favors.

She drifted to sleep filled with good feelings and good intentions, the latter being a relatively new situation for her.

It was evening in Mexico City and Bonita and Bryan were in the palatial suite of the Inter-Continental President in the Polanco District of the capital. The hotel was gorgeous and the suite's balcony was on the forty-second floor and provided a fantastic view of the city. The unlikely couple were eating in their first night, a suggestion Bonita had made shortly after their arrival.

"Tomorrow's a busy day, Bryan. You may do as you wish now, but I plan to call room service, eat in, take a long soak and go to bed."

"Sounds great. What shall I order for you? Wow! This is some room service menu. They have pheasant under glass, ostrich steaks, buffalo, rattlesnake, shark, alligator, and. . ."

"I'll have a tossed salad with oil and vinegar on the side, a broiled white fish, sole if they have it, and steamed vegetables on the side," Bonita responded.

"That's a good girl!"

"And a chilled bottle of Krystal champagne. I'll only have one glass."

"Right away and you deserve to have a glass of champagne. You've been so good about sticking to your diet and your exercise routine."

"Oh, now I understand. You didn't come down here with me to watch out for me. You came so you could make sure that I do my work out everyday."

"Absolutely, Sugarbritches, and you do know better."

"I do and I really appreciate your loyalty, Bryan."

"It's not loyalty, Sugarbritches. I loves ya."

"Bryan, I hope I'm not going to hurt your feelings, but maybe you better drop the Sugarbritches while we're down here."

"Mrs. Roberts, I would never call you that in public."

"Good. What are you going to order?"

"If it won't upset you, I think I'll have the surf and turf, a ten ounce filet mignon and a lobster tail, with baked potato and salad."

"It won't upset me in the least. In fact, I'll enjoy seeing someone relish those foods I love. Maybe one night if I exercise every day to exhaustion, you'll agree that I deserve a meal like that."

"Maybe," Bryan answered with a laugh.

In the morning, Bonita did a two-hour workout under Bryan's tutelage at the hotel spa and gym area, which was outfitted with every possible Nautilus machine ever invented along with hot tubs, saunas, steam baths, lockers, and showers. Wraps, mud baths, facials, massages, and high colonic treatments were also available and Bonita made a note to take advantage of some of the luxuries available if she had a chance.

Bonita showered and dressed and told Bryan she was going to the gallery where the Morales and Torres paintings were being auctioned.

"I'm ready to go."

"Bryan, you don't have to go with me. I'll take a cab. I'm going to an art gallery. I'll be perfectly safe."

"But I like art galleries."

"Methinks you don't trust me, Bryan."

"It's not that I don't trust you. It's just that I know how very clever you are and you might get a wild bee in your bonnet to do some investigating and you just might forget to call me and take off on your own."

"All right. Come along. If I find what I want at the gallery, maybe this afternoon we can take a cab out to the San Mateo Hills and find Delilah's sister."

"And I'm definitely going with you to that desolate place."

Bonita loved all the paintings she saw by the two masters and bought four. Bryan didn't bat an eye as she told the gallery where to ship over sixteen million dollars of artwork. Working for Bonita Roberts had inured him of being surprised at the vast amounts of money she spent. It meant nothing to her. The rich definitely did not live as did the rest of the world.

"Are you ready for some lunch, Bryan?"

"I can always eat."

They left the gallery and walked a little more than a half a block when they saw a sidewalk café.

"Want to eat Mexican?" Bryan asked.

"It's fattening!" Bonita responded.

"Let's get a burrito and an enchilada," Bryan said excitedly.

"You're on!" Bonita agreed.

After lunch, Bryan hailed a taxi and Bonita told the driver in perfect Spanish where they wanted to go.

"No, cuidado!" responded the driver signifying it was dangerous.

"Why doesn't he want to go there?"

"He says it's dangerous," Bonita translated.

Bonita flashed a wad of bills at the driver and told him "Mucho dinero."

The driver agreed to take them, but he didn't seem too happy about it. Bonita gave him half the money and then explained to him that they wanted him to wait and when he delivered them to the Inter-Continental President, she would pay him the remainder.

"You drive a hard bargain, Mrs. Roberts," Bryan said obviously impressed.

"I'm of Spanish heritage, Bryan. I know how the Latino mind works."

An hour later, the driver came over a hill and there was the area of San Mateo where Delilah's sister, husband, and five remaining children lived. Against the brown hills were gray blurs; concrete houses that seemed to be unfinished boxes. As they moved closer, they realized that interspersed with the concrete boxes were wooden shacks and in places, there were wooden slats propped up between the concrete houses with only a tin door leading to someone's or a family's habitation. Most of the abodes did not have doors or if they did, they were simply curtains that were pulled back. Looking into them as the taxi drove on dirt that wasn't really a road, they could see the dirt floors, the old clothes hanging inside the houses, and the swarms of flies that were everywhere.

Bryan could not believe people lived this way.

"Mrs. Roberts, I don't think coming to this place is a good idea. You could catch some kind of disease here. I don't want you to get out of the car."

"I've seen worse than this."

The taxi driver began to speak rapid Spanish. Bonita translated.

"He says some of those who are well off have a faucet for water and maybe a single wire for electricity, but most have neither running water or electricity."

They passed a wooden shanty with curtain doors. There were seven children running around in the dirt in front of the one-room house.

"Do you think they all live there?" Bryan asked.

"I'd bet a great deal of money on it," Bonita responded.

The driver started talking again and Bonita explained to Bryan.

"He says that at night it gets very cold here and the winds threaten to blow off the tin roofs of the houses, so the men and boys throw rocks and tires or whatever they can find that is heavy up on the roofs to keep them secure. He says cardboard boxes are at a premium here. They are never thrown away because they can be folded and put in the ceilings of the houses to keep out the cold."

Bryan noticed a group of women, babies on their backs and small bundles in their arms with children by their sides, descending one of the hills.

"Ask him where they've been," Bryan said.

Bonita asked and then said, "They left before six o'clock this morning to head up the big hill to the food aid line. Even if they get there at six, the line is usually a block long. Sometimes, they'll stand in line all day and when they finally get their turn, all the food is gone. He says that food prices are high here and the salaries are about $3 a day. It's impossible to feel a large family on that amount of money."

"I've never seen poverty like this, Bonita. It's blowing my mind."

"Bryan, we need to educate you. Do you know that 42% of Mexicans live on an average daily income of two dollars or less a day and 18% live on a dollar a day or less. I guess you can understand why they do anything they can to get to America."

"Yes, but then they really get on the gravy train, don't they? Free food at schools, free education, food stamps, welfare programs, free tuition, free medical, free everything."

"What we do for them in the US is not right either, but at least you can now see why they're anxious to get away."

The driver stopped in front of a wooden plank house that was simply planks propped up between two other houses. He indicated to Bonita that this was where she wanted to go.

Bryan jumped out of the car and opened Bonita's door. Immediately forty children surrounded them. All were dirty while some were naked. They were all begging for money. Bonita reached into her purse and removed a stack of one-dollar bills. She handed it to Bryan and told him to give one bill to each child.

"You came prepared, didn't you? How did you know?" Bryan asked.

"Spanish heritage," and Bonita tapped on the door of the house.

Minutes passed and Bonita tapped again. A tired woman with sunken eyes, one child at her breast and another hanging onto her arm, came to the door.

In Spanish, Bonita told the woman that she knew her sister Delilah in Wilmington, North Carolina, and she wanted to talk to her about her child that was going there. The woman wanted to know if Bonita had seen her Yolanda. Bonita told her that she hadn't, but she wanted to find her, and that Delilah wanted so much to see her niece. Bonita explained to Delilah's sister that if she could tell her something about Consuelo, perhaps she could find the woman and then she could find Yolanda. Delilah's sister, Angelica was suspicious, but Bonita kept talking in her soothing tones speaking to the woman in her native tongue. Angelica told Bonita that Conseulo was very pretty, well-dressed like Bonita was, that her last name was Souto, and that she had given them a piece of paper that Angelica and her husband had signed. When Consuelo Souto came back and got Yolanda, she had paid them $500 in American money.

Bonita asked Angelica if she still had the paper and Angelica went to get it. She showed it to Bonita and Bonita asked her if she could borrow it and that she would return it. Angelica said she had no need for it and that Bonita could keep it.

Bonita asked if the woman had gotten children from any neighbors and Angelica said she had. She told her that many children had gone to America to be adopted by rich people in Wilmington, North Carolina.

"But she didn't ask for any boys?" Bonita asked.

"No, she said no one wanted boys, only pretty little girls. She only wanted little girls between six and eleven years old," Angelica answered.

Bonita finished questioning the tired woman and told her about Delilah, where she lived, who she worked for, and that she was happy and doing fine except for her concern for Yolanda. Bonita told Angelica that she would be staying in Mexico City for a few weeks and she would be back to see her again.

Back in the car, Bonita told Bryan that when they returned they would bring clothing for Angelica, her husband, and her children along with bedding, sheets, towels, bottled water and sacks of groceries.

"You're a kind lady, Mrs. Roberts," Bryan said and patted her hand.

I'm learning to be, Bryan. I'm learning, Bonita thought.

The driver returned the twosome to the Presidente and Bonita gave him the other half of the money and instructed him to come back in the morning. He agreed.

CHAPTER FORTY-THREE

The Plan In Motion

A few days passed. The evening of their fourth day in Mexico, Bryan and Bonita had returned from dinner and Bryan was in his room watching television on CNN, the only station that was in English, when he heard activity in the living room of the suite. He walked into the room to find Bonita as he had never seen her before. She was dressed in a very short, black mini-skirt, fishnet hoses, a red, extremely low-cut organza blouse that was see-through, and four-inch black heels with straps around the ankle and almost up to the knee. Her hair was combed in a bouffant style and she had on enough make-up to open a Merle Norman studio. A small black sequined purse was slung over her left shoulder.

"Mrs. Roberts, what in the world are you doing and where do you think you're going in that get-up?"

"To the red light district, Bryan. I think that's where I'll have the best chance of finding someone who knows this Consuelo woman."

"Sugarbritches, you definitely look the part, but you can't go to the red light district by yourself."

"I was coming to tell you, Bryan," Bonita said, but Bryan knew she wasn't. She had planned to go by herself.

"I'll get my jacket," he said.

"But Bryan, you can't stay with me joined at the hip. I'm going to have to act like I'm plying my trade. You'll have to stay in the shadows and be invisible."

"I can handle that."

"You might get propositioned, you know?"

"And I believe I will say *no gracias*, wrong sex for me."

"Just warning you."

They got out of the taxi two blocks away from the famed red light district of Mexico City. Bryan crossed the thoroughfare and Bonita walked by herself down the sidewalk. She had hardly moved into the area when a car pulled over to the curb and she was offered money for her services. Bonita turned the prospective john down. Another half a block and another car pulled over. Again, Bonita refused. Once she got to where a group of prostitutes were standing, she spoke to them, "Hola, mi nombre es Bonita."

No one spoke to her. In fact, they turned their backs.

She tried again to talk to the girls, but they were not interested, so Bonita moved on to the end of the block when suddenly a large Mexican male stepped out of an alley and grabbed her by the arm.

"Puta, este es mi lugar!" (Whore, this is my place.)

"Deje van de mi!" Bonita yelled. (Let go of me!)

Bryan crossed the street in a flash and told the Mexican to back off in English. Bonita said to the man, "Retroceda!"

The man let go of Bonita and asked, "Es el su alcahuete?" (Is he your pimp?)

Bonita responded, "Si!"

"Usted lo dice esto es mo lugar y usted mueve ahora!" (You tell him this is my place and you move now!)

"What's he saying?" Bryan asked.

Bonita nodded to the man and took Bryan's arm and started walking away.

"Wait a minute! That man accosted you. I'm going back there and lay him out."

Bonita held on to his arm. "Bryan, keep walking. He's a pimp. I was in his territory. What he was saying to me was that I was in the section of the street he controls. He asked me if you were my pimp and I told him you were. Now keep walking. You lay someone out here and the *federales* will be here in a heartbeat. You'll be locked up and they'll misplace the key until I can find some high-powered lawyer and pay a jillion dollars to get you out. We're not in the US of A."

"Mrs. Roberts, how do you know so much about a section of town like this?"

"I read a lot."

"I saw a few guys pull up. Were they interested in your services?"

"I suppose, but I gave them the signal that I was off duty."

"That you were off duty? What is the signal and how do you know it?"

"You pass your flat hand in front of your throat. That means you've finished working for the day, are taking a break, or have an appointment already. And I know that because a friend of mine was a prostitute."

"You were friends with a prostitute? I find that difficult to believe."

"She worked for me for a time. She had been a prostitute in her youth. She told me a lot about her prior career."

"Why?"

"I asked her."

"Why?"

"I was interested, Bryan. You know there are prostitutes who stay in hotels and their pimps bring the men to them; there are prostitutes who walk the streets, some in seedy areas like here, and some in very high-class settings like the finest casinos and hotels in Las Vegas; then there are the women who are school teachers, flight attendants, nurses, and some of them are married, who respond to their pimp's phone call and go to the home or motel room of the client; they even take credit cards nowadays."

"I had no idea. So what are some of the signals the girls here would be using for instance?" Bryan asked.

"You can watch them. Most of them will stand with their legs further apart than normal. Some will fondle their hair or toss their heads. Interestingly, some of them who fondle their hair pull on it. Johns should stay away from a hair puller because it's a nervous habit that usually signals child or physical abuse. Other signals are hands on hips, the adjusting of clothing particularly bra straps or garter belts, sideways glances, and hip rolling. I've heard that if a man engages in hip rolling he is usually gay. Is that true?"

"Yep, it's one of the gestures male prostitutes use?"

"Why Bryan how do you know that?"

"Well, I've seen male prostitutes, Bonita."

"And I've seen female prostitutes, so why the third degree?" Bonita asked.

"Your knowing anything about prostitutes is so amusing to me. You're such a lady. I had no idea you would know anything about the seedier sides of life."

"I haven't been living in a bubble all my life, Bryan."

"I see you haven't. Are there any other signals?"

"The only other one I recall is either lots and lots of lipstick or constantly wetting the lips."

"Is that why you applied a whole tube of 'Fire and Ice' to yours?'"

"Precisely, but I only want to *look* the part."

"Well I certainly didn't think you were going to participate."

"Good. I'm glad we have that straight. Now go back across the street. Here's another group of girls. I want to see if I can find out anything."

"Okay, but have you noticed everyone's giving us the eye?"

"New blood; they don't like it nor do they like competition and you're obviously not a Mexican, so they're immediately suspicious because you're not soliciting any of them for their favors. Now cross the street and be a good boy!"

"I'm crossing."

Bonita intentionally stayed in a very specific area where no pimp had confronted her yet. She talked to girls who were waiting for johns, girls who had actively solicited a john and been rejected, and girls who were returning from servicing a john. Her task was difficult because almost all prostitutes are drug users, so all of the deals that were going down weren't about sex; some were about drugs, and many of the girls were high. It was the only way they could perform some of the disgusting tasks for which they charged, so trying to talk to them was like trying to catch a firefly and have a meaningful conversation with the insect.

Finally, an older prostitiute who'd been talking to a younger group of girls, approached Bonita and asked her what her deal was. Bonita said she was trying to find someone she had known many years ago. Her name was Consuelo Souto.

"You la se!" (I know her!) the woman said. "Que quiere usted con ella?" (Why do you want to find her?)

Bonita answered, "Fuimos anos de amigos hace." (We were friends years ago.) "Le hace sube donde yo la puedo encontrar?" (Do you know where I can find her?)

"Yo no la he visto proanos." (I haven't seen her for years.) Ella solia poseer un aproximadamente dos bloques abajo, la Zapatilla Aterciopelada, una de las mejores casas en toda Ciudad de México, pero ella lo vendió. Tal vez los nuevos dueños sabrán ponerse en contacto con ella. ¿Va usted a comenzar a trabajar este latido?" (She used to own a place about two blocks down, the Velvet Slipper, one of the best brothels in all of Mexico City, but she sold it. Maybe the new owner knows where she is. Are you going to start working this beat?")

"No, trabajo in America," Bonita answered. (No, I work in America.)

"Si, dinero es bueno ahi?" (Money is good there?)

"Mucho bueno. Gracias,"(Very good. Thank you.) Bonita said and started across the street to Bryan.

"What's up?" Bryan asked.

"We're going two blocks down, but we're going to walk together so no pimps come out of the woodwork to grab me because I'm trespassing into their space. Consuelo used to own a brothel down the street called The Velvet Slipper. I want to find out if the new owners know where to find her."

"The Velvet Slipper. Was it a brothel for guys with a foot fetish?"

"Bryan, you are so funny!"

The new owners didn't know where Consuelo lived, but they had a phone number and they were more than willing to give it to Bonita. In fact, they offered her a job.

"You've still got it, Sugarbritches," Bryan said as they went out to hail a cab.

"Bryan, some of the ugliest and most pitiful women in the world are prostitutes. Most of them are drug addicts and if you ever decide to switch over to heterosexuality and employ a prostitute, you be very careful because a large number of them have AIDS. That's another thing that bothers me so much about these children that I think are being shipped somewhere for prostitution – most of them will contract AIDS eventually."

"I don't think I'll be switching over and employing one, but AIDS is a scary thing. The very thought that one might *sleep* with another person, male or female and *DIE* because of it is pretty serious, I'd say."

"Very serious. Grab that cab. I'm tired and ready to go back to El Presidente."

"You'd have to work a lot longer than we've been here to make a living."

"And aren't we glad I don't have to do this for a living? I'm a lot older than I look, Bryan, don't forget! You saw the real Bonita and she ain't no spring chicken."

"But she had that beautiful bone structure that's supporting the new Bonita. You're beautiful now and I bet you were a showstopper in your youth too!"

"There were those who thought so, Bryan, but as we all know beauty fades and there has to be something there besides what's visible to the naked eye. That's the part of Bonita Roberts I'm working on now that I've gotten the outside under control."

CHAPTER FORTY-FOUR

Mission Accomplished

*B*ack at the hotel, Bonita undressed, cleansed her face, ran a brush through her hair, moisturized her skin and fell into bed exhausted and thankful that she did not have to walk the streets to make a living. After a good night's sleep, she dressed for the day and entered the living room. Bryan, fully dressed, was sitting on the sofa watching the ubiquitous CNN.

"Good morning, Mrs. Roberts. What happened to that tart I escorted to this suite last night?"

"She's gone for good, Bryan. Shall we order breakfast? Then I want to make a call to this number the good folks at The Velvet Slipper gave me and see if I can track down Consuelo."

"And what are you going to say to her if she answers the phone? Hello, Consuelo, or Mrs. Souto, my name is Bonita Roberts and I'm from Wilmington, North Carolina, in the United States. Are you purchasing children in the poor districts of Mexico City and selling to a white slavery ring?"

"Of course not, Bryan. It could very well be that I may know Consuelo."

"What? How would you know her, the owner of a brothel?"

"I knew a Consuelo Romirez when I lived in LA. She was a lady of the evening, one might say. I'm hoping this is the same Consuelo."

"Do you know what the chances of that are? Zero to none."

"You may be right, but stranger things have happened, especially in my life experiences."

"This would be the strangest of all, I dare say."

"Maybe yes and maybe not!"

They ate and Bonita punched in the number. The phone rang for about ten rings and there was no answer and no machine picked up. Bonita replaced the receiver.

"No luck?"

"I would say good luck. She didn't answer and no machine picked up, but I didn't get a message that the phone was no longer in service or that the number had been changed, so perhaps Consuelo is out. I'll try to reach her later today."

"What shall we do to amuse ourselves then?"

"We can take a walk and then I'll do my exercise with you this afternoon. I peeked outside. It's a beautiful day."

"A walk it is then," Bryan agreed as he hit the remote and turned off the TV and stood.

They walked out of the hotel and stayed on the main drag for about twenty blocks and then Bonita suggested that they take some side streets,

"One can always get a better feel for a place, especially a city, by getting off the main streets."

After several meandering blocks on side streets, they found themselves on a quaint street closed to motorized traffic where everyone was on foot and merchants had their wares displayed on the curbs and in the street. They amused themselves for a few hours examining the arts and crafts of the local artisans. After making several purchases, Bryan, who was carrying all the packages declared that he was hungry. A search began for a nice outdoor café. A few blocks more and they came upon a delightful outdoor café with a Mariachi band in full swing, margaritas at half their usual price and large bowls of tortillas and salsa served gratis to each table.

Bryan stacked the parcels next to a table, seated Bonita, and pulled out his chair to sit.

"Mrs. Roberts, look!" He pointed to a table on the other side of the restaurant's outdoor patio.

Bonita looked where he was pointing and said, "What? What do you want me to see?"

Bryan sat and leaned over to her and said, "Look at the table right under the marquee of the restaurant. There are two women sitting there. Isn't one of them Kim Bartlett?"

Bonita turned slightly and said, "Why, Bryan, it certainly is."

"Shall I go over and invite her to join us?" Bryan asked.

"Not just yet. I can't tell anything about the woman with her except she has dark hair. Her face is turned toward the building."

"Probably one of the merchants she buys from, don't you think?"

"Perhaps."

"Aren't you going to speak to her?"

"Of course I am, but let's order first."

As they placed their order, the woman with Kim rose and walked toward Bonita and Bryan, but right before reaching them, she turned and entered the restaurant. Bonita had watched her closely from behind her Jackie O dark glasses. She was almost positive the woman was Consuelo Romirez whom she had known at the Beverley Wiltshire. She had aged, of course, but was still a very attractive woman and she had a beauty mark above her left eye, as had Bonita's old acquaintance.

When the woman was in the restaurant, Bonita told the waiter that they wouldn't be staying and handed him a large bill. She turned to Bryan and said sotto voce, "Bryan, ask questions later, but right now, get the packages and follow me, but not too closely in case Kim recognizes you. I'm going to get up and walk out of here and go to the left. Wait a few minutes and then get up and leave walking to the right. If Kim Bartlett should see you, tell her you're here on vacation. I do not want her to know I'm in Mexico City,"

"But, Mrs. . ."

"Questions and explanations later. Please do as I say."

"You got it."

Bonita tied a scarf on, picked up her purse, left the restaurant patio, and turned to the left. As the woman who had been seated with Kim Bartlett was returning to her table, Bryan walked out with the pile of packages practically concealing his face and took a right. He and Bonita met in the middle of the block on its backside.

"Did she see you, Bryan?"

"I don't think so. If she did, she didn't say anything. I was walking out when that lady with her was coming back to the table. I piled the packages up so my face was partially covered. Mrs. Roberts, what is going on?"

Bonita relieved Bryan of half the packages and said, "I'm not sure, but I think Kim Bartlett may be involved in the white slavery trade. That woman she is with is Consuelo, the Consuelo I knew in LA, and I'm pretty sure the Consuelo we've been pursuing. In fact, I'm sure of it. The day my furniture arrived, I know I heard children's voices crying and asking for help in Spanish. I went to Joey Scappaticcio and told him what I heard. He went on the ship and assured me that there were no people on board other than the crew. If you'll recall, Kim Bartlett's shipment of Mexican goods came in that same day for her store. On his way to the ship, Joey stopped to talk to Kim who was on the dock. It looked to me like they were having some kind of argument. I'm sure you know too that it was rumored for years before I moved to Wilmington that Kim was running a prostitution ring on board that barge, but that she cleaned that operation up before she got caught. With all that in mind and seeing Kim with Consuelo and if Consuelo is the one buying the little girls, I'm simply putting two and two together."

"And getting ninety-five, I think, Mrs. Roberts. Kim Bartlett is on your Magnolia Ball Committee with you; she and her husband are members of the Wilmington Country Club; he was a captain for United Airlines; they're pillars of Wilmington society; they own an extremely successful gift shop and an extremely successful restaurant; and you think Mrs. Bartlett's trafficking in young girls for prostitution? I don't think your twos are adding up too well."

"We'll wait and see, Bryan, but I'll bet you dollars to doughnuts that I'm right."

"Let's head back to the hotel. It's time for your workout. I can't control that brain of yours, but I do know how to put your body through its paces."

After dinner, Bonita tried Consuelo's number again.

"Hola, digame!" a female voice answered.

"Consuelo, esto es Bonita de Los Ángel. Hacer recordáis me del Bebida Wiltshire? (Consuelo, this is Bonita from Los Angeles. Do you remember me from the Beverly Wiltshire?)

"Bonita? Bonita, Enriquecer Dubras número un chica? Claro Recuerdo usted. Dónde are usted? Qué are usted haciendo? Are usted aquí en México Ciudad? (Bonita? Bonita, Enrique Dubras number one girl. Of course, I remember you. Where are you? What are you doing? Are you here in Mexico City?)

"Soy y Amaría ver usted. Quedando al Intercontinental President. Por qué no seas venís hasta my juego por almuerzo mañana." (I am and I would love to see you. I'm staying at the Intercontinetal President. Why don't you come for lunch tomorrow in my suite?)

"El President! Y un juego! Yo oído usted golpe el grande tiempo y casado algunos rico Juan. Adivino ella must ser verdadero. Amaría venir por almuerzo mañana, pero yo tener una cita. Yo trabajando, pero no en nuestro nuevo antiguo línea de trabajo. Somos un poco largo en el diente por ese ahora, arena nosotros? Qué tal si cena mañana nocturno? Would ese estar bien?" (El President! And a suite! I heard you hit the big time and married a rich john. I guess it must be true. I would love to come for lunch tomorrow, but I am working and I have an appointment. I'm not working in our old trade. We're getting a little long in the tooth for that, aren't we? How about dinner tomorrow night? Would that be all right?)

"Ese ser explendido. Por que no sea venis a siete y haber tragos y cena y evocar el pasado acerca de antiguo tiempos. (That would be splendid. Why don't you come at seven and we'll have drinks and dinner and reminisce about old times.)

"Bueno, enfermo ver usted a siete. Qué es el número de su juego?" (Good, I'll see you at seven. What is the number of your suite?

"Está el Presidencial Juego. Decir them al frente escritorio usted deseo hasta vaya Senora Roberts' juego. Notificaré them usted are eyaculación y ducharán usted hasta el privado ascensor." (It's the Presidential suite. Tell them at the front desk that you are here to see Mrs. Roberts. I'll notify them that you are coming and they'll show you to the private elevator.)

"Bien. Cómo hacer dicen ella en Americano Bonita? Habéis venido un larga distancia, Bebé!" (All right. How do they say it in America, Bonita? You've come a long way, Baby!)

"Enfermo ver usted mañana nocturno, Cónsuelo. Adiós." (I'll see you tomorrow night, Consuelo. Good-by.)

Bonita tapped on Bryan's door and told him that Consuelo was coming to the suite the next evening for dinner and she wanted him to be out.

"She'll be much more willing to talk to me if no one else is around."

"You'll be talking in Spanish. I wouldn't be able to understand anyway."

"Find someplace to go, Bryan. I don't need any protection from Consuelo and I want to talk to her privately."

"I gotcha."

The next morning Bonita called Roberts' Publishing and asked them for the name of the very best detective agency in Mexico City. Once she had the name, Privado Ojo de Lujo, she called and told them where she was located and that a woman by the name of Consuelo Souto would be coming to her suite that evening. Bonita wanted surveillance in the hotel lobby or outside from 6:30 on that evening. The woman would be arriving at seven. She was to be followed and watched twenty-four hours a day from the moment she left Bonita's suite and they were to provide Bonita with daily reports. She ordered the surveillance for five days definitely and perhaps more. She gave the agency her credit card number and told them to spare no expense and to use as many detectives as necessary.

"I want to know everything she does, everywhere she goes, who she talks to, and what she talks about."

Promptly at seven the following evening, the front desk notified Bonita that they were directing Consuelo Souto to her suite's private elevator. The door slid open and there stood Consuelo, older, but still quite an attractive woman. She wore a black Valentino suit, perfectly matched black pearls at her neck and ears and carried a Little Edie purse with matching pumps.

"Bonita, no habéis variado a todo. Por cierto, Penso su reloj must corrido hacia atrás. (Bonita, you haven't changed at all. In fact, I think your clock must run backwards.)

"Consuelo, está así bueno ver usted y arena usted clase. Usted aspecto fantástico se. (Consuelo, it's so good to see you and aren't you kind? You look fantastic yourself.)

The women embraced and kissed the air on either side of their heads. Bonita invited Consuelo to sit and poured a glass of Krystal for each of them. They caught up on the past fifteen years or so, ate a delicious dinner together, and enjoyed each other's company. Bonita, without any success, tried several times to find out what

Consuelo's business venture was, but all her guest would divulge was that she was in the business of finding merchandise for a wealthy American and that she was compensated with a finder's fee. She did acknowledge that her business was extremely lucrative.

Bonita picked up her mental pencil and added two and two again and decided the merchandise was young girls, the finder's fee was so much money per child, and the wealthy American was Kim Bartlett. However, she kept her calculations to herself, at least for the moment.

At approximately 10:30 p.m., Consuelo took her leave and Bonita began her anxious wait until she received the first report from her hired gun, the detective agency. The next two days' reports proved to be disappointing. Consuelo had lunched with an Oriental woman on the first day, but they had eaten outside and there was too much noise for the surveillance team to pick up the conversation even though the women's waitress had been an operative who, when she bent over to take the ladies' menus, planted a mike under the table. The second day Consuelo left her house only once and that was to purchase fresh fruit and vegetables at the local market. She had made no phone calls and the two incoming calls had elicited no useful information. The agency had managed to get into her house and tap her phone line.

Bonita was getting antsy and she was getting on Bryan's nerves.

"Sugarbritches, let's get out of this suite. We can go to the zoo, an art museum, a movie even though I won't be able to understand a word they're saying, anywhere so you'll stop pacing."

"I wouldn't be able to concentrate, Bryan. I know Consuelo is hooked up with Kim and I know they're trafficking in young girls. I just have to wait for Consuelo to make a move."

Late in the afternoon, the agency called. Two men had followed Consuelo to the San Mateo Hill District where she had gone to approximately twenty houses. They made notes of all the habitats she visited and an operative would be going to the homes the next day to see what he could find out.

"Bonanza!" Bonita said to Bryan. "She went to the San Mateo District where Angelica, Delilah's sister, lives. She's back to buying children."

Bonita's suspicions were confirmed the next day when the detective told her what he had learned. "She's offering poor families $500 per young girl. She's telling them the child will be adopted by wealthy Americans and will have a wonderful life."

"Good work! Stay on her tail because eventually she'll return to collect the children and then somehow get them to a boat to ship them out of the country. I need to know how she manages that, the name of the ship, who she pays off at the docks, and anything else you can find out. I plan to leave Mexico City tomorrow now that you've done such an excellent job for me, however, I will deposit $25,000 in American money in your account tomorrow morning. Stay on this woman and if my bill exceeds the money I've left, notify me and I'll send more. Remember, daily reports to me in the US and of course, call me collect."

"All right, Mrs. Roberts. I'm glad you are pleased with our work."

"I'm extremely pleased and if I can ever give anyone a recommendation for your agency, I certainly will."

Bonita placed the receiver in its cradle and said, "Bryan, call room service. I'm going to eat a colossal meal tonight because tomorrow, we're going home!"

"Hooray, Sugarbritches. I won't even fuss at you. Let's order everything on the menu. I feel like pigging out too and I can't tell you how glad I'll be to be back in Wilmington."

CHAPTER FORTY-FIVE

Get The Goods And Arrest'em

*T*hree weeks after Bonita'a return, she got the call. Detectives had discretely followed Consuelo when she had driven a van to the San Mateo district and picked up ten young girls. She then drove them for six hours to the port of Zihuatenejo where she met another woman. That woman got in the van with the children while Consuelo went to the dock master's office. Almost immediately, Consuelo returned to the van and she, the children, and the woman headed for a container in a secluded area of the pier, hidden by several storage buildings. The dock master met the group and opened what looked like a pocket door in the container. The group was ushered in. After ten minutes or so, the dock master returned to his office and Consuelo returned to the van and drove the six hours back to Mexico City. Once back in the city, she returned to her home. For three more days, Bonita got the same report each day. Consuelo picked up girls, drove them to the port, where she was always met by a different woman and the ten girls she transported were showed to another container by the dock master.

Bonita decided it was time to make a move. She called the CEO at Robert's Publishing Company and told him she had information for the Department of Immigration and for the FBI. She planned to fly into New York the following day and she wanted representatives of both agencies to meet her at the publishing company's offices.

"I'll try to arrange that, Mrs. Roberts. Can you tell me anything that I might tell them as to what this regards?"

"I cannot. You tell them Mrs. Joshua Roberts is requesting their presence and that she has vital information regarding a horrible crime, one that is in progress as you speak, and will continue for only a few more days, so time is of the essence."

"I'll get right on it. I'll call you back this evening if I can't get anyone to come, Mrs. Roberts."

"Morey, I will not be expecting that call. Get the agents there. That's a direct order."

"Yes, Mrs. Roberts."

Fortunately for the CEO, Bonita did not get a call from him that evening and she was in New York the next day by noon. At 1:30 p.m., representatives from the FBI and The Department of Immigration filed into the conference room of Roberts' Publishing where Bonita presented them with her information. She told them what she had uncovered and provided them with written reports from the Mexican Detective Agency.

"Who paid for this surveillance, Mrs. Roberts?"

"I did."

"Why?"

"Because innocent little girls are being bought and shipped someplace, not to be adopted, I'm sure. I believe they're being sold into prostitution."

"We're going to get right on this. The United States Government is eternally grateful to you and I'm sure you'll be reimbursed for your expenses."

"I don't want to be repaid. I want you to stop this horrible crime against these children and I want you to put those responsible in prison and throw away the key. I suggest you get operatives down to Mexico City and let them witness the operation down there. The ship the containers are going to be eventually placed on is named 'El Chúpon.' I don't know if you speak Spanish or not, but it means 'lollipop' in English, but I don't imagine it's the 'Good ship Lollipop,' is it?"

"I would think not, Mrs. Roberts. How may we get in touch with you?"

"Through Morey Westin, the CEO here at Roberts' Publishing. He can convey any messages to me."

"Thank you, Mrs. Roberts."

"It was my pleasure, gentlemen. Please save this load of probably one hundred little girls."

"We will, Mrs. Roberts. I give you my word."

Bonita felt as if a huge weight had been lifted from her shoulders as she eased into her first class seat on the plane for her return trip to Wilmington. She could get back to living her life again.

During Bonita's absence, the Magnolia Ball Committee had been busy. Several members had spoken to their husbands and to community leaders. Jackson Tighman, one of the most influential attorneys in town, had written up the papers for the Foundation that the proceeds from the Magnolia Ball would fund. Brant Jansson, President and owner of the Wilmington Bank had agreed to chair the Foundation Board, its name to be the Cape Fear Foundation. Numerous charities had been selected to receive donations from the do-good organization. The young ladies had been selected at the meeting at Kim Bartlett's house and the invitations were in the mail. In two months, the young ladies would come together for the first time at the tea in their honor at the Wilmington Country Club, an event all the committee members would attend.

On November 15, at six in the morning, the Mexican registered ship El Chupon pulled into the Port of Wilmington. Bonita had been notified of its arrival by Morey at Roberts' Publishing Company. Hank accompanied his love to the dock at *O dark thirty*, but he didn't know why.

"Are you expecting more furniture, Bonita?"

"No. There's far more precious cargo on that ship than any furniture I may have, Hank."

Kim Bartlett waved to Bonita and Hank as she started down the dock,

"More furniture coming, Bonita? You're giving me a race for my money with exports from Mexico."

"I think not, Kim. You have a shipment coming in for your store?"

"Yes. I found beautiful things on my last trip. I heard from Fabiola that you were in Mexico City the same time I was."

"I think so. I stayed at the Inter-Continental Presidente."

"Ooo la la! Very pricey. I was at the Hilton in the next block. Wouldn't it have been fun if we had run into each other?"

"Definitely!

"Gotta run. See you soon," Kim called as she moved on down the dock.

Just then, Joey Scappaticcio and Norman Masterson came out of the dock master's office and began descending the steps to the dock area. Norman's foot hit the bottom step at the same time sirens blasted from some ten state trooper vehicles pulling into the dock area. A SWAT Team truck braked to a stop and at least twenty other men ran down to the pier area all wearing navy blue jackets with FBI on the back. All the men had their weapons drawn.

"What in the world is going on? Bonita, let's get you back to the car. I don't want anything to happen to you."

"Nothing will happen to me, Hank. I don't think the people who are about to be arrested are armed."

"People about to be arrested? You know what's happening then?"

"I certainly do. Kim Bartlett and Joey Scappaticcio are about to be arrested. Kim Bartlett has been procuring young girls between the ages of six and eleven from Mexico. She's selling them into prostitution in Bangkok."

"That's a very serious accusation, Bonita. How do you know that?"

"Because that's what I was doing in Mexico City. I found Kim's procurer there and had her followed. That ship El Chúpon is taking quite a circuitous route from Zihuratanejo, a port six hours away from Mexico City, to Bangkok where Kim sells each child for fifty to one hundred thousand dollars to a syndicate that runs houses of prostitution in Thailand, houses who specialize in child prostitutes. They're treated no better than slaves."

"My God!"

"Joey Scappaticcio is on the take from Kim as is the dock master at the port in Mexico. He was arrested yesterday and so was Consuelo, the procurer in Mexico City. Joey is about to be arrested now. Interestingly, while the FBI and the Department of Immigration were investigating Kim's ring, they got some additional information about the kidnappings of young Mexican men who are sent by ship to little old Wilmington, North Carolina. Those men are illegals who are brought here by Norman Masterson to work in his plant. He treats them like prisoners and houses them in a compound at La Reina de la Mar."

"You have to be kidding. Norman is the salt of the earth."

"He's also a kidnapper and he's been using illegal labor for years."

"Norman is always so sure to let everyone know that his Mexicans are legal. He gets papers for them before he brings them to the US."

"Yes, for some, but not for the majority. He has men in Mexico who literally kidnap them at gunpoint and ship them up here. Fabiola, Kim's maid, saw her brother Manuelo riding a school bus and got Kim involved. They went out to La Reina de la Mar and found the compound. Kim did one good thing in that she somehow convinced Norman to get Manuelo his papers and to not only free him from the compound but also from the slave labor he was performing at Seafood World."

"And here I thought I'd moved to a sleepy, little Southern town."

"Not by a long shot, Hank."

While they were talking, two agents had handcuffed Norman and Joey and were reading them their rights. Kim had turned to see what was happening when she first heard the sirens. She jumped into the Cape Fear River, even though it was a cold winter day. Unfortunately for her, the US Government was on its toes and within minutes, she was apprehended by two Coast Guard officers in a twin-engine powerboat who were on alert in the port area. Now, soaking wet, Kim was returned to the dock where she was handcuffed. During the arrests, the SWAT Team had stood at the entrance to the dock area, weapons drawn.

The three were escorted to waiting police cars and taken to jail. Bonita turned to Hank and said, "Shall we go, dear, and have some breakfast?"

At home, Bryan, Hannah, Felice, and Raven were all ears about what all the sirens had been. Bonita simply told them there had been a disturbance at the docks. Hank, however, told them the entire story about his beloved Bonita blowing the whistle on the white slavery ring and saving children.

By that evening, the children had been rescued and their chaperones had been arrested. The Wilmington Hilton was treating all the children to free dinners and their best rooms while the FBI booked them on a cruise ship out of Miami the next afternoon to take them home. They would be flying to Miami by chartered jet in the morning.

When the excitement subsided, Hannah retreated to her basement apartment and called Izonia.

"You ain't never gone believe what happened here in Wilmington today."

Hannah regaled Izonia with the entire story and how her Miz Bonita knowed she heard children's voices crying and calling for help in Spanish when her furniture arrived at the docks and then Alexa Masterson had told her about her maid's niece being sold to a woman in Mexico City and how Bonita had gone there, found the woman, hired a detective agency, told the FBI and the Department of Immigration and saved all them children.

"Why, they had shipped them babies here in containers, Izonia, with bunk beds and chemical pots. They was gone send them over there to Bangkok and sell them to dirty old men as prostitutes. Miz Bonita is truly a hero today!

"Kim Bartlett who own the barge and the gift shop in town was runnin' the ring and sellin' them children to some Chinese men in Thailand. She was arrested. So was Joey Scappaticcio, the dock master. Kim was payin' him off to keep quiet and then, surprise, surprise, Norman Masterson, what owns Seafood World, got arrested too. He been havin' guys down there in Mexico kidnappin' young Mexican men at gunpoint and bringin' 'em up here to work at his seafood plant and keepin' 'em in some kind of prison like place out on his land outside town."

"Lawdy. Lawdy! I done heard it all now."

"It'll be in all the papers by tomorrow, I reckon."

Hannah was right about that. The arrests were in every newspaper in the South the next day; however, Bonita had made sure that the FBI and the Department of Immigration did not mention her part in the sting operation. She didn't do it for fear of anyone accusing her of having some of Wilmington's most prominent citizens arrested. She did it because she felt that it's best when one does a good deed and does it anonymously. Hank tried to convince her to take the credit, but she wouldn't hear of it.

"The only people who know, Hank, are you, and my staff, and that's enough," and that was how it was with the exception of telling Izonia, but Hannah had warned her not to tell anyone. Izonia, loyal to her friend, kept her word and didn't tell anyone. Well, she did tell Anthony, but what difference could that possibly make?

What Izonia didn't know as she repeated Hannah's story to Anthony was that Celestine, who was upstairs napping as far as Izonia knew, had come downstairs to get a glass of orange juice. She was about to enter the kitchen when she heard Izonia talking to Anthony.

Isn't that cute? Izonia's talking to my sweet little Anthony while she irons his clothes, Celestine thought.

She started into the kitchen when she heard Izonia say Bonita's name. Celestine stopped short. She hadn't thought of Bonita Roberts for at least a year. *Whatever would Izonia be talking about her for?* Celestine did something she'd never done before in her life. She eavesdropped on Izonia's one-sided conversation with the doll. Her mouth dropped open more than once at the tale Izonia told. In fact, Celestine was so surprised at everything she heard, she tiptoed back to the stairs and returned to her room without any juice.

CHAPTER FORTY-SIX

The Ball Approacheth

*P*lans for the Ball were in full swing. Bonita and Hank went to New York where Bonita visited the houses of couture to select her gown for the fabulous event. She decided on an emerald green one-shouldered column. A swatch of material trailed behind the covered shoulder and was secured with a diamond brooch. The dress was simple but elegant. Bonita planned to wear diamond clips in her hair, a diamond bracelet, and no other jewelry.

Norman's arrest had meant no more to Alexa than if she had broken a plate on the tiled floor of her kitchen. She didn't let her husband's notoriety or his disgrace bother her one bit. She was still going to the ball and she planned to ensconce herself in a canary yellow Balenciaga gown she had purchased the year before but had no occasion to wear. It had a low neck, see-though cap sleeves, a slit up the side, and fit her like a glove. Her accessories would be gold. Alexa loved the effect yellow and gold made together – she would positively glitter!

Several hundred thousand dollars had been spent by the fathers of the ladies' to be presented, not only for their gowns, but also for the parties each was required to host.

A series of parties had taken place during the weeks preceding the Ball. Featured were a masked ball, a famous lovers' party, a high tea, a sock hop, a formal dinner dance in the ballroom of the Wilmington Hilton, an indoor picnic on the USS North Carolina battleship which was permanently docked in the Cape Fear River in Wilmington, and a wine and cheese party held in the old Cotton Mill that had been converted into a quaint shopping mall. There was even a cocktail party at the railroad museum. The girls and their parents had been most creative in their venues and ideas for entertaining. Bonita was thrilled. There were no functions resembling that horrible oyster roast in Montiac and there were no illiterate parents and grandparents whose daughters and granddaughters had somehow made the list.

A week prior to the Ball, Izonia called Hannah.

"Hannah, this is Izonia. I got somethin' to tell you and it ain't good."

"What is it, Izonia? Is Miz Celestine sick or somethin'?"

"No, ain't nothin' like that. You knows Miss Celestine is the daughter of the first Queen of the Magnolia Ball in Montiac, right?"

"Yes."

"And you knows she was the Queen of the Magnolia Ball herself when she come out?"

"Yes."

"Miss Celestine is good friends with Sally Ann and Sally Ann be the chairperson of the Magnolia Committee in Wilmington. Sally Ann thought it'd be a wonnerful idee for Miss Celestine to speak at the Ball in Wilmington. She ain't told none of the other committee members about it. It's sposed to be a big surprise! We's coming to Topsail Island tonight one week from now, Miss Celestine gonna be speakin' at the Magnolia Ball there before the presentation of them gals begins."

"Oh my Lawdy. I knows she's gonna bring Anthony. You think he gonna start runnin' his mouth again?"

"Well, I don't know that. You said Miz Bonita don't even look like she did, but her name ain't changed. I don't know what's gonna happen, but Miss Celestine still ain't got over that sweet Sandy killin' herself. She still thinks it was Miz Bonita's fault. I jest wanted to let you know."

"Well, I'm gonna have to tell Miz Bonita."

"You do what you has to, but keep me out of it. Miss Celestine loves me like her own flesh, but she would fire me in a New York second if she knew I told this secret."

"I'll keep you out of it. How am I gonna say I found out?"

"I don't know, gal. I just had to tell you. I knows how you loves your Miz Bonita."

"Thank you, Izonia. You's a good and true friend."

Hannah stewed for hours until she decided she'd just have to trust Miz Bonita if she asked her to make a promise to her. She went up the stairs and knocked on Bonita's door.

"Come in."

"Good evenin', Miz Bonita."

"Hello, Hannah. I thought you'd be in bed by now."

"If'n I gone to bed, I couldn't of slept."

"Why is that?"

"'Cause I done somethin' awful, somethin' you didn't want me to do."

"What could you possibly do that's awful? Did you make some yummy dessert that's going tempt me?"

"That ain't it. You know how you didn't want nobody from Montiac to know where was and that I wasn't even to mention Montiac, Dorchester County or South Carolina."

"I certainly do."

"Izonia that works for Miss Celestine is a good friend of mine, Miz Bonita, and I been talkin' to her on the phone ever since we moved from there."

"Hannah, how could you after I asked you not to let anyone know where we were."

"I's sorry, Miz Bonita. Izonia is a good person and we is such good friends. Sometimes, I jest felt like I gotta talk to her, but she ain't never told anyone, not Miss Celestine or nobody where we are."

"How do you know?"

"I jest knows. Now I got to tell you somethin' bad, but first you gotta promise me that you won't never let Izonia get in no trouble because of it."

"How can I promise that, Hannah, if I don't know what it is."

"You jest have to or I can't tell you what it is and I promise you this, Miz Bonita, it's somethin' you definitely wants to know."

"I'm losing you, Hannah. What are you talking about?"

"First you gotta promise me you ain't gone let no one know Izonia told me."

"Hannah, what could Izonia possibly tell you that I would want to know?"

"Somethin' real important. It affects you directly, Miz Bonita. I know I shouldn't ask this question, but 'cept for what I jest told you about talkin' to my friend Izonia, I ain't never done nothin' to hurt you, have I?"

"No, you haven't, Hannah."

"Then you gotta promise me, Miz Bonita," and by this time Hannah was crying.

"All right, Hannah, I promise. Now stop blubbering and tell me what this is all about."

"Me and Izonia been talkin' on the phone ever since we leff Montiac. Bryan took me to the market a few months ago and Izonia was there. The Peirsalls owns a house out at Topsail Island."

"I know. I saw Celestine and Jamison at Elijah's when I met some friends there. They had that stupid doll with them and Celestine, poor pathetic thing, asked the hostess to seat three of them."

"Did she know who you was?"

"No. I passed right by her in the ladies' room later and she didn't know me."

"That Sally Ann who's heading up the Magnolia Committee, she's a good friend of Miss Celestine's. Sally Ann decided to plan a surprise for the committee and the guests at the Magnolia Ball here and she invited Miss Celestine to speak at the Ball before the gals is presented. Izonia called and told me 'cause of what happened at the Ball in Montiac, but Izonia knows Miss Celestine would fire her if she found out she told. She called me 'cause she knows how much I loves you and she wanted to protect you."

"Why in the world does she want Celestine to speak at this Ball?"

"'Cause Miss Celestine was the Queen of the Magnolia Ball in South Carolina and her grandmother was too and her great grandparents started the Ball there."

"Of course. Well, she can't speak. That's all there is to it. You know she'll bring Anthony and God only knows what'll happen when she starts talking in that high squeaky voice and spills her guts."

"How you gone stop her? It's a surprise. You can't let Sally Ann know you knows Then Izonia'll get in trouble. You said Miss Celestine don't recognize you, Miz Bonita."

"And you think she won't think it's a big coincidence that my name is Bonita Roberts. I'll just have to resign and tell them to get another mistress of ceremonies. I can't take being disgraced again after all the effort I've put in to remolding myself inside and out."

"Oh, Miz Bonita, you can't resign. This is what you've always wanted and this time you didn't start the whole Magnolia Ball thing."

"I suggested the name. Oh, why couldn't I keep my mouth shut? If it weren't the Magnolia Ball, then there would be no reason to have Celestine Piersall speak?"

"Please don't let Izonia get in no trouble."

"I won't. I promise. I appreciate your telling me and I am thankful to Izonia for being such a good friend to you."

"I's sorry I brung you bad news, but you had to know."

"I did, but now I've got to figure out what to do," Bonita answered.

"Call me if I kin help you. I think I can sleep now that I got that off my chest, so I'm going to head for my bedroom."

"Good night, Hannah, and thank you."

For the next few days, Bonita tried out various scenarios of how she could keep Celestine Piersall away from the Magnolia Ball, but none of them worked. She decided she would have to resign. She called Sally Ann and told her she would not be able to participate in the Magnolia Ball and that Sally Ann would have to find another emcee.

"Have you lost your senses, Bonita? The rehearsal is in two days. Where do you think I'm going to find another emcee in that time? What is the matter with you? You were one hundred percent behind this entire Magnolia Ball thing. Why, you even suggested the name. I will NOT accept your resignation. You are the mistress of ceremonies. It's in all the press releases. The gold nametags have been engraved. The place cards have been printed."

"Let's go over the agenda of the Ball again, Sally Ann," and Bonita began to list the events.

"There's one little thing that's not on the agenda, Bonita. It's a little surprise I have planned for the guests and the committee. You know how interested we Southerners are in history and the significance of various events, so I have a surprise just before I introduce you and we begin the presentation of this year's debs."

"A surprise? That's very unprofessional, Sally Ann. This event has been planned down to the tiniest detail. You can't have a surprise in the middle of the Ball."

"Well, I think I can, Bonita. I am the chair of the committee."

"And the chair of the committee discusses everything with the committee. The chair does not make any decisions on his or her own without the approval of the committee."

"Then I'm going to use my poetic license."

"Poetic license has to with literature, Sally Ann, not with heading a committee."

"It's a great surprise. You'll love it! Everyone will love it!"

"I'm calling the other committee members."

Bonita called the other members, but none of them were upset in the least that Sally Ann had planned a surprise. Bonita had no allies. She didn't know what to do. However, Bonita was a woman of limitless depths. An idea finally came to her and it just might work.

"Hank, this is Bonita. Have you told your children about our forthcoming nuptials?"

"I have."

"And are they planning to attend our wedding?"

"I'm sorry, Sweetheart, but I've never been close to my children and and I don't believe they'll be coming."

"Splendid!"

"I beg your pardon?"

I said, "Splendid! They're not coming and I don't have anyone that will have to travel to come, so let's get a blood test in the morning and get married the morning of the 28th of December."

"The morning of the Ball? Won't you be too busy?"

"Too busy to get married to you? Absolutely not! We'll get married by a justice of the peace, go to the Ball, and then leave early for a fantastic honeymoon in Jamaica. What do you think?"

"I think I'm in love with a fantastic woman, one who constantly surprises and delights me. I'll be at your house at nine in the morning and we'll go get those blood tests."

"Perfect."

There, Celestine Piersall. Bonita Roberts will not be the mistress of ceremonies at the Magnolia Ball. By the time you make your speech at the Magnolia Ball in Wilmington, my name will be Bonita Asbury. You might think twice about the name Bonita, but you won't realize I'm the same one you knew in Montiac.

Bonita took the elevator to the basement.

"Hannah," she called.

"Right here, Miz Bonita."

"I figured it all out. Hank and I are going for our blood tests tomorrow and we're going to be married the morning of the 28th. At the Ball, I won't be Bonita Roberts any longer. I'll be Bonita Asbury."

Hannah hugged her employer, "Oh, Miz Bonita, you is one smart cookie. I knew you'd figger it all out and you did! I bet Mr. Hank is thrilled, ain't he?"

"He is. Thank you again, Hannah, and my thanks to Izonia too. Have you told her you were so clever to extract a promise from me before you told me her secret?"

"I told her. She real nervous though that Miz Celestine gone find out what she done."

"Put her at ease. There's no way Celestine will know what Izonia did and there's no way she'll ever know me. Now, the Magnolia Ball will really be fun!"

CHAPTER FORTY-SEVEN

Wedding Bells

December 28 dawned bright and clear. Bonita was up before the birds. She was   meeting Hank at City Hall at nine and she wanted to make sure she looked absolutely perfect. While Bonita bathed, Hannah laid out an off white Robert Cavelli sheath dress trimmed in seed pearls at the neck and the matching jacket trimmed in seed pearls at the mandarin collar and at the edges of the sleeves. Jimmy Chu had come through again with a pair of off white, dyed to match Bonita's dress, strappy pumps with a tiny wedding bell embroidered on the top of each shoe. Robert, Bonita's favorite Milan designer, had enclosed a gift with her wedding outfit. It was a perfect hat Robert had made out of matching material with a tiny veil just below Bonita's eyes trimmed in seed pearls and tiny diamonds.

Once dressed, Bonita accessorized with small clusters of diamonds at her ears, Jimmy Chu's purse that matched the shoes, complete with the tiny bell and her engagement ring as her only other piece of jewelry.

"You looks gorgeous, Miz Bonita. I don't think I ever seen you look this pretty," Hannah cooed.

"Thank you, Hannah. Now run get yourself dressed."

"For what?"

"For what? Why you're coming to my wedding, of course."

"I is?"

"Absolutely, now hurry. Bryan is driving all of us there in a half hour."

Hannah didn't waste any time getting downstairs and putting on a fashionable red suit trimmed in mink Bonita had given her for Christmas. *She must have bought me this here suit just for this occasion*, Hannah thought. *And it shore nuff is fantasmagoric!*

When Hannah entered the living room where all were assembled, everyone told Hannah how lovely she looked and then Bonita handed her a box. Hannah opened it and saw the most beautiful hat she had ever seen her life. A big picture hat trimmed with mink to match her suit – she was going to wow everybody at church next Sunday in this outfit.

"Oh, thank you, Miz Bonita. It's the prettiest thing I's ever seen."

"It's my pleasure, Hannah. Well, everyone, shall we go?"

"In just a minute," Bryan answered. "I have a little surprise for you," and he pulled a lovely bridal bouquet from behind his back. Bonita gasped when she saw the single magnolia surrounded by gardenias with off white ribbons flowing from beneath the flowers.

"Bryan, it's perfect. Wherever did you get a magnolia and gardenias in December?"

"You're not the only one who can get flowers sent here from Hawaii, Sugarbritches. Now let's get you in the Rolls."

Hank was waiting for Bonita in front of City Hall. His good friend Neville Smythe accompanied him to serve as his Best Man.

"Miz Bonita, you don't have no Maid of Honor," Hannah whispered.

"Oh, but I do, Hannah. You're my Maid of Honor."

Bryan had to catch Hannah who almost fainted.

"Miz Bonita, I ain't never been so honored in my life."

"It's traditional for one's Maid of Honor to be either a relative or a best friend and I consider you both."

And Hannah just bawled.

Hank ushered everyone in, and within fifteen minutes, Bonita Roberts was Mrs. Hank Asbury the third, that's Mrs. Asbury number three, not be confused with the possibility of Hank being the son of Hank Asbury, Jr., which he was not.

The entourage returned to Bonita's for a champagne brunch prepared by Hannah and for once, Felice let her do whatever she wanted and did not fuss when there was not a single nut, berry, or tofu square in any of the assorted dishes. Hannah prepared a sausage, cheese, and egg casserole, scrapple, sausage, bacon, Eggs

Benedict, homemade cinnamon buns, orange rolls, Belgian waffles with heated syrup, ambrosia, hash browns, grits, homemade biscuits, jellies, jams, and preserves and heaps of real butter all to be washed down with either mimosas, champagne only, or her wonderful hand ground coffee.

After brunch, Bonita and Hank retired to the upstairs suite. No one saw them again until they emerged dressed for The Magnolia Ball. Bryan was at the ready to chauffeur them to the festivities.

As soon as Bonita stepped off the runabout onto the barge, she headed to find Sally Ann.

"Sally Ann, I have something very important to tell you."

"What is it, Bonita?"

Holding her husband's hand, Bonita announced that she and Hank had been married that morning and that tonight she wanted to be introduced by her new name as Bonita Asbury.

"Congratulations to you, Hank, and best wishes, Bonita. How lovely! I'll make that change in my notes right away. By the way, you look smashing, Bonita."

"You too, Sally Ann."

Sally Ann was in an Oscar de la Renta willowy off-shoulder gray dress with gray accessories and she did look quite lovely. Other members of the committee drifted in with their escorts and all of them were beautifully coiffed and costumed. The debutantes, their fathers, and escorts arrived en masse on a yacht that one of the local well-to-do citizens had volunteered for the event so that all of the debs could arrive together.

Bart and the committee had outdone themselves with the decorations. Real tree boughs hung from the ceiling frosted so they appeared to have ice crystals on them; a snow machine was in constant motion making a quite realistic snowfall on the stage area; columns that replicated ice were strategically placed around the huge room that served as the main dining room of the barge restaurant; the tables were covered with shimmering silver cloths and huge Lucite vases were in the center of each table with faux snowballs, icicles, and snowflakes cascading from them; twinkling lights were everywhere; and the sound of chilling winds played over the sound system. It was indeed a winter wonderland.

After a few minutes of mingling, the debs, their parents, escorts, relatives, committee members, and their escorts were directed to their tables and the banquet began. Bart's highly trained wait staff served the soup course, a chilled split pea soup topped with slices of smoked salmon accompanied by a Pinot Grigio. Salad followed consisting of sliced Granny Smith apples on a bed of mescaline topped with walnuts and blue cheese and drizzled with a teriyaki and balsamic vinaigrette. The wine for the salad course was a Sauvignon Blanc. The main course was Beef Wellington done to perfection, baked asparagus, Duchess potatoes, and Parker House rolls accompanied by an exquisite Merlot. Everyone exclaimed over and over how delicious everything was. Dessert was Baked Alaska flambé served with heated plum wine. Before dessert was served, the lights were lowered and the wait staff came out of the kitchen in single file with the flaming dishes held above their heads. It was quite spectacular and the guests burst into spontaneous applause.

When the tables were cleared and removed and the debs had been ushered into a private room, the barge was abuzz with all of the other Magnolia Ball guests who had been invited. Over four hundred guests had descended upon the barge and the band struck up with a medley of swing tunes. About an hour into the Ball, Sally Ann strode to the stage and picked up the hand microphone.

"Good evening, ladies and gentlemen. Welcome to the first annual Wilmington Magnolia Ball."

Lengthy applause followed. When the noise died down, Sally Ann began to speak again.

"As you all know, the proceeds of the Ball will go to the Cape Fear Foundation and over the next year, we will be making donations to worthy charities throughout New Hanover County."

More applause.

"We wish to thank Jackson Tighman who drew up our incorporation papers and our by-laws pro bono and I wish to thank the members of the Magnolia Ball Committee who have worked so hard to make this evening a success. As I call your name, would each of you please stand?"

Sally Ann called each committee member by name. When all had been introduced except one, she said, "And last but not least is our mistress of ceremonies for the evening, Bonita Asbury. Until this morning, she was Bonita Roberts, however Bonita and Hank Asbury were joined in matrimony this morning at City Hall."

Bonita stood with her heart in her mouth. *Sally Ann, you are such a dunderhead. Why did you have to mention anything about my marriage and particularly why did you have to make sure that everyone knew my last name had been Roberts? Well, there's nothing I can do now. I'll just have to sit here and when Celestine gets on stage with Anthony, the show will be over. Maybe Hank and I can move to the Virgin Islands. It's going to be all over in Wilmington in about fifteen minutes.*

"And now without further ado, I would like to introduce you to Brant Jansson, the Chairman of the Cape Fear Foundation whom I've asked to say a few words."

Chairman Jansson spoke and there was polite applause. The crowd was getting restless and wanted to get on with the presentation of the young ladies. Sally Ann took the stage again.

"As you glance at your programs, I'm sure you see that the next item on our agenda is my turning the program over to the mistress of ceremonies for the evening and the presentation of our own Wilmington debutantes. However, I have a little surprise before we begin. I'm sure many of you have heard of the famed Magnolia Ball held in Dorchester County, South Carolina, for well over a hundred years. Sadly, there was some misfortune there and the giant magnolia tree that had stood in front of Beechland for hundreds of years developed a disease and died. The Ball is no longer held in Montiac, but we are very fortunate here in Wilmington to have with us this evening a former queen of the South Carolina Magnolia Ball. In fact, her grandmother was the first queen of the Magnolia Ball and her great-grandparents initiated the Ball. Our guest is now a summer resident at Topsail Island and a great attribute to our community here. Ladies and gentlemen, may I present Celestine Piersall."

Applause and Celestine walked to the podium on the stage and yes, she had Anthony in her arms.

"Good evening, friends. Thank you so much for this invitation to attend your Magnolia Ball here in Wilmington, my second home. It is my pleasure and my privilege to be here. I'm not going to keep you long, but I do want to tell you just a little about how the South Carolina Magnolia Ball began."

Celestine paused. "Not now, Anthony. Mother told you that you could come up here with her but you'd have to be quiet. This is my son, Anthony. Please forgive him, folks, he always wants to talk."

There were some coughs, some embarrassed laughter and one huge guffaw from the ballroom.

Celestine began again, "My grandmother was not the most beautiful girl who ever lived in Dorchester County. . . .Anthony, stop."

And then the high-pitched voice began, "See that lady in the green dress. Her name is Bonita Roberts or at least it was until she got married this morning. My mother and I knew another Bonita Roberts one time and she was a very mean lady. She lived in Montiac. But this is a different Bonita Roberts. This lady is kind and good. None of you know what she did, but I do. She was down on the docks when her furniture arrived from Mexico and she thought she heard children's voices crying and calling for help in Spanish. Then when Mrs. Masterson's maid Delilah heard from her sister that a woman had come and offered $500 for one of her children, Mrs. Roberts heard about it at the beauty parlor and she took off to Mexico. Mrs. Roberts found the lady that was buying the children and hired a private detective agency and had them follow that woman. She paid for all that out of her own pocket. Once she had the goods on the white slavery ring, she contacted the FBI and the Department of Immigration. Mrs. Roberts, now Mrs. Asbury, is the woman who saved all those young girls from being sold into prostitution. This Mrs. Roberts is a heroine!" and Anthony took a little bow.

There was a big hubbub and then applause. Sally Ann rushed over to Bonita and took her by the hand and moved her to the podium. She received a long and loud standing ovation.

Bonita moved toward Celestine and took her hand and then she took Anthony's little hand in hers and said, "Thank you, Anthony. What a fine young man you are."

As soon as Celestine heard Bonita's voice, she realized that this woman had the same voice as the Bonita Roberts she used to know.

"You are the same Bonita, aren't you?"

"No, Celestine, I am definitely not the Bonita you knew."

Bonita acknowledged the applause, went back to her seat, and Celestine continued her speech, uninterrupted by Anthony. Once she had finished, Sally Ann said, "And now the woman who needs no introduction, Bonita Asbury, our own Good Samaritan!"

Bonita began, "Ladies and gentlemen, from the House of Montclair, Miss Liberty Sampson Montclair, presented by her father, Admiral Thames Smather Montclair, and escorted by Alden Sweet Forte, IV. Miss Montclair," and the first debutante to be presented in Wilmington, North Carolina, came into view.

Bonita was home at last!

Epilogue

*C*elestine was so touched by Anthony's speech at the Magnolia Ball and his kindness to Bonita that she took him out and bought him an entirely new wardrobe. It included new underwear, sweaters, a fur coat, jeans, shirts, a new tuxedo, tie, vest, studs, and cummerbund, Bermudas, T-shirts, swimming trunks, cowboy boots, a new cowboy suit with holsters, six-guns and a tiny Stetson hat, suits, monogrammed shirts with French cuffs, tiny cuff links, ties, tennis shoes and ten more pairs of shoes so he would be properly attired for any occasion

After Scappaticcio's arrest and trial, Nina resigned from the Committee and sold the completely renovated house in which she and Joey had resided. She moved to her family's estate with momma and daddy, a disgraced Southern belle "who couldn't hold her head up in public," a common malady in the South when anything happens to bring one personal shame. Nina did not visit Joey in prison nor did she accept his weekly collect phone calls. In fact, six months after his incarceration, Nina filed for divorce. She will no doubt live the remainder of her days as a "grass widow," another mark against her in Dixieland.

Alexa donated the compound and the land where the Mexicans had been housed at La Reina de la Mar to a Christian camp. Each summer inner city children are brought to Wilmington to enjoy two weeks of hiking, swimming, horseback riding, campfires, ghost stories, vespers and "Kum Ba Ya."

She made up with her daughter Jennifer and then sold Seafood World for an obscene amount of money, divorced Norman, and lives happily spending his money. She continues to serve on the Magnolia Ball Committee in Wilmington.

Superintendent Zarot, Coach Cliff, and Nuts'n were all found out by the investigation into Norman Masterson's doings. They were fired and prosecuted. The local Sports' Club members are devastated; they don't think they'll ever find another coach like Coach Cliff. Therefore, the scouts won't be coming to their little waterfront town anymore.

Luzanne managed one by one to have all of Ralph's teenage children put away while simultaneously salting away thousands of Ralph's dollars into a separate account in her name. When she left Ralph, after officially resigning from the MB Committee, she had amassed a fortune plus she got half of Ralph's assets in the divorce settlement. She and Dr. Turner moved to California with the future Dahli Lama. It wasn't until some months later that Dr. Turner came to realize that Luzanne suffered from a severe personality disorder, an incurable psychological anomaly, with secondary narcissistic undercurrents. He was doomed to live with a psycho as he had given up his license to practice when the threesome ran off together to live the easy life on Ralph's money.

Raven continued to serve as Bonita's personal secretary while being courted by the owner of the construction company who renovated Bonita's "tear-down."

Celestine and Bonita became close friends, and Hannah and Izonia were able to see each other and talk to each other freely. Bonita always remembered her manners and carried on long conversations with Anthony when she and Celestine were together.

Felice made Bonita a last shake and tofu delight and left for New York City where she was to be Ivana Trump's nutritionist.

Donnice continued to yell and scream at her servants and to stew about what Bonita Roberts was doing and where she was. All her money and Donnice couldn't find the fat, Mexican whore.

While on another Sotheby's foray to New York, Precious Woodson ran into yet another old college friend and mentioned that on her previous trip she had seen Twyla. Her friend said, "Oh yes Twyla. She's been working for Roberts' Publishing Company ever since we finished school and is still there today. The rumor for eons was that she was Joshua Roberts' mistress until he left his wife and married some Spanish royalty he met out in California."

Precious called Bonita on her cell phone and chatted. Bonita had kept her cell with the Spencer area code, so Precious had no idea where Bonita was even though she attempted to wheedle it from her. After having no success at finding out Bonita's whereabouts,

Precious told her about running into Twyla and how she had lied about where she worked and had asked many questions about Bonita.

Bonita placed a call to the company and told the CEO to give Twyla a handsome settlement, a generous pension, and her walking papers. When the CEO did as Bonita requested, Twyla reminded him of Joshua's will and that she could stay there as long as she liked. The CEO told her that he answered to a new boss now and her services were no longer needed as of that moment.

Twyla took a final ride to her apartment in the chauffeured limo and immediately placed a call to Donnice who dropped her like a beaker of sulfuric acid. "Well, there's nothing I can do, Twyla. I don't have anything to do with the company, as you well know, and as you are also aware, I don't even know where the bitch is. Good-by, Twyla. Have a nice life," and Donnice hung up on the pitiful woman.

Twyla was devastated. She had never looked beyond her daily routine and what she would do when she no longer went to Roberts' Publishing five days a week. She couldn't very well knit all day long. What was she going to do with all this free time? She had no friends, no family, and no real interests other than Roberts' Publishing Company, getting even with Bonita, and her felines.

After a few months of forced retirement, Twyla went to her hair appointment, came home and soaked in a relaxing bubble bath, dressed in her most beautiful negligee and peignoir with matching satin mules, and carefully applied her make-up. She went into the kitchen and called to the kitties. She picked up Tristam and Isolde in turn, cooed to them, petted them, and then set their food dishes in front of them. The expensive Pretty Kitty cat food was heavily laced with rat poison.

Miss Twyla went to the bathroom and dumped a handful of Valium and Percoset into her hand and washed the pills down. She had amassed her stash over the last month by going to different emergency rooms in the city and displaying symptoms of acute pain and overwhelming anxiety. Miss Twyla walked into her bedroom, pulled back the covers, and lay on her pristine sheets for her final rest before the eternal dirt nap.

Bart continued to manage the barge restaurant that had become even more in vogue after it had served as the venue for the Magnolia Ball. He visited Kim once a month at the maximum-security prison in Butner, North Carolina, a seven-hour round trip from Wilmington by car. Kim had been sentenced to thirty years.

Bart sold the gift shop to Kim's assistant and it continued to do well. Having sold his Baron when he lost his job with American Airlines, he purchased a Cessna 182 RG, a six-passenger plane with a retractable gear, and in his free time went out to the local airport, climbed in his plane, and bored holes in the sky.

Fabiola and Manuelo got a loan from Bart and opened a profitable cleaning and landscaping enterprise. They paid Bart back in a timely fashion.

Bryan stayed with Bonita cracking the whip in the gym and serving as her bodyguard when Hank wasn't available. Bryan had found several *friends* of his sexual preference as Wilmington had become the "Hollywood of the East Coast" and there were many artsy-craftsy types about.

Xandi's summer concert had been a sell-out and a huge success. Wilmington matrons were at a loss for their weekly "Dos" as Xandi sold Hair tdf and returned to the music scene. Her first CD "Washing Him Out of Your Hair," a medley of songs about broken hearts and how to recover from them, was well on its way to becoming platinum.

And Bonita? She and Hank are immensely happy together. They left on New Year's Eve for a trip to Jamaica, and entertained at a posh reception at the Wilmington Country Club upon their return. Bonita is indeed a changed woman. Let us hope that the woman who began her life as a poor Mexican in the brown hills of Texas will be happy in her new body, in a new city, and in her new life, for she definitely has "Come a long way, Baby!"

And by the way, if you happen to be in Wilmington, North Carolina, during the Christmas season, be sure to call 252-555-1886 and ask to speak to Sally Ann. She will provide you with tickets at $150 each to this year's Magnolia Ball. You should go! The barge transformed into a winter wonderland is definitely eye candy; the food is delicious; the girls are lovely; the men are stud muffins; the jewels and gowns are spectacular; and Bonita, yet again risen from the ashes, will be there as the reigning queen of Wilmington society in her dual capacities as mistress of ceremonies and emcee. Everyone who's anyone will be there!

And of course, Anthony will be there in his *new* tux!

Afterword

*I*t has been my distinct pleasure to create Bonita Roberts, to spend so much time with her, and to watch her transformation. I decided she was too much of a character to "kill off," so I now plan to leave her in Wilmington with Hank to spend the rest of her days doing good works! I wish both of them much happiness and I hope to see all of you at the Ball!

About the Author

*R*ebecca Tebbs Nunn is a native of Virginia and holds a BA Degree in Dramatic Arts and Speech from Mary Washington College of the University of Virginia. She has acted with the Helen Hayes Repertory Theatre, several dinner theatres in and around Washington, DC, and in community theatres up and down the Eastern Seacoast. While she has appeared in over 40 major productions, she has directed close to 50 including the critically acclaimed Save Me A Place At Forest Lawn while studying under the tutelage of famed director Marc Connelly. In addition to making numerous radio and television commercials, Ms. Nunn was the national voice for Oldsmobile Cutlass automobiles. The Magnolia Ball III is her fourth book and the last in the Magnolia Trilogy. Her other books include The Magnolia Ball, The Magnolia Ball -dash- Two, and Stolen Sons. She lives in Kilmarnock, Virginia, with her husband Spike, a retired American Airlines Captain, and her Sheltie Cluny. Ms. Nunn currently serves as a Councilwoman on Kilmarnock's Town Council.